Visibility

FICTION BY
SARAH NEUFELD

Illustrated by D. Meister

Bowler Hat Comics
Portland, Oregon

FIRST EDITION
June 2008
10 9 8 7 6 5 4 3 2 1

A Bowler Hat Illustrated Novel

STORY	Sarah Neufeld
ILLUSTRATIONS	D. Meister
BOOK DESIGN & LAYOUT	Bo Björn Johnson
AUTHOR PHOTO	David Neufeld
EDITOR IN CHIEF	Linda Meyer
EDITOR	Jenn Crowell
PROOFREADER	Malini Kochhar
DIRECTOR OF MARKETING	Allison Collins
PUBLICIST	Emily Reis
MANAGER OF MISC. WONDERS	Jen Weaver-Neist
PUBLISHER	Bo Björn Johnson
CEO	Cameron Marschall
SPECIAL THANKS	Cassie Richoux
	Chris Huff
	Betsy Strobel
	John Peetz

Set in 9.75/14.5 Dolly

Bowler Hat Comics
1825 SE 7th Ave.
Portland, OR 97214
www.bowlerhatcomics.com

For Meera (and Ryan)

Mae mo, ima mo, kore kara mo

前も、今も、これからも

p r o l o g u e

Peter came the fall I was six, in the middle of October. It was a steel-grey, windy day, dry as bone and freezing cold. I sat in the window seat, my back to the window, because if I couldn't see the weather, I could pretend it didn't exist. Peter's suitcase sat on the floor beside his feet; he didn't look very comfortable. I didn't know what to say to an adult who was uncomfortable—or to a kid, or anyone, for that matter—so I asked him what I asked everyone I met that year. "Do you know my dad?"

Peter shook his head. "No."

"His name is Roger Kreidi. He's a photographer. He's famous," I said, even though he wasn't famous, really.

"I'm sorry," Peter said.

He didn't look sorry. I scuffed my heels against the wall, staring at him, eyes narrowed. I wasn't very fond of strangers. Peter's one asset was that he might know my dad, and if he didn't … "You can go away," I told him. "I don't want you here."

"I can't leave," he said. No excuses. Just, *I can't.*

"I don't need you. Nobody needs you. You're no good." I didn't know any swear words, but I knew it hurt to hear those things. If I hurt him enough, he'd get mad and leave.

"You need me," he said. He didn't sound mad at all.

"Do not."

"Do too."

"Why?"

"Because I can draw."

He'd caught me off guard. *Why would I want that?* I thought, but what actually came out was, "What can you draw?"

"What do you want me to draw?"

Something impossible. "Anything?"

"Anything."

"If … if you can't do it, you leave. Okay?"

Peter nodded. He pulled a pencil out of his pocket, as though that was a normal thing to have there, and turned one of his reference letters over to the blank side, bracing it on his knee.

"Draw my mom. Draw Jadyn." He nodded again, pencil already dipping down toward the paper. "Invisible," I said, hastily. The pencil hesitated. "Invisible, but you have to make it look like her."

There. *That* was impossible. But Peter didn't even look up. He smiled and started sketching. After a few minutes, I got bored trying to pretend he wasn't there. I slipped off the window seat and went over, watching his hand skate across the paper.

"Here you go," Peter said, turning the paper around and holding it up so I could see. I stared. He'd drawn the desk in my mother's

office, and the leather swivel chair behind it. There was a deep dent in the back of the chair, very definitely person-shaped. A pen hovered just over the desk, aimed accusingly at the man standing opposite the big chair. He stood with his shoulders hunched as if for protection, his head lowered as though he was too cold—or too frightened of whoever was behind the desk—to lift it.

"That's…" I started, then trailed off. "Don't make him stand there. He's scared."

"Why?" Peter watched me, light brown eyes interested.

"Because Jadyn's mad—" I bit my tongue, realizing I'd just admitted Peter had won.

"If I make him safe, then I can stay?"

I nodded, slowly, and watched as Peter drew a solid-looking door between the man and the desk. "Make it locked," I said, automatically.

Peter smiled. "Already done."

c h a p t e r   o n e

66 ... of trafficking in drugs, but we have no proof. As far as we're concerned, Javier Nadal has been seen at the edges of these things once too often, and we know he's fairly well-acquainted with your family."

I'm sitting across a flimsy metal-legged table from a policeman named Officer Reinhold in a back room somewhere on the top floor of the courthouse. It's really a break room; no one wants to insult Jadyn by putting her proxy under unneeded pressure, and besides, we all know nothing they say is going to change her mind. No need to waste an interrogation room on me. There's a bank of half-size lockers against the wall opposite the door, and someone's left a mostly-eaten carton of boysenberry yogurt on the table by the policeman's elbow. I'm glad they did, because it's bothering Officer Reinhold. He keeps glancing down at it, and I can tell he just wants to get up and throw it away, but he can't do that and still look scarily official. He's settled for edging it away with his elbow every time it catches his eye. Any minute now, it's going to fall off the edge.

"You were at his house with your mother recently...just last week, in fact. I don't suppose you heard anything."

I keep my eyes fastened on his chin, where they won't complicate things, even though I've decided I don't like this guy. I've been coming here once a month for five years, since I was twelve. Most of the time, the personnel are at least polite, as if I were here on business, but this one is making me feel like a shoplifter. He's staring at me so hard, trying to force me to look at him, that I'm seriously tempted to do it. All his questions come out sounding like demands, and his statements are just accusations in disguise. I keep expecting him to slip a pair of handcuffs onto the table as a sort of visual incentive.

I *was* at Nadal's house for four hours, at a dinner party with my mother, Jadyn Irving. Even Officer Reinhold should know what that means—I wasn't allowed to talk to anyone for longer than the time it took to say hello, that nobody talked to me, and that I was too busy trying not to see Nadal flirting with my mother to feel even remotely like eavesdropping. Even if I'd managed, and I had heard something, there's no way I'd tell this loser about it.

I've been quiet too long. "Miss Irving." Officer Reinhold reaches over and taps his thick fingers on the table in front of me. "We know you could get the proof we need."

That's *it*. That is absolutely all I am taking from this man. I glance up. "How?"

His eyes lock on mine. For a split-second, a reflexive kind of satisfaction skates across their ice-blue surface. Then the satisfaction flickers, melting into something fearful. The next second he's yanked his eyes away, flustered, and there's an unhealthy chalky smudge across each cheekbone. I lean back in the metal chair, forcing myself to keep a straight face. My eyes are the same as Jadyn's, although she uses hers more. They're a strange metallic color, eerily reflective, and they seem to pull you in somehow so that you can't look away. It's like trying to ignore something fluorescent. If anything, they're too striking: when people look at my mother's face, all they ever remember is her eyes. The only thing visible in those eyes is what she thinks of whoever she's looking at, and, since Jadyn rarely likes people in a genuine way, seeing yourself through her eyes can be devastating. She's been known to make veteran TV talk show hosts break down and cry on the air. Her eyes give her a definite advantage, and she doesn't mind using them—she does it all the time, in fact—but she's gorgeous, and sometimes I think she resents people never noticing the rest of her.

I, on the other hand, am not gorgeous. I rarely get a chance to use my eyes, at home or anywhere else. I don't have a vendetta against anybody, really, but I have no qualms about practicing on a policeman who should have known better.

"Excuse me?" Officer Reinhold is rallying, albeit sluggishly.

"For one thing, I'm useless as far as you're concerned. You know that. So we're really talking about my mother. Second, how do you know she could get your proof? What would you expect her to do?" Hearing Officer Reinhold say this stuff, as though it's something I could actually do and am only being stubborn about, hurts more than I'm willing to let him see. Even worse is the fact that, when I correct him, he doesn't even blink. He was only trying to be politic, and is willing to admit it was a bluff. He probably *would* rather talk to Jadyn, but there's no chance of that happening. Jadyn Irving has refused to have anything to do with the police or the city council for years. Unfortunately, they're almost as stubborn as she is. They took her to court a couple times and lost, hired people to follow her and got sued for it, then started calling her and begging. Finally, just to get rid of them, she agreed to compromise. She's free to ignore any requests, but she must at least hear them once a month, or send someone suitable in her place. So she sends me. She could just as easily send her secretary, but I think she likes sending *me*, specifically. Being useless, I'm a pretty blatant reminder to everyone concerned that there really is no alternative to Jadyn.

Oddly, this part doesn't bother me as much as it should. I'm not allowed to give interviews, because I might say something wrong and accidentally give people something to use against Jadyn. I'm not allowed to go to any social event unless she's there, for the same reason. But, because she can't be bothered to come down to the courthouse, and because they won't give up on her, I'm allowed total freedom—sort of—once a month. Having to listen to a creep like Officer Reinhold is a small price to pay. Especially when I know he's just wasting his time.

"Well…uh…" Officer Reinhold is having trouble refocusing. He stares down at his hands as though he's not sure he recognizes them. He clears his throat. "You know. You could—er, *she* could—just watch his house for an afternoon; he'd never see *her*. There wouldn't be any danger. Heck, she could go in and look for the stuff while he was *home* and he wouldn't know."

"Except it would be illegal," I point out.

"It was just an example," he says irritably. Even though it wasn't. The yogurt jitters a quarter-inch nearer the edge of the table. "I'm just pointing out how easy it would be. All we need is for someone to see something. It would be nothing to her." I shift restlessly, getting ready to say no. "And of course, if there was anything we could do to help her out—"

"I'm sorry." I've cut him off, and I watch his jaw muscles clench. "She won't do it. First of all, Javier is a friend of hers. Second, they asked her to do this *last* month, and she said no then."

A deep flush creeps up his neck. I hope they don't normally assign him to anything gang-related, because Officer Reinhold is terrible with teenagers. "Do you have any idea how *important* this is? This guy could be supplying half of Chicago!"

"It's always important," I tell him. Because of course it is. Just not to Jadyn.

Officer Reinhold slams his hand down on the table. The yogurt jumps; I don't, because this happens a lot. "She *has* to help! It's her civic duty; if she won't help us, she's helping him. *Everyone* knows they're friends. When he gets caught, if she's been... Is that what she wants to be known as, a drug dealer?"

He wishes. Jadyn employs her own publicist. She will never be seen as anything she doesn't want to be. I just watch him, waiting. He can't do anything to me. Peter Maraszek, my bodyguard, stands just outside the plate-glass window that looks onto the hall. Normally he keeps his back to the window, to give the impression that he's not a party to anything that happens inside. When he doesn't want to be seen, he can be almost as invisible as my mother. Right now, though, he's half-turned toward us, watching Officer Reinhold through the glass. I can see the white edge of the mini-notepad, half-hidden in his square hand; Peter sketches the way normal people fidget. I wait, wondering what he's found to draw out there, until Officer Reinhold notices him and realizes who he is. "She can't…" he starts, his voice quivering with the effort to sound reasonable. "It isn't legal not to—"

"It's in the Bill of Rights," I point out. I'm pretty sure it is, anyway. "Jadyn doesn't have to do anything unless you get the federal government to draft her somehow. And even then, you know she'd just disappear." She would. As far as I know, no one has ever managed to get the better of Jadyn. By the time she was nineteen, she'd earned enough money from "private work" to buy her resort, Isole; that's where our money comes from now. She keeps better tabs on the people around her than the CIA ever could, just in case, so she won't be caught off-guard. During the last war, the President herself asked Jadyn to spy for the US. Jadyn could have gotten into any building, learned troop movements, shortened the war, and saved thousands of lives. She refused. As far as my grandparents are concerned, she died then; they haven't spoken to her since.

Officer Reinhold obviously thought he'd be the one to finally talk her around. *It's going to take a lot more than that,* I think, but out loud I say, "Is there anything else you need to ask?"

His jaw tightens. His eyes flicker up to meet mine, then slide away. "Nothing else," he mutters, grudgingly. Then, with a glance at Peter's blunt, deceptively calm profile: "Thank you, very much, for coming. We'll see you again on July nineteenth."

I nod and stand, grabbing the typed summary—which I'm supposed to pass on to Jadyn's secretary, who won't even bother to give it to Jadyn, since it would only be in the garbage five seconds after he did—off the table. Peter opens the door for me, and Officer Reinhold pushes himself to his feet, deciding at the last minute that it's safer to be polite. It isn't. The motion finally sends the yogurt to the floor. He flinches, staring down at the mess as

though he'd like to kill it. I slip away, shielded by Peter's shadow, before the officer looks up.

*　　*　　*

"New guy?" Peter asks as we pass the front desk. He's tapping the notepad significantly against his leg as he walks; he's going to ask for my opinion on whatever he's drawn. I nod. I always try not to talk until we're out of the courthouse, and preferably safe in the BMW. It's pure superstition, like whistling when you walk past a graveyard. When I'm in this building, I am not me, and that's an advantage. In all other places, I am a failure. I don't fit in with any of the groups at my school; I've been kept so close to home that the few things we have in common only highlight the differences. Most people don't know whether to treat me as Jadyn's daughter or ignore me completely, and when they do pay attention it's generally the wrong kind. The courthouse is the only place I ever feel remotely in control of anything, and I'm afraid that, if I talk to Peter about things that matter to me, they'll realize who I really am, and I'll lose this place, too. So I don't talk.

The lady police officer who's generally up on the top floor when I come in stands by the front desk, gossiping with the receptionist, as we walk past. She turns to watch us, and I can feel her eyes on me, prickling my spine. Peter glances over at me, making sure this is normal silence and that nothing's wrong, then deliberately looks away, focusing on the corridor ahead. He's used to me; he's been my bodyguard for almost eleven years. Jadyn hired him right after the war she refused to help with, because she was getting a lot of threatening mail, and some of it was directed at me. He goes everywhere with me: to school, to interviews, on any vacations or field trips, and, of course, to the station. I don't mind all that much; it would be awkward if I had friends that I wanted to hang out with, but I don't. Peter's much better company than most people, anyway; he generally knows what to say and when to say nothing.

I step through the heavy glass doors into the cutting sunlight, and feel myself relax. On the stairs, Peter keeps half a step ahead of me, deactivating the BMW's alarm and unlocking it with the little remote that came with the car keys. He always claims he's a "protection professional," not a bodyguard, insisting that there's a difference. If anyone else said that, I'd consider it incredibly picky, but, really, Peter deserves to be called whatever he wants. I know what he's capable of; I checked the settings on the weight machine once, after he'd gone through his exercise regimen in our home gym, and it was almost scary. I know he's more than a match for anybody who might come at me, but he says it's asking for trouble to walk around an American city with someone who looks like a pro wrestler, and that he'd be useless that way. So he doesn't really look like anything. Even coming out of the courthouse, walking to a car so expensive most people wouldn't dare back it out of their driveway, he looks bland and forgettable. I doubt anyone could even take him for an undercover cop, although he's probably risking being mistaken for my dad.

My real dad isn't here, of course. He and Jadyn divorced when I was one, and I'm not sure whether the few memories I have of him are real or remembered stories from other people. He never comes to see me, and he stopped sending postcards before I turned three. I keep track of him as well as I can; lots of his pictures turn up in *National Geographic,* and that's how I usually know where he's been.

"Natalie." Peter holds the car door open for me, and I duck

inside. The leather armrest is sticky and soft, and the air in the car is so hot it smells as though someone's been running a hairdryer.

Peter slides into the driver's seat, shutting his car door. Somehow, the notepad lands facedown in my lap. I turn it over, and there's an absolutely priceless caricature of Officer Reinhold. The man's beefy face is split down the middle: one half smeared with a sickly grin, the other so twisted with rage it doesn't even look human. It would be a little creepy if Peter hadn't drawn a collar around his neck and chained him to a doghouse labeled "Jail." I bite my lip, trying not to grin. Peter's dream job is to be a penciler for P.I. or Excelsior comics, but I think he should go straight to *The New Yorker*. "Okay, but I think you made him too friendly," I say, because he'd be disappointed if I just told him it was great.

Peter's mouth twists wryly. "I just might have. Nice way to kick off a birthday party, hmm?"

What? My fingers are suddenly as limp as cooked spaghetti. The notebook slides through them, bounces off my knee, and lands on the floor mat. "Oh, geez, Peter … Tell me that's not tonight."

He raises his eyebrows, but doesn't look at me. "Yep. Don't tell me you forgot. Seventeen's a big one." He hesitates. "Offhand, I can't think why. You already drive, and you still can't vote. But it's big."

The small glow of importance from the courthouse is dying, and I can't pull it back. My fingernails press painful dents into my palms. *The party. The stupid party.* "No, I *know* that's today, but she was going to let me have my birthday, at least, wasn't she? Before … the party isn't actually *tonight*, is it? Say no," I beg, as he starts to nod.

He shoots me a sidelong look. "I can say no until we get to the house. After that, it isn't going to matter what I say, because they aren't going to leave you alone for a minute until the party starts. Which it will, tonight, at eight."

Well, of course. This party was Jadyn's idea, not mine. She invited most members of the junior and senior classes at my school, along with every remotely famous person who's close to my age and several who aren't, and sent notices to every major news station. She isn't even going to be here; it is, as she told me when she started to plan it, a very obvious gesture of trust. Or it's supposed to be. From anyone else, it would be. But Jadyn knows I haven't talked to a single journalist in at least five years, if not longer. I have minimal experience with parties like this, since she's never let me go to one without her. To make matters worse, all the people she's invited are professional partygoers, including—and especially—the people from my school. I am positive—and I have been, ever since she started planning this—that I will end up frozen in a corner, or, worse, hiding under a bed in one of the guest bedrooms for the duration of the party. Instant countrywide humiliation, when the invited journalists and news crews report back to their offices. It's a gesture, all right: a slap in the face. I squeeze my eyes shut. The sunlight felt nice until a minute ago, but now it's starting to give me a headache. The quivery, weak feeling I sometimes get at the base of my skull when I'm stressed is going to start any minute. "Couldn't I just skip it?"

"Jadyn would make things pretty unpleasant if you did."

That's one thing that bugs me about Peter: he never really argues. He just states facts, and, somehow, they always happen to be against me. "This party is going to be far from pleasant anyway, and she won't even be here. She's still at Isole." Isole is Jadyn's resort on the other edge of Lake Michigan, less than a hundred miles from Ontario; she spends about a week out there once every couple of months, and she won't be back for two more days.

Peter shrugs. "It would be worth my job."

"Great. This party could kill me, you know that? I could die, and you're worried about your job. What kind of a bodyguard *are* you?"

"One with a comfortable, well-paid position. No one ever died from an overdose of insincerity. You'll live."

If you can call *that* living. I scowl, working my fingernails into the minuscule crack between the armrest and the leather door padding. I *will* salvage something from this. "Fine. If I go, will you let me go to Toronto next week? You can come too."

"Have you asked Jadyn?"

"No." There's a huge photography conference in Toronto next week, and I'm pretty sure my dad will be there. Last I heard, he was living in Peterborough, which is only an hour or so away from Toronto, and I can't see him missing something this big. "But Jadyn wouldn't let me go without a reason, and I don't want her to know I'm trying to trace him."

"Then, no."

If I try to argue with Peter past this point, he'll just stop talking for the rest of the evening, and I don't need that tonight. I give up, glare out my window, and try to tell myself it doesn't matter. It isn't for much longer, and I've got a plan. Next May, I will graduate from high school. Next September, I will be shipped off to Columbia University, and then I'll disappear. I will dye my hair, buy some nice coffee-brown contacts to hide my Irving-trademark eyes, and run away to find my dad. If he won't come to me, I'll go to him. He'll see I'm nothing like Jadyn, and that whatever it was about her that made him crazy and drove him away isn't in me, that it's driven me away, too. He'll let me travel around with him to all the places he photographs, and teach me how to use a camera, and introduce me as just his daughter. Not his daughter, the failure, or his daughter, the only boring person in the family. Just his daughter. And I'll leave Natalie Irving behind forever, packed away in a box in my dorm room at Columbia with the rest of my junk.

c h a p t e r   t w o

I t's a great party, or so I'm constantly being told. The dusky backyard of my house is a sea of satin and chatter and faces like carnival masks. Someone ran a string of white circus lights around the terrace sometime during the afternoon. Reflections glare from the guests' too-bright eyes and make the punch glasses look like they're filled with blood. I keep hearing my name, slipped from person to person under the polite party chatter, but I can never tell who's said it, or what they're talking about. I feel as though everyone is watching me out of the corners of their eyes. My fingers are clamped around my punch glass so tightly they're starting to lose feeling.

"I can't believe it! I'm so glad I was invited; I would've *died* if I hadn't been able to come!" Robyn Scoville stands in front of me, gushing. Her dress is this season's shade of pink, with a puffy, gauzy skirt, and her dark eyes glitter like glass beads. I watch her, numbly, not sure whether to feel amazed or sickened by her acting skills. She's in my chemistry class at school, and on the track team; last year, she organized a school-wide protest to try to get Jadyn drafted. Everyone watched me then, too, and whispered to each other behind my back. My locker was papered with slogan stickers by three o'clock, and my homework binder vanished. Except for the missing homework, it feels a lot like that today.

"I'm glad you could come," I manage. My fingers squeeze the punch glass, reflexively, and a tiny, protesting flicker of pain sparks in my wrist. *Just lie. You can do that. She can't tell, and anyway, it's expected.* But I'm pretty sure she can tell. There's a malicious sheen of laughter in her eyes, like an oil slick on a puddle. "So many people have gone on vacation, I wasn't sure who'd be able to make it."

"Oh, I wouldn't have missed it for anything! Tell your mother I said hi-and-thanks when you see her, 'kay?" She smiles a covergirl smile, showing exactly the right number of even white teeth, and then she's snagged by a couple of her friends and disappears in a swirl of pink. I feel the tense place between my shoulder blades loosen, just a little, but two more girls I don't recognize rush to fill Robyn's place, and my heart sinks.

You shouldn't be afraid of this. Normal people aren't afraid of parties.

I can't convince myself. Anyway, I'm not *that* normal. Everybody knows that.

Just remember, then: for every time you fail and freeze up, you're proving Jadyn right. You think she isn't counting on that? She'll be checking the papers tomorrow, just to make sure this didn't go well. Do not let her win. You're better than that.

The stressed-out trembling at the back of my head is making me a little dizzy. I'm wearing a pale lavender silk dress that Jadyn picked out for me before she left, and I wish I wasn't. It's gorgeous—necessary, considering the number of photographers here—but it's tight where I'd rather it was loose, there's an uncomfortable slit up the back, and it's very hard to walk in. I'd never be able to run in it. I know it's a great dress, and that it makes me look passably decent, but it won't help here. It's much too late for me to make a first impression. There are more than two hundred people here; they all know Jadyn in some way, and they know all about me. Most of them are comparing me to their favorite celebrity, and some of those opinions will be written up in newspapers and magazines for people all over the country to read and snicker at. Across the terrace, a woman gives a high, artificial giggle, and I feel the short hairs on the back of my neck stand up. I want to hide.

In the dusk outside the square of lights, other people mill around: reporters and photographers, a few notable adult guests and their bodyguards. Peter's there too, somewhere. I haven't seen him since we both came out here, and I know I won't be able to spot him, but I let my eyes drift across the shadowy crowd anyway. Just knowing he's out there helps a bit. Peter is the one fragment of normalcy at this party, and, wherever he is, he's probably sketching. There's plenty of material here. If he's drawing, he'll show me what he's done later. *Later,* I tell myself. *Just think about later. All you have to do is hang on until then.* Considering the fact that Peter specializes in caricatures, it's a little like picturing your audience in their underwear to combat stage fright. I let myself pull back into my mind, paying just enough attention to the people around me to avoid saying anything blatantly rude, and I wait.

Time runs the way it sometimes does in dreams, so slowly it's almost moving backward. I'm watching the swarm of people over the shoulder of a woman in a navy-blue sundress when, through a tiny gap between a man with two punch glasses and a brunette woman holding a cigarette, I see someone familiar. Ari Foster, from school. He isn't really a friend of mine, but it doesn't matter; everyone knows Ari. He transferred in from Boston in January. He's an artist, a pretty good one, although not in Peter's league. The only class I have with him is history, but I see him in the halls quite a lot. He's good-looking enough that most of the cheerleaders are after him, even though he doesn't play sports. Better yet, he's smart, one of the kids who can unsettle any teacher in any class in three questions or less. And, best of all, I really don't think Jadyn invited him. Did he gate-crash?

I'm surprised at how much that thought helps. The gap closes, but it opens again a few seconds later, and he's still there. He's wearing a dark jacket, but it's leather, not part of a tuxedo. His hair falls in his eyes, like it always does: no gel. Definitely a good sign. *She can't control everything,* I think. Incredible how much of a difference that makes.

"…isn't it?"

I blink, turning hastily back to the person in front of me. A tall guy, a few years younger than Jadyn; I don't know him. "I think so," I say, noncommittally; he smiles wryly, nods and moves away, so I guess it was an okay answer.

When I look back, my eyes snag on Ari's so suddenly I flinch. He's been watching me for a while, I realize. His eyes are steady and focused, as though he's trying to figure something out. I'm not quite sure what to do; it's disconcerting. Almost no one looks at my eyes this long. *His* eyes are bright and, somehow, deep, and

SARAH NEUFELD

I feel my face flush without knowing why. Is he going to come over? I don't think I'd mind talking to him, and it would give me an excuse to avoid everyone else. Then, just as I think that if one of us doesn't move soon I'm going to go crazy, he... *winks*. Just like in an old Cary Grant movie. Before I can react, someone grabs his arm and tugs him away, toward the corner of the terrace and out of sight around the side of the house.

I feel a little dizzy. No one's ever looked at me like that before, let alone *winked*. He can't really be hitting on me, can he? The crowd has melted into a muttering, faceless blur that doesn't seem to matter all that much anymore. There must be some mistake. Any guy who comes here, no matter how old or young, is interested in some aspect of my mother. Not me. They generally don't even *see* me. But...

It's no good. He's wrecked it. Trying not to think isn't going to work anymore. My eyes keep drifting back to the corner of the house, as though that wink still tugs at them, and finally I can't take it any more. I excuse myself from the girl who's trying to explain why, exactly, I should convince Jadyn to help with a benefit for the animal shelter, and make my way across the terrace to the corner.

The strip of yard on that side of the house is dotted with tall, thin, evergreen topiaries trained into flame-shapes; I've heard the gardening crew complain about how hard it is to steer a riding lawnmower around them, but they're definitely handy for hiding behind. That's evidently what Ari and his friends are doing. There are five guys back there in a tight circle, and I can smell that at least one of them is smoking. Not Ari; I can see him from where I'm standing. That's a relief. I don't think I could date a smoker.

I don't want to go closer, although I should; I won't find out anything for sure if I don't go talk to him, and if someone sees me here it'll look like I'm eavesdropping. But I can't help it. It would be hard enough to talk to Ari alone. Talking to him in front of his friends is so impossible it's ludicrous. So I stay where I am, half-way behind one of the topiaries. I'm not exactly *listening*; I'm just waiting until Ari comes back, so I can talk to him. That's all.

"…perfect. Shoulda seen him," one of the smokers says, punching Ari lightly on the shoulder.

Ari shakes his head, grinning, and mutters something I can't catch.

"Naw, it was great! She totally saw. Give it a couple of days, then call her."

I squeeze my eyes shut, biting my lip hard. *Please let this be what it sounds like…*

"Those eyes are majorly spooky, though." I can't see who's spoken; he's out of sight behind one of the topiaries.

Ari shakes his head; "Spooky is good, man. Seriously. Think how those would show up in a photo; almost like cat's eyes. And, a-*hem*, she probably prefers 'striking.'"

Well, that's something. He really doesn't mind the eyes. I relax a little, flexing my toes to try to relieve the ache in my feet.

One of the smokers coughs. "What are they buying?"

Wait a second. Buying?

"Anything I can get. The ad just said photos."

Photos. Ad. I swallow hard, unable to look away. Maybe I heard wrong. Maybe they changed the subject and I missed it.

The guy closest to Ari snorts. "You mean they'd pay you ten thousand bucks for a picture of the Irving fridge?"

Ari shrugs. "They said they'd take anything. Hope I can get more than that, though."

"How long've you got?"

"A month. If nobody else gets in first."

Someone snickers. "Into *that* house? Doubt it. You'd better move fast, though, and hope the invisible woman doesn't catch you at it. She'd probably make *you* disappear."

I can't take it any more. My chest hurts. The dark yard is bright-edged and sharp; if I don't get away, I'll get cut. I could bleed to death out here. I back away, slowly, feeling the heels of my stilettos snag in the grass.

*   *   *

As far as I'm concerned, there is only one advantage to having a mother who could be anywhere at any time: you learn not to be noticed. It's not so much how quiet you are or how slowly you move. You keep your eyes vague and turned away from people, and move as though you haven't quite decided where you're going. You make yourself so boring that people are forced to overlook you. It's never failed to fool anyone, except for Peter, and it doesn't let me down tonight.

I slip into the house through a side door and cautiously work my way through the main rooms. I'm relieved that the lights are dimmed, so I don't have to deal with the rooms themselves. Jadyn's last decorator was a skinny, flamboyant man who was thrilled to be working for her, and who decided that the entire house should act as a showcase for her personality. Since, on top of that, each room was designed to have its own "mood," I live in the most colorful house in Burr Ridge. The ceilings are white, but the walls are green and gilt and cerulean blue, wine red, and aubergine. Jadyn stands out against them like a fountain pen in a box of magic markers, but no one else can. I feel myself fade every time I walk through those rooms.

Tonight, though, Jadyn isn't here to fill them with personality; they're just hollow, angled pockets of air, jumbled with furniture. I hurry through them as fast as I can, watching the floor. All I want is to get to my room. It's at the end of the third-floor hall, far enough away from any regularly lived-in rooms that it's always quiet. There's a window at the end of the hall, only a few feet from my door, but I'm too high up for anyone on the ground to see. What worries me is the thread of light that gleams under my door. Did I leave that on? If there's someone in there … I can't even finish the thought. I ease the door open very, very slowly. The room is empty.

I don't have enough energy to search more carefully. I dart inside, remembering just in time not to slam the door. Then I lean against it and slide down to sit on the floor. I think I'm going to be sick. I double up, resting my forehead on my knees, and squeeze my eyes shut against the brightness. I need to calm down; there are two hundred people out there, and, sooner or later, they're going to notice I'm gone. Good hosts don't disappear. If I do, the journalists will pick up on it, and Jadyn will know. Even before she gets back, she'll know. I can't let her win, but I can't go out there again, either. I just can't.

You can't do anything. My head feels like it's full of wet, knotted black yarn. Every thought I have dead-ends into another equally depressing one, and my neck hurts. I open my eyes, resting my chin on my folded arms, and stare at the opposite wall, trying to stop thinking entirely. My room has almost no color. It's just white. I specifically asked for that, and, fortunately, the decorator decided I was right. It looks like something off a *Better Homes & Gardens* cover: white walls, beige carpet, maple furniture, wicker accents. It's not my ideal room; I don't care much about it either way. If I had a real, private room, I'd want it to be all earth tones, but that will have to wait until I have real privacy to go with it. No place in this house can be truly private or safe.

When I was younger, I was panicked with the idea that my mother might come into my room while I was sleeping. All the little noises houses make—floors creaking, doors moving ever so slightly, a magazine slipping off a stack—were, to my mind, my mother's doing. She lurked in the hallways, watching me. She made noises when I was putting off my homework, so I'd know I wasn't alone. She didn't trust me. After a while, it didn't even take a noise to make me nervous. I could be totally absorbed in a book or TV show, and all of a sudden this twinge of fear would jerk me out of it and set me staring around the room.

Feeling unable to have secrets makes you positively determined to keep everything you can to yourself, and that leads to interesting habits. The year I turned five, I started hiding anything and everything of mine that I could. Letters, doll clothes, jewelry, report cards, crayons, candy, and interesting rocks. I had stashes all over the house, most of them safely away from my room. There's a wide crack at the top of a window in a room down the hall, just wide enough for a necklace, and a shadowy corner in the back of a games cupboard downstairs in the rec room that no one uses anymore which is perfect for books and trinkets and my marble collection from second grade. I can't go anywhere without automatically noticing hiding places.

Any remotely normal person would have outgrown that habit years ago, but I still use the places, sometimes. I can't even remember all of them anymore. I try to tell myself that I'm still the most normal member of a family that sets the standard for weird, but on nights like tonight I know that's no excuse.

My head hurts. I reach up, gingerly, but my hair is stiff with mousse, and thinking about touching the tacky, sticky stuff makes me feel queasy. I let my hand fall. Photos. Ari wanted *photos*. I don't even want to know what he planned to get pictures of. The tabloids already have a huge file on us, courtesy of my mother. I can't imagine what else they'd need. Pictures of her medicine cabinet? The cereal cupboard? Her underwear drawer? *Well, it's progress. Last year, no one would have been caught dead dating you. Now someone's willing to do it for ten thousand dollars.*

I didn't need this tonight. Worse, since I didn't make a noise when I heard, Ari's probably still planning to ask me out. The safest thing to do would be to go along with him until I found a good time to ditch him, and then do it quietly. Jadyn could do that and like it; I'm pretty sure she's actually done it several times. I couldn't. The next time I see Ari, I'm probably going to throw up.

My feet are throbbing. I shift position, awkwardly kicking the shoes off and shoving them under the bed with my toes. The dress makes an ominous stretching noise. It isn't made for sitting on the floor. I edge away from the door, deciding at the last minute not to stand up, since my window overlooks the backyard and someone might see me. Instead, I half-slide half-crawl across the floor to the other side of the bed. It's too late to go back, even if I had the courage to. Now that the nervous tension has mostly drained away, my body is one big ache, and I seriously doubt I'll be moving any more tonight. I lie down on the carpet. Anyone who finds me there will have to be seriously looking for me.

I shut my eyes, hoping that maybe I'll just fall asleep, but it's no use. Why couldn't Jadyn be the kind of parent who's too busy to remember when their kid's birthday is? If she'd forgotten, I could probably have talked Peter into driving me someplace quiet for dinner, and I might actually have had fun. It isn't fair. The people down on the terrace don't have any reason not to like me. True, they don't have any reason to *like* me, either, but lots of people are rich or famous without having done anything, and they get by just fine. The problem is that the people who don't like Jadyn—and there are a lot of them, because Jadyn isn't the type to bother much about keeping people happy—are too afraid of what she might do to take it out on her. She isn't a safe target. So they take it out on me instead. And some days, when I'm really, really depressed, I think Jadyn keeps things that way on purpose. It's fairly convenient for her.

She's done worse. They say, when I was younger, I did something to injure myself, which is why I can't go invisible the way Jadyn can, but I know better. I haven't told anybody, not even Peter, but I remember. Sometimes I still dream about it.

"Okay, Natalie," my mother says, absently twitching a piece of lint off the sleeve of my pajamas. "Show me."

I giggle at her; I'm in one of those moods. "No, you!"

"Natalie." She raises her eyebrows at me. She gets tired a lot faster than I do. I squeeze my eyes shut, folding my hands pretend-seriously in my lap, and make the funny, loose-feeling muscles at the back of my head pull tight. It's as easy as blinking. I open my eyes, looking for my mother, but of course she's disappeared. Everything's gone except me. I am the only person in this room, in this house, in this city, in a thousand black miles of nothing. But it doesn't bother me. It's my nothing.

Something's changing in the darkness. It draws together around me, curdling, and a weird buzzing hums in my ears. I wince, slipping my

*hands over the muscles at the back of my skull, but someone's fingers
are already there, in the way, and then the buzzing shrieks and splits,
and there's a flash like fireworks in the blackness. In the instant before
the pain hits, I hear my mother's voice, sharp and worried and loud, but
then the shock tears through me, wiping out my hearing. My throat is
suddenly so tight it aches, and I'm scrabbling with my stubby little-kid
fingers, trying to rake the pain away. Large hands grab my wrists, forcing my hands down. I fight, but she catches my shoulders and pulls me
onto her lap, holding me tight and rocking back and forth, just a little
too fast. Her hand cradles the back of my skull. I can feel her heart hammering through the silk of her dressing gown.*

*The pain bleeds away, grudgingly. Through the ringing in my ears, I
can hear myself crying, hiccupy, hysterical gulps; that's why my throat
hurts. "Natalie?" My mother's voice vibrates in her chest. "Natalie,
what did you do?"*

No one can figure out exactly what's wrong with me—mainly
because no one's figured out what makes Jadyn the way she is in
the first place—but whatever happened left the skill stunted or
damaged; the only signs of it now are occasional dizzy spells and
the weird feeling at the back of my head when I'm very tired or
stressed. And, of course, my eyes. If she hadn't done that—hadn't
dislocated whatever it is, broken me—who would I be?

The trembly feeling isn't going away. I put a hand behind my
head, trying to ignore the stickiness, and rub at the place carefully; it twinges alarmingly, and I force myself to stop. It's dangerous. Every doctor I've talked to thinks the places are weak spots in
my skull, and I've been told that if I do the wrong thing I could put
myself into a coma. I'm supposed to take aspirin, and use a hot
pack, and either fall asleep or try to ignore it until it goes away.

But it's impossible to ignore. Medicine will take at least fifteen minutes to work, and I *really* don't want to get up. By now it feels as though my head is going to shake apart. I bite my lip hard, trying to distract myself, but it doesn't hurt enough. Warm, sticky tears slide down my cheeks. On top of everything else, a migraine is far too much. I can't take much more of this... *Stop it*, I tell myself. *You're being stupid. Deal with it.* I slip my hands over the shivery patches, trying to force them to hold still. It works for a second, and then my vision starts to grey. I stop, panicked; it's never done that before. *I have to calm down...*

But why? The tangle of wet black yarn has dried into a solid snarl, and it sucks the fear in, leaving me empty. Why should I worry about potential medical problems, when I've just proved that Jadyn's right, that I *am* incompetent, in front of the entire city of Chicago? It might be better if I *did* send myself into a coma, or worse. At least then I wouldn't have to hear what people said about me over the next few days. I wouldn't see Jadyn come back to find all the bad reviews of the party in the newspapers, or have to deal with Ari or any of the hundreds of social piranhas outside, or try to find a balance between hating Jadyn in private and defending her in public, because, whatever else she is, she's all the family I've got. There's really no good reason not to do this.

Peter would mind.

Of course he'd mind; protecting me is his job. But he can find another job.

If Peter's art gets accepted, you won't know about it.

Like it would matter.

You won't get to see Dad.

I probably wouldn't be able to find him anyway.

The tiny, arguing voice is losing; it doesn't help that it doesn't really want to win. My mind feels fuzzy and vague. I let my fingers creep back to the place, and feel the annoying, exhausting quivering under my fingertips. I know I can stop it. It won't take much...

Jadyn will be mad.

I won't be able to hear her.

I let the muscles pull tight...

...and everything goes black.

chapter three

For a heartbeat, every sound and feeling and idea inside me seems to hang suspended. Then, in a rush, it all crashes down. Panic shrieks through my mind, tearing the few solid thoughts I have left to shreds. I open my mouth but can't manage to draw in enough air to scream; it's a full second before I realize that I'm hearing myself gasp for breath. *If I'm hearing myself,* I think, *it can't be that serious a coma.* My heart hammers so hard it's a wonder I can hear anything else. Maybe I've just scared myself into believing I've done something awful. I lie still, trying to force my breathing to slow, because maybe if I calm down I'll be able to see again.

My heart slows. My ears stop ringing. But the light doesn't come back.

I put my hands up to my face, gently, just to make sure my eyes are open. They are. I still feel a little dizzy, but I'm not sure now whether it's physical vertigo or just confusion. I remember reading somewhere that blind people actually see cloudy white, not black. In this room, anybody should be able to see white. The last shreds of panic turn in on themselves, fading to worry. Things are unnaturally clear. I can feel every individual carpet fiber pressing into my shoulders. I know by the way the air moves that I could touch the ruffle at the bottom of my bedspread by moving my index finger an inch to the left, and that I couldn't touch the ceiling without standing on a ladder. There's a faint, sharp smell to the air, like the aftertaste of cinnamon.

And then I realize, with an unexpected jolt of fear, that there's someone in the hall outside my door. Several someones. Clumsily hushed voices beat against the ceiling like moth's wings.

"You knock!"

"No, *you*."

I'm paralyzed, too confused to know what I'm afraid of, but I remember I came here to get away from the people outside. A hunted feeling squeezes the inside of my chest, and it's hard to breathe.

A soft, hesitant tap on the door. A pause. Then another tap, slightly more confident. "Natalie? Are you up here?" There's a false, hurried edge to the voice that tells me the girl isn't really expecting an answer.

They'll find out I'm here no matter what I do. I've got to figure out a way to turn it to my advantage. Could I pretend I've passed out? It feels as though I might do that anyway.

The door swings open, although I'm not quite sure how I can hear that; it's something about the way it skims over the carpet. I squeeze my useless eyes shut, fighting to ignore the panicky reflex that's screaming at me to move. Someone tiptoes in, scuffing her shoes a little. "Clear," she hisses, and then the others—two? three?—tumble into the room in a rush, almost slamming the door in their hurry to get it closed.

I blink, forgetting about the coma I'm trying fake. Something changed with the noise, but only for a second. It's fading fast, and I can't tell quite what... Wait. Fading. Did I *see* something? But everything is still black...

"Bathroom," I hear, and someone runs to check that door, too. It's near the head of my bed, on the other side. The knob rattles as the girl opens the door, and then I see it again: a faint, misty line tracing the mattress edge above my head, and, far above that, a pale smudge that has to be the ceiling light. The lines are smoky and brittle, but whoever's trespassing in my room has decided it isn't quite so important to keep quiet, and the noise they're making seems to keep the lines steady somehow.

Stealthily, I turn my head. The smudge that's the lamp slides out of view, and the outlines of the window—uncovered, with the curtains bunched at the sides—and my bookshelf, my desk, and the knob on the closet door creep into my line of sight. The corners of the room and the lines along the ceiling are brighter, drawn in chalk instead of smoke, but of course they would be: angles collect sound. I'm *hearing* the room. On impulse, I shut my eyes, and then cover them with my hands. The outlines stay. My heart beats in my throat. I don't understand this at all. Blind people can't see like this. Maybe I really am in a sort of coma, and this is a dream.

One of the girls runs past the end of my bed, her puffy gauze skirt rustling like crumpled newspaper. The movements seem jerky and a little blurred, almost like flip-book animation, and at first I think something's wrong with her. But the footsteps sound normal. Probably it's something to do with the way sound bounces off her. She pulls the curtains shut, then turns back, into the room.

Toward me.

Too late, I realize my hands are still over my eyes. There's no way I can pretend I'm unconscious now. I'd better switch to being hung over or something, and hope someone managed to spike the punch. Gingerly, as though I'm afraid the light's going to hurt my eyes, I lift my hands away from my face.

But she doesn't see me. I don't know how she could miss me; the stupid dress is lavender satin, and everything else in the room is white. Not to mention the fact that I'm in plain sight, and moving. But when you discover there's someone else in a room you thought was empty—especially if you aren't supposed to be in the room in the first place—you tend to jump. Only this girl doesn't. In the next second, she's rustled past the foot of the bed again and is on the other side, out of range.

Well. That proves it. This is a dream. I stand, moving carefully; the dress is too tight to let me bend my knees as easily as I'd like. The trespassers huddle on the other side of the room, near the bathroom door. I make my way slowly around the end of the bed, the carpet cool and weirdly smooth under my bare feet.

"No, not over the seat! Idiot; what good would that do? You stretch it over the bowl, really tight, then put the seat down on top of it. That way she won't see it until it's too late."

Someone snickers. I'm very close to them now, between the group and the bathroom door, and I think I can tell which of them laughed, but I can't see faces well enough to know who they are.

"Nobody keeps plastic wrap in their bathroom," the girl in the puffy skirt says, and that voice I recognize. Robyn. "Did you bring any?"

Nobody did. It isn't exactly standard party equipment. "We could borrow some; I know they've got a kitchen." Another voice I don't know.

Robyn snorts. "Oh, right. Like no one would remember that. Clarie, what kind of soap does she have in there, bar or soft?"

"Soft," says the first girl.

Robyn grins; I can't really see it, but it's easy to hear in her voice. "That's better. There's probably a refill then, too; just pour that over the floor, and kind of spread it around. They won't get that off for years."

Up until now, I've been a little dazed. It's a dream, after all; I'm not supposed to be fully conscious. The halting, smoke-traced motion, just a fraction of a second slower than the voices, is disorienting, and the sharpness of textures and smells is almost overwhelming. But that remark snaps me out of it. It's one thing to pretend to like someone so you can come to a party and maybe get your picture in the paper. It's another thing entirely to break into that someone's room and prank her when you're planning to go back to the party and pretend again, to her face. And, for another thing, I know the woman who cleans this floor of the house. She doesn't know I watch her—she'd never talk to me; she seems afraid of pretty much everyone and, besides, her English isn't terrific—but I know she's in her forties with three kids at home. When she comes here she always looks so tired that I want to make her go sit down with a cup of tea or something. The last thing she needs to deal with is a soap-encrusted tile floor. How *dare* they? If I thought I could get away with it, I'd slap them.

And then I think, why not? They're not only in my room, they're in my dream. I can do anything I want. I stride over to the nearest girl; I don't really care who she is. "I don't know," she's saying. "It seems kinda—" My hand arcs up and back, then swings forward and down, and hits her cheek with a satisfying smack. In the instant it takes, I get the uneasy feeling that something's not right, that, somewhere, I've made a mistake. It isn't until the girl's stumbled back toward the other two, shrieking, that I realize what it is.

My hand stings.

Things don't really hurt in dreams. Even if you know that they should, they don't. I rub at my tingling palm, absently, staring at the shocked huddle of girls. The one I slapped is still shrieking in a gasping, hysterical kind of way. The other two are half-panicked by the noise; Robyn grabs the girl's shoulders and shakes her, trying to get her to stop. "Shut up, shut *up*, *shut up!* Mags, I swear, if you don't stop—"

"She—they—I—somebody *hit* me—"

"She's right," says Clarie, shakily. "I heard it. And she's all red."

I don't understand. This should be impossible. I thought…

Robyn's face tilts up; as far as I can tell, she's staring straight at me, or at where I would be if I were real. "Are you drunk? There's no one here. No one was here when we came in, and the door hasn't opened."

"Didn't you hear that? If there's nobody else here, what *did* that?"

Mags sniffles. I feel vaguely guilty. If I'd known I was actually going to hit somebody, I would've aimed for Robyn.

"Geez!" Robyn says; she takes an irritated step forward, waving her arms around wildly as though she's playing Marco Polo. The motion blurs her arms into flickering wings, the fingers into

pinfeathers. Evidently, she isn't the type to believe in things she can't see. "Define 'empty room' for me, okay? There's nobody—"

I step back, trying to get out of her way, but I'm not fast enough; her arm glances across my shoulder. I flinch back, but I don't have to; she stops as though she's been shot.

Silence.

The other two freeze, staring at her. For five long seconds, none of us move. Then, tensely, Robyn draws a quick, shuddering breath and takes a step back.

It's too quiet. The smoke-lines that trace the room are fading, and when Robyn changes position, it's as though she's blurred into oblivion. I dig my toes into the carpet, to reassure myself it isn't me that's disappearing. The dream is spinning off in all directions, and I can't understand why I'm not dissolving with it. I *should* be. Shouldn't I? Something very weird is going on. The three girls seem to know something I don't. I can still sort of tell where they are, by the small scuffing sounds their high heels make as they back up and the occasional squeak from the floor. This is far, far too scary. I just want them to leave; it was okay before they came. I start toward the wall, making a wide circle around the place I think they are. Once there, I feel my way along the wall and across the door to the doorknob. I hold it tightly, so it won't rattle, and turn it very, very slowly...

Behind me, Robyn clears her throat. "Um... Jadyn?"

I flinch. My fingers slip off the knob; it rattles, and the now-unlatched door bounces off the doorjamb, swinging slowly into the room.

"Ms. Irving?" Robyn whispers.

Why is she saying that? Jadyn's at Isole; everyone knows that. *I'm* not even really here as far as they're concerned... *You're not a ghost. This isn't a dream. They can feel you, but they can't see you. Figure it out.*

They can't see you.

I freeze. I can feel the door in front of me, blocking most of the room; it squeezes the air into a narrow ribbon that curves across my face. Robyn clears her throat again; she seems to be having some trouble talking. "We were just...that is...Clarie had to use the bathroom. Natalie said we could use hers." It's a stupid lie; the guest bathroom is ten feet from the back door. No one would have been allowed farther into the house. "The...um...the soap-thing was just...I mean, it was a joke. It's traditional; it wouldn't have hurt anything. Natalie understands."

No, she doesn't, I think.

"We were going to help her clean it up, anyway," Robyn says, and then she's slipped through the door, following Clarie and Mags. I hear them scuffling down the hall, trying to move as fast as they can without actually running. The sounds fade, and I know they've reached the stairs. In front of my face, the door moves gently, pressing the air toward me. I stare at it, or at the section of blackness where I know it has to be, feeling my mind shrinking away from the place it's supposed to go, dwindling to a distant point of light.

The darkness presses in on me. I can't take it anymore. I have to get out. I *have* to. I push the door shut—the click of the latch sends sparks of white racing along the room's outlines—sit down so I'm leaning against it, and frantically rub at the places at the back of my head. They ache, and for an awful minute or two I think they're permanently stuck that way; they feel as solid as wood. I've *got* to see again. I need light more than I need oxygen. *Please, please, please, please, please...*

With a reluctant shiver, the muscle under my right hand loosens a little. Relief sizzles through me like an electric current, and as it does the muscle gives a bit more. It's my fault they won't unlock; I'm too tense. I put my head down, resting my forehead on my knees, and take a slow, deep breath. Then another. And another.

When it comes, the light is so bright that for a second I almost wish I were blind again. My breath is a hiss of pain, and I clap my hands to my face, shutting out the worst of the glare. Pain or not, when I manage to look again, the white wall is the most beautiful thing I've ever seen.

I rub at my aching eyes. They prickle the way they do when I've just woken up. *Maybe you really were asleep,* I think, but I can't even pretend that's a logical explanation. The curtains are pulled across my window. One hangs a little over the other one, snagged by the velvet. I'm sitting on the floor in a satin evening dress that, I realize with a distant, sick feeling, I *have* managed to rip a seam on.

I squeeze my eyes shut. I can still see the blur of Robyn's face, rigid with apprehension, as she edged out of the room. *"Jadyn? Ms. Irving?"*

Jadyn. Jadyn, who will open the papers and read about my disintegrating birthday party and feel justified in her belief that I shouldn't be let out of the house. Jadyn, who is the reason I haven't talked to my father or grandparents for more than half my life. Jadyn, who's never had any competition, who made sure she never would. What if there *were* somebody else? What would she do? What would everyone *else* do?

I stare down at my feet, tracing the toenails with my index finger. *Careful. You won't be here much longer anyway, remember? What about college? What about Dad? And if Jadyn finds out you're trying* *anything...*But I can't make the questions matter. This is a new universe, and they don't mean anything in it. I can see Robyn's shocked expression, can feel the smack of my palm across her friend's face, along with the sharpness of my senses in the darkness, and, slowly, I feel a smile start to tug at the corners of my lips.

Happy birthday to me.

*   *   *

The minutes melt into one another as I sit, watching daydreams float behind my eyes like gilded bubbles. Then, abruptly, I blink. The room pulls back into focus, and I find myself staring at the curtained window. I fell asleep without noticing. Being invisible must be more tiring than I thought. My head doesn't hurt anymore, although I feel a little shaky, and my eyes sting. And I'm very, very tired. I rub my hands across my face. My fingers are cool against my eyelids, and it wakes me up a little. The hum of voices from the yard rises and falls, filtered through the window glass, fragile and artificial. I lean my head against the door again, trying to pull the daydreams back, but something's changed. They're slow to come, and when they finally do, they're tarnished and cracked. Maybe having competition *would* do something to Jadyn, but the fact that the competition would be *me*... It's been years. I have no experience with this. What made me think I could do anything? Even if I had something concrete to do, I wouldn't know where to start.

Might as well not start at all. You need to practice before you can really plan, and where are you going to do that? Not here.

It's my house.

It's Jadyn's house.

How hard can it be to hide invisibility?

From Jadyn?

Good point. If she finds out about this … I shiver. I don't trust her. Except for that one time, she's never even tried to hurt me, but I see things sometimes, when she doesn't know I'm watching. In her shadow, and the lines of her profile, and the glint in her eyes. It's nothing concrete, nothing I can pin down. It's just enough to let me know that, most of the time, I'm looking at a mask, only seeing what she wants me to see. I don't know who she really is. Maybe no one does.

I *do* know enough about her to know that, if she found out she had competition, she'd go through the roof. If she found out it was me … No. If I'm going to do this, I can't afford to make mistakes. Which pulls me, inexorably, back to the problem of practice.

Where can I go?

Maybe it doesn't matter so much. Maybe all I need is a place to run to *if* I get found out. In which case … *Go to Toronto. Find Dad. Talk to him and get his address or find out how to get hold of him. Then, no matter what happens, you'll have somewhere to go. If things get bad, all you have to do is run to him.*

But if I'm going to do that, I'll have to square Peter. Jadyn might not notice if I disappear for a few days next week if no one mentions it to her, but Peter will. And, as he's said, it could be worth his job. He's paid to protect me, but Jadyn's the one who pays him to do it. If it came right down to it, whose side would he take?

There *has* to be a way to get what I need, but I can't seem to find it, and I'm so absorbed in the problem that I don't hear the footsteps on the stairs. When someone knocks on the other side of the door, just over my head, I jump.

"Natalie?"

It's Peter. His voice, coming just after I've been thinking about him, raises the hair on the back of my neck. But then, he is my bodyguard, and I've been missing from the party for—I check my watch, then check it again, startled. It's only a few minutes until eleven. I haven't even been gone an hour.

Peter knocks again; I push myself to my feet and open the door a few inches. He's standing just outside. He looks odd in his tuxedo. Not uncomfortable or out of place, but *too* comfortable. As though he was made for the clothes, not the other way around. The dark shoulders of his tuxedo look dusty and unreal in the light from the lamp down the hall, and his face is carefully blank. "Are you okay?"

I nod, a little guiltily. For a second, I can't remember why I left the party. "Yeah, I—I couldn't handle it. I thought I was going to blow up or something."

Peter's light brown eyes are steady: not accusing, not upset, just very, very clear. I wish he was easier to read, although I guess having a good poker face is probably part of the job.

"I kept hearing people … talking," I mutter, finally, telling myself that's all the explanation I'm going to give him, no matter how he looks. Or doesn't look.

Peter nods. "Well, they tend to do that at parties." I know that. *He* knows I know that. I roll my eyes. "They're starting to wonder about you. Are you planning to come down, or should I tell them something?"

I wince, squeezing my eyes shut. That's *all* I need; something else to think about. "Ugh. Peter, I can't. Honestly, I can't take it."

"Then what do you want me to tell them?"

I sigh. My head still feels fuzzy and kind of thick. "You could tell them I'm drunk or high or something." Peter's eyes are abruptly too sharp; he raises one eyebrow. "Kidding," I say, a little quicker than I mean to.

The eyebrow returns to its default position. "Good. That's probably not something you want said around reporters." He shrugs, restlessly; it's the first sign he's given that he's not entirely thrilled to be wearing a tuxedo. "I could tell them you've had a long-distance call from someone important and won't be back."

"Who?" He's always better at this kind of thing than I am. His excuses never sound made-up.

"I wasn't planning on saying."

"Well, you should at least have an idea ready, in case you have to say for some reason."

Seriously. Anyone who's been in the Secret Service should know these things. And then, suddenly, I know what to do. I stand there, frozen, my mind racing.

"It could be the President, if you want," Peter says. "Or maybe an interested Hollywood casting director?"

"Oh, Hollywood, please," I say automatically.

"Sure thing," he says, and starts to leave. Then he hesitates and turns back, tugging the mini-notepad out of the inner pocket of his tuxedo jacket. He holds it out to me, through the gap between the door and the wall. I take it. "I needed the practice," he says. "Look 'em over for me? I expect feedback, of course."

I nod, sparing a quick glance for the notepad; he's done about half a dozen drawings. He's several steps down the hall before I look up. "Peter, wait!" He pauses a few yards away, turning just enough that I know he's listening. "I've been thinking," I start slowly, trying to fit the words together in exactly the right way, because I'm still not really sure how this is going to work, "and I still want to go to Toronto. I'm not—" I say, because I can tell he's going to ask—" going to tell Jadyn. I'm seventeen, remember? I shouldn't have to tell her everything, and it's just to Toronto."

Peter just barely manages not to sigh. "Natalie, I can't let you go alone. And I definitely can't take you without telling your mother. People have been put in jail for less."

"I know," I say. "I don't want to get you in trouble. But I want to make a bet. If I win, you let me go to Toronto for a couple of days, and cover for me here. If I get caught—which I won't—I promise I'll take all the blame."

Peter's facing me now, feet planted solidly on the carpet, his back to the hall. "What if you lose?"

"I'll pay for five hundred dollars' worth of art supplies down at Graphix. Either way, I won't ask about Toronto again."

"Ever?"

"Ever."

He quirks a skeptical eyebrow. For a second, he looks like Peter-the-cartoonist again. "What's the bet?"

"You worked Secret Service before you came here, right?"

He nods.

"Where did you work before that?"

He just watches me, wordlessly. I knew he wouldn't answer. He never does.

"Okay, then," I say, as though that's settled everything. "I bet I can find out where you worked before, and I bet I can do it before Jadyn comes home. How's that?"

Peter stares at me incredulously. Then he chuckles. I almost never see him even smile, and it startles me a little, but I know why he's doing it. It's what makes this such a great bet. "You're on," he says. "Start saving your money." I nod; he starts down the hall again, and I slip back into my room.

It really isn't a safe bet, even knowing what I know. Peter had references when he came, of course, and Jadyn ran her own background check on him, but getting into the Secret Service in the first place involves so much screening that nobody really bothered to check beyond that. The only people who'll know where he was before are the people who actually hired him then, Peter himself, the Secret Service…and Aegis, the agency that represents him now.

Aegis's offices cover a good chunk of the fifth floor of one of the Federal Center buildings downtown, in the Loop. I know because Peter and I stopped there a couple of years ago on the way back from one of my sessions at the police station. All I have to do is get inside the building, get into the offices on the right floor, find where they keep the files, unsnap long enough to find the information I need, then get out the same way I got in. Assuming I don't get caught, or locked in, or set off any alarms. As far as practice is concerned, it will be terrific. If I can't do this, I can't afford to risk anything bigger, at least for a while. If I *can* do it, I'll have earned Peter's silence.

I flip the lock on the doorknob, to make doubly sure no one will walk in on me. There's a loose panel in the back of my closet. I think maybe it was meant to be that way, because it fits so neatly with the panels on either side; it doesn't feel broken. It's the one hiding place that's actually in my room, and it's good for small flat things, like letters and postcards and report cards. And, more importantly, photos. I keep all the pictures I can find with my dad's byline here, and the two pictures I've actually got of him.

One of them is a picture I found at the end of a photo essay he shot a few years ago. The other I found behind the dresser in my mom's bedroom when I was six; it was snagged between the molding and the wall, which was probably why she hadn't found it to get rid of it. It's a picture of Jadyn, my dad, and me, maybe a year after they moved to Chicago from Los Angeles. I'm only a few months old, and my dad's carrying me in a Snugli pack. My dad. Not my mom. I've always thought that was significant. I don't look happy—the sun is pretty bright in the photo, and I'm squinting— but my dad's laughing. He's got an arm around Jadyn's shoulders, and she's sort of cuddled into his side, hugging him back. She's so young, only four years older than I am now. She's got a funny little smile on her face: half-flirty, as though she doesn't want anyone who sees the picture to automatically assume she's married, but also a little uncertain. The sun makes her dark hair gleam coldly, but my dad's hair is deep gold, and just wavy enough to trap the light.

I got his hair. It isn't as well-behaved as Jadyn's; it won't really curl and it won't lie flat, and it has a tendency to frizz when it's rainy, but I love it anyway. I wore it long for years because Jadyn said it looked better that way, but when I hit twelve and started to realize that my mother didn't have to have the last say on everything, I cut it all off. I did it myself, at home, with scissors. When I was through, it was only about an inch long.

I think what bothered me most of all was that Jadyn didn't care. Nothing I've ever done has been important enough to upset her. She had Peter take me down to her salon, where they somehow managed to even my hair out and make it fairly presentable, and I've kept it short ever since. It's easier to take care of that way, and if I have to go to a party and I gel it, it stays curly enough that I don't look like a guy. I told myself when I cut it the first time that I was doing it to make Jadyn mad, but I'm not so sure now. Maybe I was thinking of my dad's hair in the picture.

What would have happened if, instead of staying with Jadyn all those years ago, I'd been given to my dad? He looks like a nice guy, the kind of guy who'd like kids and want his daughter with him. I don't know anyone who'd trust Jadyn with their children. But Jadyn is famous and rich, and my dad is a freelance photographer. Things wouldn't have been perfect if I'd grown up with my dad; I know that. But I wouldn't have been a failure. If I'd lived with my dad, I might actually have been part of a family, not just an accessory for Jadyn. It's the *feel* of that photo I miss, more than the people.

When I was little, I used to think about my dad the way other kids think about Santa Claus. Someone distant and kind and a little magical, whom I might get to see someday if I was good enough, and patient, and clever.

Waiting hasn't worked. It's impossible to be "good enough" here. But I can be clever. And if I manage to do just this one thing, I can win: find my dad and beat Jadyn forever, at the same time.

If I don't even try … Well, I'm not suicidal. I *will* try.

c h a p t e r   f o u r

I t's odd how many things that sound perfectly reasonable when you're safe at home
turn out to be crazy once you're actually doing them. Peter had an
appointment with a friend this afternoon, since I wasn't sched-
uled to go anywhere, and he'll be out of the house until 8:00 PM
at least. An hour after he left, I told the first maid I saw that I was
going into Chicago so I could check out the main library's college
guides, and that was that. Nothing easier.

Only now it's 4:30, and I stand with my back against the glass
panels near the door of the Dirksen Federal Building, as far as I
can get from the rest of the Federal Center Plaza without actually
being inside. I wonder whether it's even possible to do this. The
building stretches up for about a mile, a humongous modern-
art sculpture of metal and glass, lines etched painfully sharp by

city noise. It's a bit easier not to think about it when I'm standing under the overhang and can't really look up, but I still don't feel good about this, even though I've been invisible ever since I left the BMW on Monroe Street, a few blocks away.

I need to make a run for it, just grab the first door I see and jump. Once I'm inside, I'll have to finish this, and it'll be okay. But I can't move. *Just take a step. One step. That's all.* I can't. I stare out across the plaza, letting my eyes skim over the blurred, seething swarm of people. The *Flamingo* sculpture rises out of the bustle in a gigantic liquid arc, the only steady thing in the plaza. Normally I like it, but right now the lines look too sharp; it feels ominous, towering over all those people. I don't know why it's called *Flamingo*. It looks more like the Loch Ness monster to me.

If I don't do something soon, I won't get to do anything at all today. The office is only open for another half hour, and I don't dare risk being locked in. My heart thuds in my chest. It's too hot even in the shade, and I'm starting to wonder whether it's possible to die from an adrenaline overdose. Which would be worse, trying and getting caught, or not trying at all? *Come on. Peter's superheroes do stuff like this all the time. It's standard. How hard can it be?* I squeeze my eyes shut, which feels weird since I can still see the lines. Sure. Maybe if I *were* a superhero, instead of just weird, and the building was something Peter had penciled.

When I was younger, Peter used to let me read the really old comics in his collection, the ones most serious collectors keep in airtight plastic bags. Breaking into a building the way I intend to would've been too boring to fit into any of those storylines. I would've had to climb up the outside of the building, at least, and possibly pick a lock or break a window with my bare hands to get inside. Compared to that, getting through a door should be pitifully easy. There is no possible way to make it exciting. That's got to be a good sign, right? I open my eyes, trying to set up a narrative for myself, just to prove how much worse it could be: *Within the looming structure lies the key to our hero's past, present and future. If she is caught, the rest of her life may be measured in seconds, but it's worth nothing if her mission fails. Tensely, she waits for—*

The door swings out sharply, ejecting someone with a briefcase who passes so close to me I can smell his cologne. Before I realize I'm moving, my fingers are clamped around the edge of the door, stopping it from closing all the way. I have to pull it open a little farther to squeeze through, but I don't think the motion is enough to attract attention.

And I'm in.

Inside the building, the lines change abruptly; I slide away to the side, my back pressed against the window glass. My throat tightens with anxiety. I *hate* not being able to see. The traffic on Dearborn Street was so deafening I could almost make out the features on people's faces as they brushed past me. It's still loud in here, but it's a muddled, echoey kind of loud. Too many surfaces, too many noises from too many directions, too much movement. Like being snow-blind. I put my hands over my ears to block some of the sound, and slowly the room fades to grey.

Blank grey.

It's just the lobby that's this loud. Get onto one of the upper floors, and you should be fine.

But to do that, I have to find the stairs.

Well, they won't be in the middle of the room by the front doors. Find a wall first.

The only way I can do that, right now, is to stumble around blind until I run into one, and before I do that, I'm sure to have run into at least twenty people. The edges of my vision flicker as the doors beside me open and shut, and I realize I've planned myself into a corner. If I'd worn normal clothes today, I probably could have unsnapped and walked through the lobby until I found the stairs. But I didn't wear normal clothes. I couldn't afford to, because I don't know exactly how much the invisibility covers. For all I know, the patch of floor I'm standing on turns transparent, and Robyn and her friends were just too dumb to notice last night. I thought tight, dark clothes would be a good idea—tight so they'd be fairly sure to turn invisible when I did, dark in case I ever had to unsnap and hide—but I don't own much black. All I could come up with was a black turtleneck from three years ago with a hole in one shoulder, a pair of leggings from an aerobics class which I quit after the first week, and my ballet slippers from eighth grade. If I unsnap in the lobby of a downtown building dressed like this, they won't just notice me, they'll lock me up. Even Peter's superheroes would be embarrassed to be caught wearing this stuff.

Someone brushes past me, pushing me so far off-balance that I stumble back into somebody else. And neither of them stops. I stand there for a second, one palm on the window brace, trying to get my heart to slow down. Neither of the people I bumped into seems to have noticed anything odd. Which probably means no one else did, either. Which means … *It means you're worrying too much again. Get moving.*

So I do. I walk as carefully as I can, feeling the air around me swirling out of the way of people passing close by. The few times I can't avoid a collision, the other party doesn't seem to notice. Maybe they just don't care. The tiny voice in the back of my head buzzes on, cheerfully: *The hulking edifice seems deserted.* "A trap?"

she wonders, but quickly discards the idea. They never could have guessed she'd infiltrate the very heart of their organization.

I know where the wall is quite a while before I reach it; for one thing, the surface grows brighter the closer I get to it. For another, there are air ducts set into the ceiling, under the first tier of balconies, and the air flows down the surface like a waterfall, pouring onto the granite floor. Then it's just a matter of getting to one of the flickering blurs that the noise turns the doors into, and I've made it into a stairwell.

It's blissfully quiet. I lean against the wall for a second, letting myself breathe. There's someone on the stairs—a woman, I think; I'm learning to tell the sound of high heels from loafers—but she's farther up. I can see the outline of the steps, but no movement on them. Good. *The corridors are swarming with guards, but our hero slips through their ranks like a shadow …*

I decide almost immediately that I like the stairs. For one thing, even the scuffing of my ballet slippers against the stone is enough to let me see the next two or three steps. And, even if I couldn't see, there's a handrail to follow. I pass the woman in high heels at the second floor, and two men when I'm almost at the fourth. None of them seem at all aware of me.

By the time I reach the fifth floor, I'm feeling pretty good. I wish I knew exactly what time it was, and that I didn't have to do all this in reverse in a few minutes, but so far, things are going amazingly well.

Too well.

Don't think that.

The door opens onto a wide balcony that runs around all four sides of the center well. The noise from the lobby echoes hollowly

up through it, but it isn't half as bad as it was on the main floor. I edge around the balcony, sticking close to the wall, and after about ten seconds, I realize I may be in trouble. It's been two years since the last time I was here. *Where is the Aegis suite?* Most of the offices are marked by tasteful plaques by their doors, with the business name etched into them. Elegant, but impossible for me to read.

This is insane. If I'd known it was going to be this hard just finding the office, I never would have come. How am I supposed to find Peter's records if I can't even find the business? I hesitate, telling myself I could try feeling the letter shapes on the plaques to puzzle out the names, but I don't want to. I really don't. Right now, the only reason I'm not turning around and going back to the car is the fact that I'll have to go through that lobby again, and I'm not quite ready to do that so soon. *I mean, really, is this so important?* If I want to go to the conference so badly, I can just sneak out, run away for a week or so. Peter isn't exactly authorized to tie me to a chair. Nobody knows I'm here, and no one else will know if I quit.

Then I realize that I'm staring straight at the word "Aegis" on the wall about two offices down. For a second, I think it must be some kind of divine omen, because there is no way a word that huge could fit on one of those plaques. But it isn't a miracle. The Aegis sign is in the shape of their letterhead: bold, free-standing, round-cornered letters. Probably silver or shiny chrome. I run my fingers lightly over the A, still not quite believing it. Then I turn to the door.

Just as I reach for the handle, the air around me is abruptly sucked toward the door. I jerk my hand back and edge away as the door is tugged inward and a man backs out. He's talking to someone inside the office, laughing, and doesn't seem to be in any hurry to leave. "No, I *did* tell him that," he says, "but you know how much he likes advice; he just…What?" The man leans forward now, bracing the door open with one arm so he can catch whatever's being said.

I drop to my hands and knees and crawl under his arm, veering off to the right as soon as I'm inside the room. As soon as I hear the door shut, I slowly stand up. I'm glad I didn't try opening the door on my own; there's a receptionist only a few yards away from me. I can hear a low, one-way phone conversation and the sound of frighteningly efficient typing. *I'm here. I've done it. From here on, it will be easy. It can't possibly be harder, anyway.* I stay where I am for a minute, trying to get my bearings.

With her pursuers moments behind her, our hero snaps into action, razor-sharp eyes scanning the baffling maze of corridors that confronts her.

Actually, there are only two halls that I can see: one by the receptionist's desk, almost opposite the office door, and one in the wall to my right. Neither one looks particularly promising. Just to keep moving, I start down the hall to my right.

The office is full of voices. The noise is muffled by the carpet and the ceiling tiles, not much louder than a stage whisper, and it only makes things as bright as a nightlight would. But most of the doors along the corridor are open; there's someone in nearly every office, and most of those people are talking. The voices hang in the air like smoke. I move from one band of sound to another, like walking under streetlights at night, and try to make sense of the fragments I hear.

"Not really coffee; it's probably watered-down ink. Totally biodegradable. I doubt there's a health regulation against…"

"I think we can get him for you. You said he's worked for you before? Could you tell me when…"

"They shouldn't be able to sue over that. It wasn't her fault she was drugged."

"Yeah, I know, but they're going to sue anyway. Already hired a lawyer…"

"Don't *believe* she expects me to handle this on top of the regular…"

The hall dead-ends at a closed door that I'm not quite desperate enough to try opening. I backtrack to the last junction and follow the new hall, up and around a corner, until it ends in a wall. The third hall puts me in the lobby again, beside the receptionist's desk. I walk the circuit again, and again, and again. After the fourth time, I've lost track of how long I've been inside; I have to hold my watch up to my ear, to make sure it's still ticking. The adrenaline that's kept me going so far is bleeding away.

Undaunted, our hero presses on, toward…

Despite the incredible power of the mind-bending thought-dispersing illusion machine, she…

Our hero is trapped.

No. Not trapped. Definitely daunted, though; also tired and disgusted. Finally, I lean against the wall in the second hall and just listen. I don't dare sit down—someone might trip over me—but I have to stop. I'm too close to leave now. There has to be something I'm overlooking. I need to think of it, and if I can't think of it, I need to give up. But I *can't* give up. I haven't been through this much stress for nothing. I put my hands up to cover my face, just to feel something normal. I've been invisible for more than twice as long as I was last night, and it worries me. So far, nothing hurts, but I'm not sure how long I'll be able to stay like this. I've got to *think*.

And, of course, I'm standing right down the hall from two

women who are having an animated conversation in that whispery, hissing tone of voice that's impossible not to listen to. I dimly recognize one of the voices as the one that was grumbling about the extra work; she's still at it. "So, I'm just wondering why she gets three weekends off in a row when she's only been here four months."

"Just one of those whiz-kids, I guess. They want to keep her happy."

"They think she'd leave if she weren't happy, huh? What do they think *we'll* do?"

"Stay. Obviously. Were you thinking of leaving?"

"I was thinking of *telling* them I was."

I wish they'd stop. I don't need to know this. What can I do? *What?* Walk by all the rooms again, and listen for one that has more paper-sounds than the others? Sure…

"Well, she's probably pretty valuable. Look at all the stuff she's handling."

"*I'm* handling *for* her, you mean." The crabby woman is holding something bulky which shifts strangely in her arms; she tries to get a better grip on it. "They wanted me to update all these today. *Today.* And I got them at three."

"All those?" The second woman sounds impressed.

"Actually, no. These are the ones I finished," the crabby woman admits, a little mollified. "I can't get them all back tonight, but I wanted to get the finished ones to Records before I left; it's no good leaving things out in the open."

My head snaps toward the woman of its own accord, and I almost stop breathing. *Records! Is she just going, or has she already been?* She starts down the hall, and I push myself away from the wall and follow as fast as I can. *Don't lose her! Don't you dare!* My heart beats so hard it makes the outlines around me skip a little.

The woman stops in front of a door near the end of the second hall. She shifts the files to one arm, awkwardly, and reaches for the door handle. There's a keypad built into it, I realize, just in time. I duck around to her other side and lean close enough that I can catch the pattern. First row, third row, third row, second. If it's set up like a phone keypad, the code is 1-7-8-4. She presses one last button at the bottom of the keypad, and before I can see what it is, she's ducked through the door and shut it in my face.

I lean forward and run my fingers across the keypad, making sure I've seen right. Then I step back, cautiously, watching the door and repeating the code to myself in my head. The woman is inside just long enough for me to start worrying that there might be another exit, then, so abruptly it startles me, she comes out again. She pulls at the door handle, jiggling it to make sure it's locked, then hurries off down the hall.

For safety, I count ten seconds and then reach toward the keypad, but there are too many people in the hall now. Doors close and people shrug into suit coats, twisting the air into eccentric little currents, saying goodbye... and leaving. It's five o'clock. Time to go home. I stand there, frozen, one hand covering the keypad possessively. *I can't be too late! It's not fair.*

The noise drains out of the office. Fewer and fewer doors are closing, and the voices trail away toward the main exit. The hall I'm standing in is now empty. Quickly, I bend over the keypad, tapping numbers 1-7-8-4, and then the last button at the bottom. The handle whirs, then loosens and turns under my fingers. *I'm staying. I've come too far not to. I'll break the glass in the front door if I can't get out any other way.* I shove the door open, stumble in, push it shut behind me, and unsnap. My fingers find the light switch mere seconds after the darkness goes from endless and white-traced to stuffy and closet-like. The lights stutter on, and I rub at my stinging eyes, impatient to look around even before I can see clearly.

This is the place. The room is small, not much bigger than a freight elevator. A computer sits on a desk to my left, clicking softly to itself, and the wall in front of me is lined with filing cabinets—six refrigerator-sized metal boxes. I glance at my watch. *Only a few minutes after five. All I have to do is find the Ms.*

The drawers have letters scribbled on the front in permanent marker, near the handle. *M* is the top drawer of the fourth cabinet, and it's only latched, not locked. Inside, things are more confusing. The files are arranged alphabetically, but it isn't just employee information. There are files on court cases; on other agencies; on cities, states, and countries; and on clients. "Maraszek" should be between "Maran, Victoria" and "Martinique, Juan" ... and it's not.

I flip through the files again, faster. Whatever confidence I had seeps away. *Where else could it be? They couldn't be insane enough to put it under P for "Peter," could they? Maybe it's a computer file, or ... Wait. The woman with the files said she had another stack in her office. Could it be with those?* My fingers fall still, then fumble into action again. I'm almost to the back of the drawer by now, but I'm not really looking at the tabs. *What if the file really is in that woman's office? I didn't see which one was hers, and by now it'll be locked up. Like everything else. Don't panic, don't panic, don't panic. All you've been doing up till now is improvising. It's worked so far. Just don't—*

There! The tab under my thumb says "Maraszek." Someone stuck it back in the wrong place; the tab after it says "Moscow." I can't believe it. My face flushes, hot with relief. My eyes can barely focus on the print. Is anything really worth this kind of stress?

I pull the file out of the drawer and open it on the desk, ignoring the strange little twinge of guilt, and fumble through the stack of paper inside. It's pretty thick; Peter's thirty-four, younger than Jadyn, but apparently that's old in bodyguard-years. He's done a lot of stuff. There's a photo of him clipped to the first page in the file, which seems to be personal stats. I skim it, looking for a list of previous jobs or employers, but there doesn't seem to be one. The rest of the file is a confusing mix of news clippings, official reports, and letters from previous employers. The letters seem like my best chance, and I'm just starting to systematically separate those from the rest when I hear a soft beep from the other side of the door.

Someone's working the keypad.

I freeze. My first thought is, *It's Peter. He's going to see this.* Then I realize it can't possibly be him, and I'm so mad at whoever it is for scaring me that everything goes dark around the edges, and then I realize I don't have time for any of this. I snap back into the darkness, letting the room shred and dissolve around me as I scoop the papers into the folder and try to get it back into the file drawer, but there's no time.

The door opens just as I touch the drawer, and I let the folder fall flat on top of it. It makes a sliding, rustling noise. I back away, as quickly as I dare, flattening myself against the wall by the door, just as someone brushes past me into the room. Two someones. The person in front hesitates just inside the door.

"No one here," she says. Then, "Do you normally leave the lights on in this room?"

"Never," says the second person, another woman. Probably a

manager. "There's enough of a fire danger that we …" She pauses. "Who did that?"

Their voices are loud enough to let me see a fairly sharp outline of her arm, pointing at the open drawer. The first woman—who has to be security of some kind, since she doesn't seem familiar enough with the office to work in it—steps forward and lifts the file off the top of the drawer, touching only the edges. She sets it down on top of the desk, then motions for the manager to come look at it.

"I don't understand," the manager says. "The alarm was triggered right after we locked up, and I kept an eye on the door until I went to let you in. No one came out."

"There's only one door?"

"Well, obviously—"

"To the office."

"Oh. Yes." She lifts the top paper from the file, then hesitates. "You mean they might still be here?"

I glare at the figures, half-heartedly wishing something nasty on both of them—*I almost had it! Just five more seconds …*—but my anger is fading fast. *I almost got caught. I should never have been here to begin with. I've got to get out of here.* There's just enough room behind them for me to squeeze through, to the door, if I'm very, very careful. I hug the wall, holding my breath as I inch along, until I feel space behind me. Then I back into the hall. Almost there …

"Why *this* file, though?" The manager sounds irritated. "Peter hasn't changed employers in years. I think he holds some kind of in-house record."

"Which Peter is that?" Something about the security officer's voice is unsettlingly familiar, but I can't place her.

"Peter Maraszek," the manager says.

"Doesn't he work for the Irvings?"

The room is suddenly so quiet I can hear the hum of the computer. I know that silence. It's the silence you hear when people walk past a graveyard, a silence that makes you want to knock on wood. The kind of silence that seeps through any room my mother walks into. Who could get into and out of a security agency without being seen? In Chicago? *If they suspect her...* I stop breathing.

"I think Jadyn's out of town for the week," the manager says, a little too brightly.

My heart starts beating again, just a little too hard, and I take two more steps back. They won't ask Jadyn about this unless they're pretty sure. Nothing's been taken, so they won't have anything to look for. But Jadyn is very good at picking up on rumors. If someone *anywhere* starts talking about this, she'll notice. *She'll* know it wasn't her. Then she'll start wondering who it was, and if she starts actively trying to find out... My throat is painfully dry. I swallow, hard.

"And anyway," the manager continues, "if she wanted information on Peter, she could just ask him, or call us. She wouldn't have to break in."

I slide away, down the hall, wondering how it's possible for ballet slippers to make any noise at all. They do, though; the soles make little scratching sounds when they snag the carpet, so I try my best to walk on the sides of my feet. The walls dim as I get farther from the voices in the Records room. I feel as though I'm about to fall down a set of stairs. I'm not even sure which way I've gone, or where the main door is. I find a wall and slide my fingers along it as I walk, feeling the tiny plaster bumps scrape my fingertips. *What made me think I could do this? I have got to get out of here.*

"Shouldn't be too hard," the security officer says from down the hall, her voice suddenly louder. "We can check it for fingerprints, although I don't expect to find any. Paper isn't a good surface for that, and anyway, everybody wears gloves these days."

I squeeze my eyes shut. *Oh, geez. No.* Something *else* I forgot. The only gloves I own are a pair of fuzzy ones for winter and a pair of padded ski gloves, neither of which are exactly stealth ware. But I should have tried *something.* Why didn't I think? Being invisible doesn't make me a ghost.

What if they *do* find fingerprints?

The voices fade; they must have turned a corner. They're going back to the main door, probably, or to the manager's office. I've got to get out before they do. I start to jog, forcing myself not to break into a run. My fingers hit a corner, skim over one door, two, six, seven, and then another corner. I can hear their voices ahead of me again, dim and a little echoey; they're around the next corner. *While her would-be jailers scour the building for her, our hero slips silently through the back door.* My internal narrator doesn't help this time. No self-respecting superhero would run, and there is no back entrance, only the door in the lobby.

I feel so disoriented, I've got to see, just for a second. I'll hear if they come any closer. I unsnap. Light floods in, streaming off the white walls and the piercingly bright ceiling... and I'm staring at an entirely unexpected hunter-green, wide-shouldered back.

Over one of those shoulders, someone is staring at me.

The eyes are deep brown and unsettlingly bright, like bird's eyes; very clear and much closer than they should be. For a second I'm paralyzed, unable to breathe, pinned by the sharp spark in those eyes. And then, mercifully, they blink. I let the darkness crash down around me, terrified. The world goes to white-traced black, and I see the owner of the shoulders turn to look behind her. "What is it?"

It's as though I'm hearing her through water. *Lobby*, I think numbly. *The room past them is the lobby. Just a few more steps.* I cross the hall, groping for the other wall, and feel my way along it. The security officer with the bright eyes steps around the manager, missing me by a foot, and walks briskly back toward where I was a few seconds ago. She waves one arm from side to side, sweeping the hall, almost like Robyn did last night. A hysterical little bubble of laughter struggles up through my chest, and I clench my teeth against it. I know her. *I know her.* I see her at the courthouse all the time. Worse, she sees me. Two days ago, she was standing by the front desk when Peter and I came out, and she watched me all the way across the lobby.

Don't think, don't think, just get out!

The manager follows the security officer into the hall, whispering something shaky-sounding about never liking to be the last one out at the end of the day. I duck around the corner into the empty, dimming lobby, and manage to find the door before the lines fade entirely. I can't afford to be careful anymore; I'm already far too close to disaster. I turn the knob as slowly as I can manage, pull the door open enough to let me out, then lean against it a little so the compressor doesn't slam it shut. The moment it's settled into place, I let go of the knob and run for the stairwell. The echoes from my footsteps illuminate the metal treads a second before I hit them, and I run all the way down.

Fortunately, the door at the bottom of the steps is the kind with a crash-bar, and it isn't locked from my side. I push through, dashing across the cavernous granite lobby to the main doors, which also open, from the inside. I squeeze through the nearest one, letting it swing shut behind me, and run across the plaza, heading for Monroe Street.

The street is blessedly noisy. Horns blare, engines growl, someone's radio blasts rap. The lines are as sharp as cut glass, but I feel as though I'm running into a chalk drawing. It's hard to remember that the shapes moving around me are real, and that I could get hurt if I ran into one. I wish I hadn't parked so far away. I can't think. My head is full of office noises and useless files and bright brown eyes. Falcon eyes. *Did she see me? She had to have seen something, she was looking right at me, but did she really see* me? I can't remember anything except her eyes. That's what people usually complain about when they see my mother or me. Maybe it worked both ways this time. If I'm lucky, and she did only see my eyes, she'll probably just think I'm my mother.

But if Jadyn finds out, she'll kill me. If *Peter* finds out... What would he do if he knew? Would he leave?

Our hero sprints through the sun-scorched city streets, all too aware of the mocking laughter splintering the air behind her...

My head hurts.

chapter five

The drive back to the house is terrible. Traffic is the way it always is during rush hour, and the sun explodes off windshields and mirrors like flashbulbs at a premiere. It's much too hot to wear black, but I don't turn on the air conditioning: I'm already shivering. Images from the office whirl through my mind, blurs of sharp white and endless black and words straight out of a nightmare, and my head still hurts.

When I finally get home, I have to force myself to snap into darkness again, since I don't want anyone to see me dressed like this and start wondering. It doesn't exactly hurt, but it feels like a very bad idea. When I'm finally in my room and able to let myself unsnap, between the headache and the heat I feel so sick that I have to sit down on the floor until the room stops jumping around. I rub at my aching temples, wondering whether my head hurts because I spent such a long time invisible, or because I was panicking for so much of it.

I can't take this. I decide, as an experiment, not to believe any of it. I wasn't seen. Things can't possibly be as bad as they seem right now. Everything will look better tomorrow; it has to. I strip off the stupid black clothes and pull on a nightshirt. I haven't eaten anything since lunch, and I should probably go tell someone that I made it home okay, but I don't have the energy. All I really want is to sleep, preferably without dreaming. *Things will be better tomorrow.* I pull the curtains across the window, locking out the sky, and turn off the lights.

As I drag the covers to the foot of my bed, something small and white slides off the comforter to the floor. It takes me a few seconds to recognize Peter's notepad, and when I do I feel another twinge of guilt. I tell myself it's because I forgot to look over his sketches. I pick up the sketchpad and turn on the bedside lamp—which, thankfully, doesn't seem to aggravate my headache quite so much—and pull the sheet back up over my lap.

Peter managed to do six drawings last night before he came looking for me. Four are simple caricatures of people I don't know: he's exaggerated a toothy grin or a squint until the owner of the face probably wouldn't want to claim it. The fifth is a sketch of one of Ari's friends, whom Peter has somehow managed to make look like James Dean and a hopeless wannabe at the same time. The last one is of Robyn, and even in this mood I can tell it's brilliant. In the drawing she's gorgeous and sophisticated, with a thinly disguised gleam of malice in her eyes; she looks almost dangerous. But Peter's penciled her shadow in, off to the side, and it's in the shape of a stumpy preschooler wearing a witch costume, broomstick and all. I start to laugh, but all that comes out is a croaking little chuckle, and even that hurts.

Suddenly, I'm trying not to cry. Why did I go after his file? I could have made another bet with him; he's a decent guy. If I'd told him I really, really wanted to see my dad, he might have helped me figure something out. It isn't Peter I'm trying to take down. I just didn't think. If the file was that hard to get to, it probably wasn't meant to be seen. Confidential. I feel dirty; I might as well have gone through his medical records to see if he had any nasty diseases he wasn't telling me about.

Well, you didn't find anything, and you got to practice. No harm done.

But I don't know that. I didn't see the file, really, but somebody saw *me* and they know whose file it was.

Forget about it. Just go to sleep.

So I sleep. But I can't forget. I have dreams all night about sharp-edged darkness, whispers that glow and fade, and a harpy with bright falcon eyes sweeping down from the sky to catch me, except she can't because I'm only a shadow, and then I'm nothing at all. Late at night—so late it's probably early morning—I think I hear a car outside. I'm not awake enough to get up and check, but when I fall back to sleep, it's changed my dream to something vague and violent and horrifying. The only clear thing in the dream is the receding car, its taillights glowing in the blackness. I know, somehow, that it's my dad's car, and that if I catch it I'll be okay, but I can't move, and he doesn't stop. The car disappears and the darkness closes over my head. The terror in the dream fades to dull, aching sadness, and then nothing.

*   *   *

I wake up at 7:30 the next morning, much too early for a Saturday in June, feeling more tired than I did when I went to bed. The headache, at least, is gone. The clothes I wore yesterday afternoon are lying in a black, twisted heap at the foot of my bed, like some burned-out wreck. With a shiver, I remember the shadow-dream from last night, but refuse to think about it. I kick the clothes under my bed where I don't have to look at them, open my dresser drawer, and grab a pair of shorts and the first T-shirt I touch.

Now that I think about it, I'm sure the woman didn't recognize me. How could she have? It all happened too fast; she probably thought she was hallucinating, and I'm not going to worry about it any more. Today is a whole new day. I am going to pretend that yesterday never happened.

I go to the breakfast room in the back eastern corner of the house, mainly because it's always empty on mornings when Jadyn's gone. I like to give myself a long time between waking up and having to talk to people, even when I haven't had a rough week. Anyway, I love that room; it has a high, white ceiling that catches light, sandstone tiles that are great for bare feet, practically a whole wall of windows to let the sun in, and two palm trees in brass pots. I plan to sit on the floor by the windows to eat breakfast, so I can try to tan and maybe pretend I'm somewhere exotic, on vacation.

Except, when I get to the breakfast room, Jadyn's there. It's impossible, because she isn't due back until this evening, but there she is. My feet falter and I stop, staring. She sits at the table, with a glass of orange juice at her elbow and so many magazines and newspapers spread across the glass top that I wonder if she's writing a research paper. Her dark head is bent over the magazine in front of her, and for a moment I think maybe she doesn't know I'm there, but of course she does. She always does.

"Don't lurk," she says, still scanning the magazine.

I take a few reluctant steps into the room, realizing that the car I heard last night must have been hers. "You're early," I say, because my mind is perfectly blank and it's all I can come up with. *Not fair. I should have had another twelve hours to myself.* As I'm thinking that, she glances up, catching me in her clear, bottomless eyes, and for a second I can't breathe.

"Yes," she says. "Is that a problem?"

"No," I mumble, staring at the floor. So much for my relaxing morning. I start to back away. Jadyn folds the magazine and sets it down, still watching me.

"Why are you here?"

"Just for breakfast. I'll go somewhere else."

"There's food here. Sit down."

I don't want to. I really don't. But leaving requires more courage or a better excuse than I can manage after yesterday, so I stay. There's milk in the mini-fridge and cereal in the cupboard by the door. I pour myself a small bowl so I won't have to stay long, then sit down across from Jadyn. A warm rectangle of sunlight stretches across the floor, stopping just a few inches from my toes, but I can't reach it.

"Apparently it didn't go well," she says.

My heart gives a nervous thump. She can't possibly know about … *No. Innocent until proven guilty. Pretend you're Jadyn.* "What didn't go well?"

"The party."

Oh. Of course. I knew she'd do this. The twinge of annoyance that comes is only a ghost of what I was expecting, and the predictability of the conversation is reassuring. I know how to deal with this, even if I don't like it. "It went okay," I lie.

Jadyn arches one dark eyebrow, rechecking the article in front of her with a little too much dramatic flair for me to believe she needed to. "Strange. This says that you left around ten and never came back."

"Oh. That." I stir the cereal, carefully. I don't want to talk about this. It would be hard even if I were discussing it with Peter. With Jadyn... There are so many ways this could turn ugly. But if it helps me avoid other subjects... "Well, there was this... guy. From school." Somehow the explanation comes out, in ragged bits and pieces. Jadyn watches me the whole time. She isn't usually interested in the reasons behind my mistakes, and I find myself trying to read her; what is she *really* listening for? The light in her eyes is fierce and loose, like sunlight through the surface of the ocean, and it keeps changing. When I first mention it sounded as though Ari might be interested in me, the lights sharpen, intrigued. When I tell her about the conversation I overheard, and about the photos, they flatten and dim. She looks away.

"Typical," she says. She sets the magazine down, and fiddles with the almost-full glass of orange juice, finally deciding to take a sip. "So you left."

I shrug. "What else could I do? I didn't want to start something in front of... everyone."

I'm expecting a lecture on why that would have been the best course of action, but, weirdly, Jadyn is nodding. "That was right. Especially since you had Peter cover for you." *How many articles has she read?* "What are you going to say next time you see the boy?"

"I was planning on never seeing him again," I say, too startled to make up something more Jadyn-friendly. *She thinks I did something right?*

"He goes to your school."

"It's a pretty big school." I really don't want to talk about this.

Jadyn's glass clinks sharply against the tabletop. "Avoiding him isn't an option."

I flinch; I should have nodded when I had the chance. "But he doesn't know I know. He's going to want me to date him—"

"Then do it, if you want, and get rid of him later. Or turn him down. Or tell him flat-out that you know what he's planning and that you won't stand for it. I don't care what you do, but you must not avoid him. Now tell me why."

I stare at her. I have no idea. Fragments of yesterday spin through my mind, and it's getting very hard to concentrate. "I—I'm not good at that. I just want to be left alone."

"If you avoid him because of something he's done," Jadyn continues, as though I haven't said anything, "you're telling him he can control you. Never give control to anyone. Ever. It's much too hard to take back. Do you understand me?" I nod, staring at her chin; her eyes are too harsh now, even for me. "You have nothing to be ashamed of. He does. Let him know you know that, and there won't be a problem."

I shift uncomfortably in my chair, knowing I'll never do it. School is months away, and by then, hopefully, Ari will have forgotten about everything. It shouldn't matter. And it's not like I have any control to give away. I make a noncommittal, vaguely positive-sounding noise, and change the subject. "How's Isole?"

Jadyn recognizes why I've done it. There's a sharp, wry glint in her eyes, and for a second I'm sure she's going to twist the conversation back on me, but she doesn't. "Oh, fabulous." She twitches a newspaper over to her and rattles the pages open. "As always. They're running a little below capacity this season, but that means the facilities aren't crowded. People tend to enjoy themselves more when they think they have some space, and then they tell their friends about it, so we'll probably be at capacity by mid-July."

"What did you do?" I ask, hoping to keep her on a relatively safe subject.

"Reviewed the new staff. Talked to the managers. They had three big dinner parties while I was there, so there were lots of people around all the time. That newsman was there one night—the decent one, Arthur what's-his-face—and the governor's wife. Oh, and Javier made it up on Wednesday."

I have to force myself not to scowl. I told Officer Reinhold that Javier Nadal is my mother's friend, but he definitely isn't a friend of mine. He's quite handsome and even richer than Jadyn—I don't think she'd be seeing him otherwise—but he gives me the creeps. I've never seen him be anything less than polite, and yet it's easy to picture him slipping out of a reception, knifing somebody in the next room, then rejoining the party, wearing that diplomat's smile of his and gloves to hide the bloodstains. Not a problem for Jadyn, of course. It may be one of the reasons she likes him. But Officer Reinhold was right about one thing: Nadal is at the edges of a lot of things, and nobody could possibly be as perfect as he manages to seem. I glance at Jadyn's face as she says his name, hoping to see what she really thinks of him, but her eyes are shuttered, as opaque as I've ever seen them. If she looks up, I know all I'll see is myself.

After breakfast, I walk down to Peter's room, carrying the mini-notepad by the edges so the pencil lines won't smudge. The door is shut, but Peter's always awake by 5 AM, so I knock. Inside, I hear a chair squeak, papers being shuffled, then footsteps across the floor. The door swings open, and Peter's standing there. His hair is sticking up a little around the edges, but his eyes are focused, as though he's trying to read an eye chart on the other side of the house, so I know he's been drawing and that I've interrupted him. "I'm sorry," I say, holding out the notepad. "I didn't mean to keep this so long."

He glances down at the notepad, then smiles and takes it from me. "Good morning. It's fine. Come in."

"I didn't mean to interrupt," I say, even as I follow him into the room. I like Peter's room better than mine. It's smaller, and the walls are a weird green that's probably supposed to be "sage" but looks more like "army," and it feels like a cave on cloudy days. But it only looks that way from the door. The back of the door and the wall it's set in are plastered with Peter's drawings. So are parts of the ceiling and the inside of his closet. Any surface that isn't visible to anyone standing in the hall is, by now, covered in art.

He should probably be more careful. He's always drawn superheroes for fun, but he's been drawing more of them in the past six months, ever since he decided to try to get work at P.I. or Excelsior. Jadyn doesn't mind his drawing as long as it doesn't interfere with his real job, but one drawing of anything remotely resembling a superhero would be enough to get him fired. She's hypersensitive to stuff like that.

"And?" he prompts.

Peter's sat back down in the chair by his drafting table, watching me as though I should know what he's talking about. "Sorry?"

"You brought back my sketchpad. What's wrong with this set?"

"Oh." I have to scramble to find a problem with any of them. "Um. Can I see … ?" He hands the notepad over wordlessly; I flip through it until I find the drawing of Ari's friend. "Yeah, here. This one's pretty good, but his teeth stick out too much."

"It's a caricature. They're supposed to."

"I know, but look." I point at the line, "See how this slants out? If you angled it in, just a little, so it looked less cartoony, I think it would be even funnier." Peter cocks an eyebrow, still examining the drawing. "I mean, I can tell right off that the guy's a hopeless wannabe, but if he looks dumb on top of that, I start to feel sorry for him. If you just make him a poser who should know better, I can't sympathize at all."

Peter nods pensively. "Okay. I can see that. What about the others?"

I turn the pages. "Well, the one of Robyn is absolutely perfect. Seriously, you need to send this to somebody. The others were harder. I didn't know any of them, so ... " I shrug. "Sorry."

Peter leans back in his chair, relaxing ever so slightly. Getting his drawings critiqued is tough on him, although he never says anything about it. "Did Robyn stop by your room on Thursday?"

He's caught me off-guard. "Yeah ... I mean no ... um ... why do you want to know?"

"I saw her come out of the house with Clarissa Bennett and Margaret Fujita around ten. When I went in to find you, you acted a little ... unnerved, and you've been jumpy ever since."

"Have not."

"Your hands were shaking the whole time you held that notepad, Natalie. What's wrong?"

"Nothing! I just ... "

Just what? Just think I might have gotten caught trying to steal your personal information from your office, Peter?

"It ... wasn't such a great birthday," I say, finally.

He watches me silently.

"I mean, it was a good party and everything, it just wasn't my idea of fun. And then Robyn and the others tried to get into my room to prank me, and it got embarrassing. And I just finished talking to Jadyn. Why is she back early?"

Peter's eyes are sympathetic. "I don't know. I haven't seen her yet this morning, and no one's mentioned anything. Maybe she felt guilty about missing your birthday."

I snort. I can't help it. "Yeah, right."

"Why wouldn't she?"

"Peter, she doesn't like me. I'm useless to her, so she doesn't have to like me." He knows this. He's seen her in action.

Peter starts to say something, then hesitates. He's quiet for so long that I've almost decided to change the subject when he finally starts again. "Your mom...is very good at controlling people, but people who are wired the way she is...most of them aren't good at discussing what they think or feel. They see it as a compromise, and they don't trust people enough for that. It's the one thing they can't afford."

"Are you saying my mother secretly loves me and would do anything for me, even though anyone on the street could tell you she doesn't?" I'm being sarcastic, and a tiny part of me feels guilty about sassing Peter, but I'm not in the mood for this.

Peter's lips twitch a little at the corners. "I'm saying that you probably shouldn't assume you know what she's thinking about anything. She doesn't trust anyone enough to be that transparent."

I shrug. "Maybe if she were trustworthy herself... Anyway, she doesn't seem to have a problem showing Nadal how she feels about him."

Peter's eyebrows go up. "Was he at Isole?"

I nod, fidgeting with the edge of the notepad, rubbing it between my thumb and forefinger. "I wish she'd get rid of him. I know she can't date just anybody, but why can't she find someone who's scared-and-in-awe of her instead? He gives me the creeps. And his name came up during the briefing on Thursday, too. They think he's got drugs up at his house."

Peter makes a little disgusted noise in the back of his throat. "I wouldn't be surprised. But even if he does, they'll never prove it." He notices what I'm doing to the notepad and reaches for it. I hand it to him, a little sheepishly. "And anyway, if your mother ever decides that being with him is not to her advantage, she'll dump him."

I nod, although that isn't as reassuring as it should be. Things that are to Jadyn's advantage aren't necessarily good for anyone else.

"Oh…Peter?" He's looking down, tapping the notepad against the heel of his palm, but he glances up at that. I clear my throat. "I—um—I owe you five hundred bucks."

He's forgotten. I can see in his eyes that he doesn't know what I'm talking about. Then the confusion shifts to recognition, then to something that, on anyone else's face, would have signaled an *I told you so*. But that's another thing I've never heard him say. "Oh, the bet. Forget about it. I knew you'd never find out when I took it, so it wasn't—"

I shake my head, emphatically. "No, no, I want to." It might help me stop feeling guilty. "You're not supposed to let people off when they lose bets; how else are they going to learn? It's not like I can't pay up or anything."

Peter watches me for a few seconds to make sure I'm serious.

Then he nods. "If that's what you want. You do realize this means you aren't going to—"

I cut him off before he can finish. "I know. I knew that." I don't want to think about Toronto anymore.

"Well. Just so you know." Abruptly, Peter stands up. "I've got something to show you, by the way. I started it yesterday evening, but since you weren't around…"

He turns, snags a slim sheaf of papers off his drafting table and holds it out to me. I take it, uncertainly. "What is it?"

Peter doesn't answer. I glance up, realize I'm supposed to guess, and look back at the papers. The top page is set up in panels, like a comic book. There are no words, only pictures: a city at night, a lone, worried-looking man pacing under a streetlight, an ominous shadow blocking half of the next panel, and then…a very familiar, caped figure.

I frown; Peter doesn't usually copy other peoples' characters. "Isn't this Domino Rey?" Peter nods; I can't read his face. "But he's Excelsior's."

"Yeah. They prefer I use their characters."

"For…Wait a second." I check the papers again: nine paneled pages and three cover mock-ups. I glance up, eyes wide, and this time I recognize the tension behind his eyes. "Peter. Is this what I think it is?"

"It is if you think they're samples. I'm sending them to Excelsior today or tomorrow. If I'm good enough, they'll call me."

I flip through the pages, critically. I don't think it's the best stuff he's ever done, but then, I'm not partial to superheroes. I think his caricatures are better. At least these aren't all action drawings; the last mini-story is set in a restaurant kitchen, apparently a conversation between a busy short-order cook and her boyfriend. "If they don't hire you, they're crazy," I say. Then, very carefully not looking at him, I ask, "Are you going to have to move if they do?"

"No," he says, and I relax. "They'd mail assignments to me, and I'd complete them and mail them back. Distance doesn't matter much anymore, although postage might get to be a headache." He's fidgeting, tapping his thumb and fingers together restlessly. It's funny what scares some people. Peter wears a gun on the job sometimes, which would make me too shaky to move, and he doesn't seem to care about that, but sending out cartoon sketches…

"They'd better pay you enough to cover *postage*," I say, handing the test back to him. "Have you sent in any of your own characters?"

Peter grimaces. "Not yet, no. That's not a good idea right off." He starts to bend the sheaf of paper, then realizes what he's doing and hastily puts it back on the drafting table. "Excelsior has close to four thousand characters licensed to them already. Four thousand! Can you imagine trying to come up with new superpowers for that many characters? I don't know how anybody does it."

Peter's looking a little dazed, even a bit intimidated, and I decide he needs to stop thinking so hard about this. Just the fact that he's *able* to take things like X-ray vision seriously…

"I bet it's easier when you're actually working at the company," I tell him, even though he knows so much about comic books and the business of making them that he could probably teach a yearlong graduate course in it, and I could be completely wrong. "And, you know, it's mostly just combinations or variations of a few basic superpowers, like flight and telepathy and such. Besides, is it even possible to write *exactly* the same character as someone else? Everyone's brain is different."

"Especially mine, huh?"

That wasn't what I was expecting. I scowl at him, pretending to be annoyed, but the fact that he's being sarcastic is a good sign. "I didn't say that, and you know—"

The intercom by the door beeps, interrupting me. Peter strolls across the room, pointedly ignoring me, and presses the button. "Maraszek. What do you need?"

I can't hear the voice on the other end; it's too scratchy and distant. Then Peter says, "The courthouse? Are you sure?" Scratchy, garbled noise. "She was just there two days ago, I don't see—" He breaks off, listening. Then he looks back at me. "Were you expecting a call from the courthouse today?"

I stare at him. The room is suddenly very, very quiet.

"Natalie?"

No. This is not happening. I don't move, and Peter turns back to the intercom. "She wasn't expecting a call."

"Wait, Peter—" my voice is a croak, but I can't make it louder. "Who is it?"

He shoots me an I-know-you're-brighter-than-this look. "The courthouse."

"I mean, who exactly is making the call?"

He relays the question to whoever's on the other end of the intercom, then waits. "She won't say," he says, finally.

She. Abruptly, things snap into focus. I have to get to a phone. But Jadyn's home, and if she should happen to pick up an extension…

The hiss of intercom static, Peter's bland telephone voice, and the floorboards creaking under me as I step around him are abnormally clear, almost as though I've let myself go invisible. With a flash of panic I glance down at my hand, but it's still solid, still there. "Natalie?" Peter watches me, eyebrows drawn together in something that isn't quite worry, not yet, his hand over the intercom speaker.

"Tell her not to hang up," says someone who sounds quite a bit like me and seems to be using my throat. "I'll get the call in my room."

"You don't have to," Peter says, or maybe he's said something else. Either way, I'm not listening. I have to get to my room.

I walk for what feels like forever. I don't even recognize some of the rooms I hurry through, and I'm starting to think I may be lost when I realize I'm standing just outside my door. After locking the door behind me, I pick up my extension. "I've got it," I say in that voice that can't be mine, and there's a subdued click somewhere along the line.

"Natalie Irving?"

"Yes," I say, warily. Is it her? I can't remember what the woman's voice sounded like. Just those eyes…

"Officer Carmichael," the woman says. "Do you remember me? I don't think we've spoken more than once, but…"

"I'm sorry, I don't," I say. Maybe it'll be okay. It's just her word against mine, after all. Maybe I can convince her that she was seeing things. If I'm lucky. Even I don't think that's likely. My heart feels like it's stuck in my throat; it's making it hard to talk.

"It doesn't really matter," the woman says, briskly. "I was calling to make sure you remembered about our meeting today."

"Meeting?"

"You agreed we'd meet at The Pastiche down by the courthouse today at 1:30. I'm on my lunch break then, so we'll have time to talk."

"When did I agree to this?"

"Last night, when you ran into me downtown. Don't tell me you don't remember."

I don't say anything.

"I did see you, you know," Officer Carmichael says.

"Not possible," I tell her, firmly. "I wasn't downtown yesterday. Maybe you were hallucinating."

"That's strange. There are really only two people who could have been where I saw you, when I saw you there, and I believe your mother was out of town."

"You've got no proof," I manage, realizing a second later that it was probably the dumbest thing I could have said. If she wasn't sure I was hiding something before, she is now. My heart is beating much too fast.

"No, I don't," she says agreeably. This is unreal. She sounds like someone's grandmother. "And you're right. I have no legal right to accuse you of anything until I'm sure your mother was out of town at the time. If you'll just put her on the phone—"

"No!"

Silence.

That's it. I'm cornered. She'll get what she wants either way, and she knows it. "What do you want?" I ask.

"Just to talk. That's all." There's a brisk, satisfied note running under her words that sets my teeth on edge. "So, I'll see you down The Pastiche at 1:30. I suppose you'll have to bring your bodyguard, but it would probably be best if he wasn't in a position to overhear anything." And she hangs up.

I sit on the bed with the phone in my hand for almost a minute before I realize there's no point in holding it anymore. The sky outside my window is a fierce blue, and the white walls shine like the inside of a cloud. I could just wait here and hope it all goes away.

But if I listen really hard, I can almost hear Peter's voice, still echoing somewhere in the angles of the house: *You probably shouldn't assume you know what she's thinking about anything.* Jadyn is downstairs, right now, somewhere below me. Waiting. Everything around me feels strangely shaky, as though it's just a reflection of the real thing. Any motion, any loud sound, could shatter it into a million pieces. Whatever this woman wants, I'll have to do it. *Anything* is better than having Jadyn find out about me.

c h a p t e r   s i x

I stare out the window of the BMW all the way to the Loop, letting the streets and high-rises blur into one long, bright smudge. So far Peter hasn't asked me any questions, but he keeps sneaking much-too-casual glances at me. I'm pretty sure this is how he used to size up potential assassins when he did crowd-work, and I'm scared of the things he might be able to see in my face. So I don't look at him. And, for the length of the drive, neither of us says anything.

Peter leaves the BMW at the courthouse because it's the closest place to The Pastiche with any decent parking, and we walk the rest of the way. It doesn't feel real, and I think that if I keep thinking that, maybe I'll wake up. But I don't. When I can see the cafe sign a few doors down, I realize I don't dare let Peter sit close enough to overhear, which means I have to say something now. "Peter?"

He's silent; it takes me a minute to realize that he's heard and is only waiting for me to finish.

"I—I'd like to talk to…this woman…privately. I mean, she'd rather I did."

Peter nods. As long as he's able to see me, he's doing his job. I feel my heart drop a couple of inches lower in my chest; I was almost hoping he'd argue. I have no idea what to expect from this woman, and I'd much rather Peter was standing right behind me, ready to shut her up and get me out of there at the first sign of anything threatening. But I don't think this is the kind of thing Peter can help with. Being nervous makes me cranky, and when Peter looks over at me, I snap at him before he can say anything. "What?"

He holds a hand up, placatingly. "I just want to know if that's what *you* want. She may want to talk privately, but seventeen is still a minor, and she can't legally make you do anything. If you want it this way, fine, but don't let her push you around."

Too late. "I want it this way," I say, flatly. Peter holds The Pastiche's front door for me, then follows me in.

I've seen this place before, but I've never been inside. It's one of those dark hole-in-the-wall diners that someone's tried desperately to clean up and make appealing, and from the outside the result is a little sad. So the inside surprises me. The floor is some kind of black stone, so polished that I can see my reflection in it, and the walls are half-covered in mirrors of every shape and size. The front windows are amazingly bright, considering the surrounding skyscrapers; the light gleams dustily off the mirrors.

I look around, warily, hoping to spot Officer Carmichael before she sees me. There are several little tables—round and square and triangular, glass mosaic and varnished maple and wrought iron—

placed around the floor, most of them taken, and a sterile-looking glass-and-chrome deli counter at the back of the room. The unifying theme seems to be that there isn't one.

Officer Carmichael is already watching me. When my eyes snag on hers my heart gives a panicked lurch, as though I've seen a spider or a cobra instead of a person. She's sitting at a tile-topped table against the left wall, with a mug of something at her elbow and a sandwich she doesn't seem to have touched on a plate in front of her. My stomach clenches—with anger or nausea, I'm not sure which—but my face is the one thing I still have control over, and I refuse to look scared. I start across the room toward her, fighting the urge to watch my reflection in the floor instead. Peter follows me, and at first I'm afraid he's forgotten I asked for privacy, and that I'll have to tell him again, in front of her. But he only goes as far as the table, makes eye contact with Officer Carmichael, nods, and retreats to a table on the other side of the room.

I'm left staring down at the woman. She isn't what I expected. I thought she'd look like the Devil incarnate, but she doesn't seem intimidating at all. She's older than I remember, nearing sixty, and a bit dumpy. Her hair is permed and frizzy and an improbable rusty color, and her face—incredibly—seems honest. Her eyes are the ones I remember, but somehow, in the context of that face, they seem less threatening.

She smiles, a little too broadly. It makes her look...hungry, somehow. "Glad you could make it. Sit down."

I sit, because I can't think of anything better to do.

"Order something, if you like," she says, tapping the mug's handle with a close-clipped fingernail. "They've got some good teas here."

"No. Thank you," I manage. I don't want to be here. Now that I

realize I have no idea what to expect from her, I feel like I'm shaking apart inside. "What exactly do you want?"

Officer Carmichael lifts the mug to her lips. "I should think you'd know that already."

"Maybe. I'd rather hear it from you." I don't know how to handle blackmailers. I read somewhere that the best thing to do is to tell them to talk all they want and get lost, but that can't be right, can it? I let my eyes flicker across the patches of mirror behind our table: fragments of wall, iron chairs, black floor. It's as though someone's shattered the room. I can see Peter in one of the shards, watching us out of the corner of his eye. *Can he read lips?*

Officer Carmichael's hands encircle the mug and she rests her old, slightly saggy elbows on the table. "Familiar stuff," she says. "You know we've been having problems with drug runners here for years. We've asked your mother for help, and she's refused—repeatedly. I thought you could help us instead."

"What if I don't?" I ask automatically, even as I think, *Wait. She isn't going to ask for money? If she's saying what I think she is ... No. There has to be a catch. This can't be real.*

Officer Carmichael shrugs. "There are quite a few people who would be interested to know you've turned out like your mother after all. I assume there's a reason you haven't informed them on your own. And I'm willing to respect that, as long as you help me."

This is insane. Even if she's serious, I can't trust her. Although, if I could ... then maybe ... "Um, I'm sorry, but I don't think that'll work. If I start helping you, people are definitely going to know something's going on. They'll ask questions, and Jadyn will deny all involvement and make sure they believe her, and then they'll start looking for the next most likely person. And that's me. The minute I start doing anything out in the open, it's over."

"If you were as worried about that as you claim to be, you

wouldn't have been in the Aegis offices last night." I flush. "But you're wrong. As long as you help me, I promise your cover will not be blown."

"How, exactly? What is it you want me to do?" If this is for real, what she's offering me is a chance to practice, doing official things under official protection. Whether she knows it or not, it's precisely what I need: government-sponsored anti-Jadyn training. But I can't let her see that.

The silence stretches long enough to make me nervous. Officer Carmichael gazes down into her mug of tea for almost a minute before she answers, and then it isn't really an answer at all. "Do you know how your mother was first found to be … er … 'special'?"

"Sort of. She never talks about it, but—I mean, everybody knows that, right? There was some kind of an operation … "

"Right. Emergency surgery when she was eleven to try to head off a brain aneurysm. The tabloids started saying odd things two weeks or so after her surgery, but no one paid much attention until a national news network discovered the tabloids were telling the truth for once. Then everything went from there." Officer Carmichael hesitates. "There are some who think the operation had nothing to do with anything, that it was just a well-timed coincidence. Her eyes were always the way they are now. It's possible that her talent is the product of some kind of genetic anomaly, and, incidentally, the fact that you've inherited it seems to back up that line of thinking. Still, it was very good timing, and most people think the surgery somehow triggered something."

And how does this relate to your blackmailing me? "Is this important?"

She watches me, intently; for a second, I catch a glimpse of the falcon's eyes. "I don't think you know just how badly people want to understand Jadyn Irving. All that power, all that potential, and she does nothing with it. Or rather, nothing we can see. Do you know how much people would give to have her solidly on a side—on *any* side? The fact that she isn't helping us makes a lot of people sure she's working for someone else, and they're afraid. They want something just as powerful, someone to counteract her in case she decides to go renegade." She's trying to tell me something, but I don't understand what.

She leans forward a little, lowering her voice. "For the last twenty years, people have been trying to replicate the circumstances that led to Jadyn's ability. The same surgeon, when they can, the same anesthetic, the same tools, the same building, the same number of assistants... they even prefer that their volunteers come from families with a history of aneurysms."

I stare at her; the harsh glint in her eyes has softened into something I don't understand. "You mean they—they've been doing brain surgery on people who don't need it for twenty years... because my mother won't help you?" This is unreal. Does Jadyn know about this?

Officer Carmichael shrugs. "They might have done it even if she had helped. People are greedy, and she's proved it can happen once. But there's never been a success. In the earliest experiments, several of the volunteers died. There hasn't been a death in the last five years, but almost a third of the volunteers end up brain-damaged. Even the ones who recover completely are failures, still only human."

I swallow hard. No one's ever told me about any of this, but Jadyn *has* to know. Somehow, she hears everything ever said about her. She couldn't possibly have missed this. The deaths and damaged minds... those are her fault, indirectly. How could she let them do it? Does she think it's funny to watch them try? An image of Jadyn flashes behind my eyes, all practiced manners and cold eyes. She just might.

The woman gives a small, tight smile. "But, you know, things could always change. They keep trying. The latest volunteer is a twenty-four-year-old woman named Monica; her operation took place a couple of months ago, and she's perfectly healthy. Granted, she hasn't yet shown any signs of becoming exceptional, but no one knows exactly how long it took Jadyn's abilities to surface. A couple of months could be just what she needs."

Finally, I see what she's getting at. It *could* work. Maybe. But there are too many people involved. It's risky. "The doctors would know, though. The people who did the operation, and the ones who set it up, and—"

She's shaking her head impatiently. "It doesn't matter. That's not what we need her for. We can't even fool all the people in the police department. Monica will give us something to show the media; once they get hold of it, they'll take care of the rest of the city. We'll work it so that no one at the station ever sees you—shouldn't be hard to hide someone invisible—and we can tell anyone who's close enough to know Monica isn't the real thing, that we've managed to get Jadyn to work for us."

"There's no way you'll make anyone believe that."

Officer Carmichael's eyebrows go up in something that looks very much like sarcasm. "Oh, I don't know. It's incredible what can be done if people really put their minds to it. Let's say we've found something to blackmail Jadyn with. That way, it will be embarrassing enough to the force that no one will call her and congratulate her on coming on board, or, alternately, feel the need to brag to the press about her conversion. Monica will make appearances, give interviews, be your public face; Jadyn will be the force's internal explanation, and you'll do the actual work. Invisibly, of course. Does it really matter who people think it is, as long as no one thinks it's you?"

I guess it doesn't. There's something about the whole situation that feels wrong, but I can't find a hole in her plan. And if it works...I couldn't ask for a better opportunity. In any case, I don't have much of a choice right now. My best option is to pretend I've still got some control over the situation and hope it fools her, at least until I know more.

I shrug, trying to look as though I couldn't care less. "Fine. I'll help this once and see what happens. If anything goes wrong, though, all bets are off. And if anyone—*anyone*—finds out about me—" I catch the woman's eye and hold it, even though the obsidian sharpness in them makes me want to put a lot more than a table between us— "I'll disappear. Permanently. And I will find a way to take you with me."

Officer Carmichael nods, as though she thinks that's a perfectly reasonable bargain. Or maybe she knows I'm bluffing. "Fair enough." She fishes something small and silver out of her pocket and slides it across the table to me; I put my hands up to catch it, reflexively. It's a tiny cell phone. "I'm going to need you tonight," the woman says matter-of-factly, even as I think, *Tonight?* "I'll call you on that with specifics later. It isn't bugged, and your mother won't be able to eavesdrop on an extension." How did she know I was afraid of that? "Just do yourself a favor and don't leave it lying around."

I slip the cell phone into my pocket; my fingers feel stiff. I'm tenser than I thought I was. "Is that all?" She nods. I stand up, and, out of the corner of my eye, I see someone across the room mirror the motion. I turn, feeling my heart kick into high gear. *Oh. It's Peter.* Only Peter. Nothing to worry about, but the flash of paranoia is alarming. Last week, that was something I only felt at home.

Officer Carmichael stands, wrapping her still-untouched sandwich in a paper napkin, and nods to me. "Always nice to see you, dear," she says kindly, as though she were only my grandmother and I'd come down to keep her company. *Dear.* Who does she think she is? I glare at her, but she's already turned her back and doesn't see. When I finally look away, Peter's waiting for me near the door.

"Everything okay?" Peter asks, once we're in the car again.

I nod.

"They missed something on Thursday, then?"

"Sort of."

The wheels hum against the pavement; I can feel the vibration in my bones. The cell phone is an uncomfortable lump in my pocket.

"Am I going to have to figure out how to get you somewhere, or did you say no?"

Normally, I would have explained the situation to Peter as soon as I knew anything at all about it, and it isn't an easy habit to break. Especially not now, when I'm distracted. I can't make his question make sense. "Of course not. I mean, I said no. I don't know why she couldn't talk about it over the phone. It's just annoying."

Silence again.

I come in through the front door, since I'm pretty sure there won't be anyone watching it at this time of day. The entryway is cool and dark after the bright car ride, and the glassy green marble floor reminds me of a Japanese koi pond. The bright purple afterimages, residue from the sunlight outside, seem to dart through the greenness under my feet, so that for one dizzy moment I think it might really *be* a pond. I sit down on the stairs and squeeze my eyes shut, resting my head in my hands.

I'm going to need you tonight.

Am I going to have this figured out by tonight?

Footsteps click on marble at the other end of the front hall, coming toward me. *High heels,* I think, and I know exactly what the noise would make the front hall look like if I were invisible, but I forget that the shoes are most likely attached to a person.

"Natalie?"

It's Jadyn, followed by a well-groomed, overeager blond woman I don't recognize. I scramble to my feet, then hate myself for it. If the woman didn't know how awkward I was before, she will now. "I'm sorry…" I say automatically, then shut my mouth. The little voice in my head sniggers; *How many times do you have to apologize for being inadequate before they forgive you?* Jadyn is standing a couple feet behind the journalist; she seems to be watching the marble step under my sandals, and it's hard not to look down. Does she think not looking at me will help, or something?

The woman was clearly on her way out; she's shuffling papers into a chic attaché case. I can't stay; I'd rather walk away, but Jadyn is still here, obviously still in control of the floor. Which move would be the wrong one? I take one more cautious step up the stairs, but just then the woman looks up at me, beaming. "Natalie! I'm glad you're back; I didn't think I'd get to talk to you this time."

A journalist. I smile but my face feels stiff. *Too late to get away…* I've never managed to hold a coherent conversation while Jadyn's watching… But that was before. Maybe the invisibility's changed that, too. I shoot another wary glance at Jadyn, but she's gazing absently down the hall. She seems to be waiting for something.

"So," the journalist says, "seventeen, huh? What's that like? Do you feel older?"

Yes. A million years older. "Um, not really. It's only been a couple of days." That doesn't sound right. I should've just said yes; this way, I haven't left her any openings. I let my eyes flicker back to Jadyn, and feel my stomach tighten. Her eyes are focused on me now.

"Well, give it a few weeks," the journalist says, oblivious to the nightmare just behind her left shoulder. "Things really start to happen at this age. I think you'll like it."

Now, Natalie. Here's my chance to start a real conversation, tell her what I'm looking forward to, prove I've gotten better. But I can't. There's nothing to say. My mind is blank, and I couldn't open my mouth to save my life. *Come on, you're losing it! Please!* My throat constricts. The silence stretches out so long that the journalist starts to fidget a little. I can't stand it. I shut my eyes, and the next thing I hear is Jadyn's voice, as smooth and controlled as though it's been her conversation the entire time, saying to the woman, "When did you say you needed to be at Lincoln Park?"

Somehow, I find myself on the second floor landing. My heart's racing, so I know I must have run, but I don't remember doing it. My cheeks are burning. I don't believe this. How could this happen twice in one week? I can hear their voices echoing up the stairwell, and I slide down to the floor, leaning against the banister. If *she* hadn't been watching me…I'm so angry that, for a second, all I can see is Jadyn in her crimson, Asian-cut pantsuit with the high collar, so vivid and alive that she makes the Italian marble column behind her look cheap and unreal. If they didn't know better, no one on earth would suspect that Jadyn was even capable of fading, let alone disappearing entirely. Yet, somehow, she manages to do that *and* be one of the most visible people on the planet. How can she possibly have both?

Downstairs, a door shuts. They're gone. I get to my feet, wearily. The cell phone feels odd in my pocket: light, and somehow special. Like Christmas. Or a prepaid airplane ticket to anywhere I want to go. Or maybe revenge.

I spend the rest of the afternoon hiding in my room, both because I don't want to run into either Jadyn or Peter, and because I'm not sure when the phone will ring, or how loudly. It's making me edgy. Finally, after carrying it around in my hand for an hour, I put it on my bed, near the center, as though it's a bomb and the mattress can absorb the shockwave when it explodes. Then I sit down on the edge of the bed and try to read a magazine. I'm not even sure which magazine it is; my attention keeps flickering back to the ominously silent phone. Finally, just as I'm about to give up on a fourth article, the cell gives a high, adrenaline-triggering twitter. I snatch it up, too startled even to remember who's calling. "Hello?"

"Don't talk, just listen." It's Officer Carmichael, and I'm surprised to feel relief fill my chest. Who was I expecting? She doesn't give me time to say anything, even if I wanted to. "I am going to pick you up at 9:30, a quarter-mile down the road from your house. You'll have to come meet me. Alone. Don't bring Maraszek, or a driver, or anybody; if you do, you've broken your half of the bargain and left me free to break mine. Plan to be back before eleven; it doesn't matter what you tell people, as long as you can remember it later. Wear dark clothes and shoes that don't make noise. What time are you going to meet me?"

I consider reminding her she told me not to talk, but decide it wouldn't be politic. Let her be brusque if she wants; the more control she thinks she has over me, the more careless she'll be with the smaller things. "Nine-thirty. What am I—"

But she's hung up.

c h a p t e r   s e v e n

At 9:25, I'm waiting on Fieldstone Drive, a few hundred yards down the road from the house. The sun is staining the sky bright orange and dull red. *Danger colors,* I think, and then wish I hadn't. I am going out of my way to avoid bad omens tonight. I can see the roof of my house from where I'm standing, a shadow against the sunset; the ironwork along the crest of the roof looks like burnt lace. There's no way anyone could see me from there, but I still feel edgy, exposed. *Why would they be looking for me now? They mostly don't see me when I'm home.* Especially now that Jadyn's back.

I turn, letting my eyes skim across the sky, through the disquieting sunset, past the bright explosion of the streetlight above me, into the safer, luminous blue on the other side. A pair of headlights swings into view around the curve of the road, coming toward me. I wait, telling myself it isn't Officer Carmichael, until the car stops in front of me, and I can't pretend anymore.

It's a generic, steel-grey midsize that looks nothing like a police car. *If things go bad,* I tell myself, *just run. There's no way she can catch you. You can get out of this anytime you want.* I open the door and slide into the passenger seat.

In the split second the dome light is on, Officer Carmichael's gaze sweeps over me from head to toe. Then the light clicks off, and the car goes dusky. She clears her throat. "Are you sure those clothes are going to work?"

I'm not, really, but there was no way I was wearing last night's clothes in public. I decided to try the oldest, tightest pair of jeans I own and a navy blue tank top. If Robyn couldn't see the party dress, the jeans should be pretty safe. The ballet slippers worked just fine, but I didn't want to wear them out of the house, so I'm carrying them. "They were fine last night," I lie. Officer Carmichael shrugs and shifts the car into drive.

"What am I supposed to be doing?" I ask, after a long, quiet mile. She has to tell me soon. She should have told me earlier. She drives another fourth of a mile in silence. I can feel the impatience pressing at my temples, but I've had enough experience with Jadyn to know that this is a power play, and I'm not about to give her the satisfaction of asking a second time.

"We're going to Albany Park," she says, finally. "There's a talent agency down there that has heroin coming through it fairly regularly. We've been watching it for five months, and we've caught several dealers who claim they got their stuff from this place. We've gone in twice, with search warrants, but we've never managed to find anything."

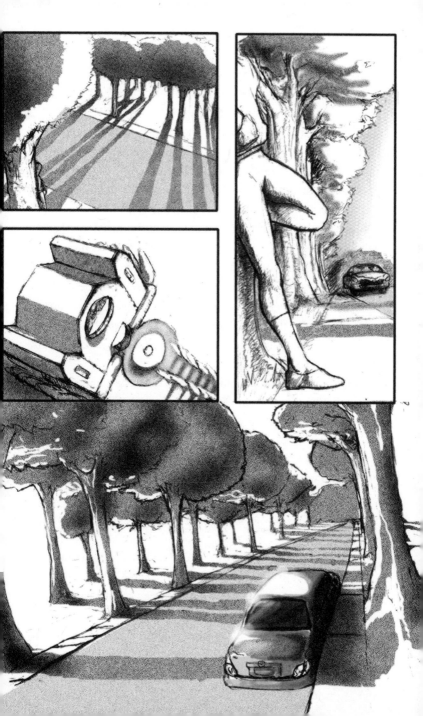

"So...you want me to get inside and find whatever you couldn't?"

She nods, eyes on the road.

"What makes you think I can find it?"

"The owner always seems to know when we're coming, so of course once we get there everything's perfect, but..." She hesitates, braking for a yellow light. "This isn't an official search. And we haven't made one in a month. It's possible that he's becoming careless, and you'll be able to see something."

See something? With a stab of anxiety, it dawns on me that she doesn't know I'm blind when I'm invisible. There's no way I'm going to tell her—it's never a good idea to fill your enemies in on your handicaps—but what if whatever she wants me to do depends on my being able to see? If I have to explain why I can't do it... *You're being stupid. She doesn't know what to expect, but she can't be expecting much from you. Just fake it. You'll think of something.* "Are there going to be people there?"

"Shouldn't be. They might have surveillance cameras set up, though." That isn't so bad. I can go through the agency and listen for people before I do anything.

"Why?"

"If somebody's going to have a gun I'd like to know now."

"Oh. I doubt it." She shoots me a sidelong glance. "Stay out of sight anyway."

Uh-huh. "So if I find something, do you want me to bring it out?"

"No! Leave it exactly the way you found it; don't even touch it if you can help it. If they find out we've been here, they'll just move it. Memorize exactly where it is and give me as many details as you can, but leave it alone."

I shrug, feeling like an idiot, and bend down to switch my

sneakers for the ballet slippers. "What makes you so sure he's got anything? Couldn't the people you talked to have lied?"

She snorts. "*They* could have, but the owner can't. He makes a point of following us around when we search, saying he doesn't have anything every chance he gets, and he always smirks—literally smirks—when we give up. He's got *something*."

It doesn't sound like concrete evidence to me, but it doesn't really matter. If she's got a search warrant, it can't be entirely illegal. All I have to do is look for someone else's hiding place. I'm not stealing anything.

After fifteen minutes, Officer Carmichael pulls over to the side of the street and cuts the engine. I glance out the window, wondering if she's gotten lost; we've parked in the middle of a small, neat business district. A couple of the buildings do have bars on their windows, but lots of overcautious people put those up. It doesn't look like the type of neighborhood that would have a drug problem.

I look back at her. She points across the street, and I follow the line of her finger. Five doors down, there's a one-story building with "Bismark Talent and Modeling" painted over the door.

Well, at least it looks safe. I reach for the door handle, but Officer Carmichael grabs my elbow. "Hang on." Her fingers are cool and her skin feels powdery, but she's got a good grip, and I can't pull loose. "Prove those clothes are going to work."

I glare; I want my arm back. "What?"

"Go invisible, or whatever it is you do. I need to make sure you aren't going to be seen."

I sigh. I've never actually done this in front of anyone, and I don't think I want to now. Especially since I don't really know what happens. *Serves her right if it's weird.* I shut my eyes, letting the other darkness close over my head. There's a sharp intake of breath from the driver's seat, which makes the lines of the dashboard flare white for a moment, but she doesn't release my arm. "Good," she says, after a minute.

I let go, and the dusky light floods back in; it's getting surprisingly easy to control this. I glance up, sideways, hoping to catch Officer Carmichael off-guard. There's uncertainty lurking behind the professional blandness in her face, and I feel a flicker of satisfaction. Anything that makes her feel shakier is okay by me.

She finally releases my arm, and bends down, tugging an object out from under her seat. "Here," she says, and tosses it toward me. I put up my hand and catch something thin and silky and dark. *Gloves,* I realize a second later. *So I don't leave fingerprints.* At least somebody remembered that. Officer Carmichael holds out a couple of plastic baggies. "This is what you'll be looking for," she says.

I take the bags, and hold them under the window so that the light from the streetlight falls on them. One has some sifting white powder in it; the other has a pinch of something dry and dark green in the bottom, like crushed parsley. "The powder is heroin," Officer Carmichael says. "There are other colors, too. It might be brownish, or possibly black and solid. The other stuff is marijuana. We're not sure whether or not he has any of that in there, but you'd better know what it looks like just in case."

I stare down at the baggies. I've never actually held drugs before, and I don't think I like it. My fingers feel itchy and restless. The plastic of the bags gleams in the light from the streetlamp, almost iridescent. There's no way I'll be able to see either of these things when I'm invisible. *Well, if you can't, you can't. That's all.* I take a slow, deep breath, trying not to be obvious about it, and hand the baggies back to Officer Carmichael. "Can we just get this over with?"

We walk around to the back of the building, where Officer Carmichael does something to a metal box which she insists has deactivated the alarm system, and unlocks the door. I don't ask where she got the key. I snapped invisible before I got out of the car, but she made me hang onto the door until she'd come around to my side, and then she held onto my wrist all the way across the street. I think she was afraid I'd run off, although it would have been a really dumb move; she definitely knows how to find me, and angry blackmailers are generally a bad thing. "Go," she whispers, letting go of my wrist and giving me a push toward the door. "If you haven't found anything in twenty minutes, come back to the car."

I nod, not wanting to make any more noise than I have to. The gravel in the alley pokes into the ballet slippers' thin soles, and it hurts. Through the door, the hall's outlines look thin and cobwebby; I'm not entirely sure they'll hold my weight. I slip through, into the building, and hear the door shut behind me.

The air inside is cold, so dry that breathing in makes the back of my throat tickle. It sounds dead. Outside, I could hear muted traffic noises from Lawrence Avenue, six blocks away, and the buzz of the transformer on the telephone pole in the alley, and the crunch of Officer Carmichael's shoes. In here, there's nothing. Not 'nothing,' as in, only floorboards settling, or 'nothing' as in only air-conditioning noises. Absolute silence. I've been holding my breath, listening for people sounds. When I let it out, the slight noise shows the pale line of a doorjamb a few feet ahead.

The silence makes me incredibly nervous. I tell myself that it's a good thing, that it's on my side, that at least it means there's nobody else here. Just me, the furniture, and—possibly—some illegal substances. I walk forward a few steps, scuffing my feet along the floor in a vain attempt to make some small noise to see by. I hesitate at the end of the hall, fingers curled cautiously around the doorjamb. The room in front of me is a hollow darkness.

This isn't going to work. I have to do something. Surveillance cameras don't pick up sound, do they? I know the ones at the courthouse don't. I lick my lips and whistle the first few notes of "Yankee Doodle," the only song I can think of. The sound rockets around the room, bouncing off plaster and tiles like a Superball. I can see almost as well as I could yesterday outside the Aegis offices. The room ahead of me is somebody's office, not terribly different from the records room at Aegis, but larger. I wait, listening for movement, but there's nothing. I start on the second verse of the song and walk across the room to the next doorway. Better to see how big the agency is before I start looking for hiding places.

It isn't that big. By the time I've whistled "Mary Had A Little Lamb," "Mrs. Robinson," and the theme song from some movie whose name I can't remember, I'm back where I started. There are three offices, a small break room, a mostly empty room with metal folding chairs stacked against one wall, which I think is probably used for meetings or auditions, and one tiny bathroom just big enough for a sink and a toilet. The office in front has two barred picture windows flanking the front door, and it's the largest. I sit on the top of the cluttered desk to think. I don't know how much time I've used up, but it must be about ten minutes. Half my time, gone. I've stopped whistling, and the lines of the room are fading. I tap my heel against the front of the desk, and the noise is just enough to keep them from disappearing entirely.

Where would someone hide drugs? All the places normal

people hide important things—locked desk drawers, refrigerators, medicine cabinets, toilet tanks—are much too obvious; the police would have checked those straight off. Loose boards, ceiling tiles, and secret compartments are probably also out.

I scowl, looking around at what I can see of the room. The office is deserted and so far I haven't spotted a camera. I could unsnap, just for a little. But I've done everything else blind, and this is supposed to be practice. It might only be discouraging, anyway; even half-blind, I can tell that the offices—this one especially— are hopelessly cluttered. It looks as though someone decided to hold a neighborhood garage sale in the building, and then forgot to put up signs telling people where it was. I can probably discount most of the things—vases, obvious medicine bottles, file cabinets—because the police will have gotten those. But what if they haven't?

Don't think like that. You'll psyche yourself out. Think creative. Where would you hide something small?

Personally, I'd duct-tape it to the inside of an air vent, but I'm not sure how protected drugs have to be; maybe the constant airflow would damage them. Besides, there's no way I can search the air ducts without disturbing things. Something with stuffing would be good—an armchair or a sofa, or maybe a coat. I could unpick the seam and hide stuff in the cotton, then stitch it back up. But I haven't seen any furniture here that isn't wooden or metal, and...

Wait a second. I stop swinging my foot, and the blackness creeps back in, dissolving the room. *Metal.*

I push away from the desk, drop to the floor and almost fall because I can't see which way is up; I put my hands back and catch the top of the desk to steady myself, then start whistling without bothering to find a song. The lines flare around me. I start down the hall toward the audition room, moving as fast as I dare.

The folding chairs are piled against the front wall, under a high row of windows. It's hard to see them with these eyes. The lines blur into each other, dizzily, and I think there might be close to fifty chairs. This is going to take forever if I can't see. I unsnap, impatiently, and am surprised at how dim the room is. The windows are too high up for the light to reach the floor, and the shapes of the chairs aren't much clearer than they were. But at least I can tell which is which. I drop to my knees, pull the first one away from the wall, and tug the rubber grips off of the bottoms of the legs.

After five chairs, I'm starting to lose enthusiasm. All the leg pipes so far have been empty, and my fingers are starting to hurt. The gloves are too thin to give much protection, and if I do all fifty chairs I know I'm going to get blisters. Not to mention the fact that it would take all night. I put the fifth chair on the stack of searched ones and pull a sixth one away from the wall. This one is very old; its vinyl seat cover is cracked, with a ragged edge of foam sticking out. The hinges feel loose, and the legs are rough and scarred. There's a dark mark on one of the back legs, like a slash of permanent marker. To show that the chair isn't safe?

Maybe. I yank the grip off and carefully poke my index finger into the pipe's opening. Something rustles. I trap the edge of the rustling thing under my finger, tugging out the corner of a thin plastic bag. I almost can't believe it. Gently, I pull it out the rest of the way; the bag is very small, maybe half the size of a sandwich baggie, and rolled up as tightly as possible. Inside are a few ounces of fine powder. I stare at it, feeling the blood pounding through my ears, flushing my face. *Impossible.* I actually found something?

I roll the baggie up again, careful not to let the powder bunch up in a corner, and feed the thing back into the hollow leg, pushing the rubber grip back on. The other three legs are empty, but I start pulling chairs away from the wall again, not bothering with the normal ones this time. The third chair has two black-marker-smudged legs, and both of them have plastic bags inside.

That's it, then. Carefully, I put the chairs back the way they were, hoping I've gotten them in the right order. I'm pretty sure the drug chairs are in the right places, and that's what's important. I snap invisible again and step out into the hall, feeling curiously detached.

The rooms feel huge, open, and empty. Before, I couldn't make enough noise to see. Now, the smallest sounds hang in the air for what seems like hours. The ballet slippers slide a little bit against the tiles, as though I'm really walking on ice, and I let my gloved fingers skim over the wall to keep track of where I'm going. I turn the knob-lock on the back door and step out into the alley, pulling the door shut behind me. It clicks, and something in the box on the wall that Officer Carmichael messed with starts to hum.

After the crackling dryness in the agency, the air outside feels humid against my bare shoulders. I lean back against the gritty wall, and let my lungs fill with warmth and alley-smells. It *worked*. I almost can't believe it, but... There's a funny, light feeling inside my chest. It takes me a minute to realize that, for the first time in months—maybe years—I'm not worried about anything at all.

The midsize is still parked across the street. I open the passenger door and slide into the seat, unsnapping as I shut the door. The look on Officer Carmichael's face is something else, but all she says is, "You're late."

"I am?"

"Ten minutes. I was about to go in after you."

It doesn't really look like she was. I buckle my seatbelt as the car's engine rumbles to life.

"You're lucky I was late," I say, because, right now, there's nothing she can do to me.

She shoots me a disgusted look; "Lucky? If you'd been on an actual job, you could have been—" Then she seems to see something in my face; her tone changes. "Why? Did you find something?" I nod. "What? Where?"

"Bags of powder like the stuff you showed me. Probably heroin, I don't know. They're in the third room down the hall, the one that looks like a mini-auditorium or something. There are folding chairs against the wall—"

She shakes her head; "We checked those."

I frown; is she putting me on? "All of them?"

"Well, of course not. Maybe ten. But they were all from different parts of the stack; it was a good sample."

"Can't have been. I found three bags with maybe four ounces in them. Some of the chairs have a black permanent-marker line on one or more of their legs, and those are the ones to check."

She glances at me, startled. "You're not... Seriously? He had four ounces back there?"

"No, twelve. Three bags of four. There might have been more; I didn't check all the chairs, either. But you might want to."

"That doesn't make sense. How..."

"You were the one who said he always knows when his place is going to be searched. Maybe he puts the drug chairs in storage when he's expecting you. But they're there now. If you went tomorrow, you could probably get him." I'm enjoying this; I'm not usually the one with information.

We're stopped at a red light. Officer Carmichael stares straight ahead, her fingers clenched on the steering wheel so hard her knuckles are white. The light changes to green, and we don't move. I count five seconds, and just as I'm about to say something, she gives an odd, dry chuckle that seems to rattle a little in her chest. She crosses the intersection, then pulls over to the side of the road, crosses her arms on top of the steering wheel and rests her forehead on her arms. I watch her for a few seconds, uncertainly; her shoulders aren't shaking, and she isn't making any noise that I can hear. Is she sick? I don't know what to do, so I wait, watching the dark street outside my window and thinking I'm not sure I like being stopped here.

Finally, Officer Carmichael raises her head. She's grinning. The faint glow from the streetlights warps the smile into something almost ghoulish, and my heart gives a nervous flutter. "You just turned seventeen, right?" she asks. "I saw the write-ups."

I don't answer. It wasn't really a question, and I've decided I'm not going to talk about my birthday unless tortured.

"Do you realize we had ten people—ten *specialists*, no less—go over that place for two hours without finding anything? And it takes you thirty minutes."

I don't say anything.

She shakes her head, her frizzy hair gleaming like copper Brillo in the light from the streetlamp, and shifts the car into drive with a flourish. "I *knew* this was a good idea."

Officer Carmichael drops me off on Fieldstone Drive again, only a yard or so from where she picked me up earlier, then pulls away down the street. The sky over my house is black now; it's almost 11:00. It's unlikely that anyone even knows I'm not up in my room, but I snap invisible anyway. I've gotten used to it. Besides, the evening's success has left me feeling a little drunk, and I don't want to lose the feeling yet. I circle around the house to the back gate; it's more heavily alarmed, but I don't have to worry about tripping motion sensors when I'm like this. Getting in is almost pitifully easy.

Inside, the air feels brighter somehow. I enter through the sunroom, which smells like plants, damp potting soil, and warm metal. It's deserted, so no one sees the door open. I hear someone moving in the next room. One of the maids is dusting, but she might as well not be there. I walk past her, so close I could whisk the dust rag out of her fingers if I wanted to, and she doesn't notice me. I was a thousand times more nervous at Aegis. *In other words, yesterday. Unreal.*

The second floor is quieter than the first. I don't bother to move carefully because I can tell from the feel of the silence that there's no one here. After Bismark Talent and Modeling, I'm pretty sure I'm an expert on how empty rooms sound. So it's a shock when, as I'm passing the door of Jadyn's study, it swings open in front of me.

I throw up my arm, reflexively protecting my face, and the door rams my elbow, hard. I stumble back, biting my lip to keep from yelling and rubbing frantically at the throbbing bruise that used to be my elbow. I'm so mad about being startled out of my mood that the lines around me shimmer. The person who shoved through the door has turned back—a woman, I think—and is standing in the middle of the hall, arms crossed. For a second, I'm tempted to push past and startle her. If anything, she'll just think it's Jadyn. But then I hear the voice and freeze in midstep.

There's only one person in Chicago who can speak that calmly and still sound as though she'd love to kill you. "I believe we've discussed this before. Any calls from him are to be forwarded straight to me. It doesn't matter where I am."

I shrink back against the wall. My heart beats so hard that the darkness is fading. The lines disappear into the haze. *Jadyn* won't think I'm Jadyn...I don't dare breathe.

An apprehensive male voice from inside the room utters something I can't quite catch, but it does nothing to appease Jadyn. She's tucked her left arm behind her back, and even through the haze, I can see that she's clenched her fingers into a fist. The man in the room can't tell from where he is. I stare at the fist, concentrating on slowing my heartbeat. She hasn't noticed me yet. Maybe—just maybe—if I stay where I am, and she stays as angry as she is now, she won't see me.

"What if he *did* mention a job? He's a friend. I might have been interested." I shake my head, slowly; she's just trying to scare her secretary now. I'm surprised he hasn't picked up on it. Jadyn, interested in a job? Since when? "You're lucky. If I hadn't run into him on Wednesday, you might have been out of a job yourself. Now get out."

The man slides warily out of the room and hurries across the carpet, away from me; his shoes scuff up a vague trail of light that follows him like a comet's tail. Jadyn turns, watching his back until he disappears around a corner. Then her shoulders drop an inch or so; she sighs, puts a hand up to her hair, hesitates, then lets it fall, looking back at something in the study.

The wall is cool under my palms. I stare at Jadyn, feeling the fear drain away from me as the seconds tick by. She doesn't know I'm here. She really can't tell. She always seems to see more than other people do but, right now, she's just as blind as her secretary.

She shuffles through the thick stack of letters on the half-table by the door, choosing three from the pile, and turns away, opening the first on her way to the stairs. She passes so close to me that I feel the air flow out of her way and hear her whispering to herself, reading the first few lines of the letter. I stare at her, openly, not even trying to lie low now. All the years I was afraid of her lurking in corners, watching me…and now *I'm* watching *her*. The strange, light feeling I felt in the alley outside Bismark Talent and Modeling floods through me, draining away the last of the tension and making me giddy. Less than an hour after my first official session, and it's already starting to work.

c h a p t e r   e i g h t

On Sunday morning, I wake up at 10:30. For a few minutes I lie in bed, staring up at the bright ceiling, trying to trace the hazy excitement humming through my mind back to its source. I don't remember dreaming. It's July, so it can't be Christmas, and my birthday's been more a source of nightmares than anything else. Is it about Dad? No ... Jadyn? *Jadyn*. Of course. Last night ...

The first thing I hear when I come downstairs is a sharp, heavy *thwack*, like the sound a window blind makes if you let it roll up too fast. I pause just outside the breakfast room, listening, but the sound isn't repeated. I can hear Jadyn's voice, low and angry, but no one else. Maybe she's on the phone. I slip through the door and grab a breakfast bar out of the cereal cupboard, feeling a little like a spy in enemy territory.

Jadyn paces from the windows to the rear wall and back, a cell phone clamped to her ear, scowling so hard I look the other way on instinct. "*No*," she spits, "I do not believe it, but I don't know. Find out, and call me back. *Yes*, now!" She hangs up, starts to dial another number, then notices me standing there. "Natalie?" Her voice is sharp, but somehow distracted; whoever she's mad at, it isn't me. I glance up, reluctantly. Her eyes are fixed on me, so fierce they make her look almost predatory. This morning, even though I'm perfectly visible and she's looking straight at me, they don't scare me at all. I let the thought drift to the back of my mind, absently turning it over and over like a mental worry stone, and shrug, raising my hands palms-up to ask what's wrong. Jadyn shakes her head, stabs a finger viciously at the table, and starts talking again. "Yes, hello, Lani? I need you this afternoon. Have you seen the paper?"

Lani is Jadyn's publicist, and from the sound of things, she's going to have a rough day. Something pretty big must've blown up. I sidle over to the table and casually turn the paper so it's facing me. The instant I see the headline, I realize that the thwacking noise must have been Jadyn throwing the paper down. The front-page headline—printed in capitals so large and dark it's a wonder the paper can hold together under the ink—screams "IRVING MONOPOLY BROKEN!"

A shivery sensation travels up my spine. This is wrong. Not just wrong, impossible. What happened? What is this? I unfold the paper.

There are two pictures on the front page. The largest one is a picture of the exterior of the University of Chicago Hospital. The second is a school-picturish photo of a pretty, Polynesian-looking girl. Neither of them means anything to me. I scan the article, looking for clues.

In what many people see as a miracle and a few call a sign of the End Times, an operation engineered to bring out the talent of invisibility—previously restricted to Chicago resident Jadyn Irving—has been successful. Two months ago, the surgery was performed on twenty-four-year-old Monica Aloia. At the time, it was considered unsuccessful; however, recent developments have led researchers at the University of Chicago to conclude that the two months were simply a latency period. "We know much more about the human brain now than we did ten, even five, years ago," says department head David Persichetti, "but nowhere near enough to analyze exactly what's happened. The basic principles are fairly straightforward, but from there you've got literally millions of variables. It may take twenty years of research before we understand exactly what's happened here. We may be able to do this a thousand more times, or we may just have gotten lucky."

The newsprint blurs in front of my eyes as my heart rate picks up. I can hear Officer Carmichael's voice, dry and tinny with distance. *Monica will give us something to show the media…*

This is not the University of Chicago. This isn't even Monica Aloia. It's Officer Carmichael. It's *me*.

My chest feels so tight with happiness that I don't dare look up. In this room, with Jadyn pacing like a caged tiger fifteen feet away, smiling at anything in the vicinity of this article would be a very, very bad idea. I skim the rest of the page. Only the last paragraph seems important:

Ms. Aloia could not be reached for comment, but at this morning's press conference, Chicago Chief of Police Reitter

> confirmed that she has agreed to work with them for a trial
> period of three months. Footage from the conference will be
> aired on Sunday evening at …

How did she manage it? She must have pulled some very ef-
fective strings. It's only been about twelve hours since my
first assignment for Officer Carmichael. But I guess if she has
convinced the right people she's managed to blackmail Jadyn
Irving … I gaze down at Monica's friendly, slightly vapid face.
She's prettier than I am; it isn't a face I'll be embarrassed to wear
in public. I don't mind if she pretends to be me, so long as it
leaves me free to do what I have to. And best of all, even if someone proves she's a fraud, they won't have found me. Monica and
the police will take the fall, and I'll be twice invisible.

"Can you believe that?" Jadyn glares at me—or, actually, at the
newspaper under my hand—as she muffles the cell phone against
her shoulder. "Some people will do anything for publicity."

Some people. Yes. *It takes one to know one.* She isn't expecting
an answer, but she's going to get one this time. Might as well
start the day off right. I look up, innocently. "You don't want it to
be real?"

Jadyn's eyes snap up to my face, hot and unsettlingly alert.
"What?"

I shrug, pushing away the little voice that's hissing at me to
stop, *now.* "Well, if she's for real, she's already agreed to help the
police out. Now they won't be after you to do it."

The silence that follows that remark is electric. For a long moment, I hold Jadyn's glare, knowing if I look away now, she'll
know I'm bluffing. Her eyes bore into mine as though she's trying
to burn through my act to the truth behind it, but I'm still not

afraid, and now I know why. Jadyn's eyes have always frightened me because she seems able to see into my mind. Now I know she can't. I really *am* invisible to her.

The seconds stretch into an age, and, finally, Jadyn's cell phone gives an irritated little beep. She flinches at the noise but holds my eyes a second longer. "You," she says, finally, "don't know anything."

Which, right now, is pretty funny coming from her. I feel my face grow hot, but she's given me an excuse to leave without looking odd, and I don't dare risk a comeback. I turn and walk out.

I'm on my way back upstairs to get the cell phone when I run into Peter coming down. "Oh, good, you're here," he says. He sounds a little surprised, as though I'd be anywhere else at 11:00 on a Sunday. "We're going downtown this morning, if you don't mind."

I look up at him, blankly. It's fine with me if he goes downtown, but I can't think why he'd need me to come. "Why?"

"Because you owe me five hundred dollars, and I'm running low on ink. I'd like to cash in."

"Oh." *Of course.* I'd forgotten about the bet. "Right. Um, you want to leave right now?"

"Now would be good."

Something's odd. Normally, this sort of thing could have waited until afternoon. Peter's expression is just a bit too blank; he's wearing his courthouse face. What is he hiding? *You're being paranoid. He did just finish those samples yesterday. He could still be feeling keyed-up about that, trying not to show it. Just like you.*

"Okay," I tell him. "I have to get something from my room first. And, um, shoes. But I'll be right down." He nods and starts down the stairs again, shoulders back military-style, walking just a little more briskly than normal.

Maybe it's the weather.

Peter's favorite art supply store is a one-room shop called Graphix, on the border between Near North and Streeterville. It's tiny, with icky fluorescent lights, minimal air-conditioning and a staff that mostly wears black, and it has every art-related thing you could ever imagine wanting to buy, not to mention a few I don't see any point in owning. Peter loves it, for obvious reasons; setting him loose in there is like taking a preschooler to Disneyland. We stop by at least twice a month, usually after a visit to the courthouse, so he can stock up on Bristol board, drafting tape, ink, this particular brand of pencil no one else seems to sell, and pens imported from Japan.

It isn't a bad store to wait in. It's interesting to look at all the supplies and try to figure out why they're called "camel hair" brushes when even the package says they're one hundred percent pony hair, and it's kind of funny to watch Peter shopping. Not to mention the fact that, although everyone on the staff knows who I am, they don't care. None of the other customers has ever bothered me either, although that could be because they're all about as crazy as Peter when they're in the store. I don't have to pretend to be someone else while I'm here, because no one will notice anyway.

Peter heads for the rack of tiny, criminally expensive ink jars the second we walk through the door; I've never been quite sure why he needs a jar of black ink, and a twenty-five-dollar paintbrush, *and* a pen, but he insists they're all vitally important. Even though he wants to be a professional penciler, not an inker. It's just one of the many artist things I've given up trying to understand.

I wander over to a wire rack that has thick sheets of very expensive paper draped across its shelves. There's rough, handmade paper with flower petals and dried grass in it, pastel card stock in pink and blue and green with furred edges and a faint shine to it, and an even thicker paper dyed to look like tawny marble. There's a wide window right in front of the stack, tinted so that the light doesn't bleach the paper; I can stand here and look through the shelves at the people outside, and no one will see.

Even though it's Graphix, I'm wearing my sunglasses today. People are talking, and even though most of the talk will be about Jadyn or Monica, I'm feeling jittery. Besides, the sunglasses ensure that Peter can't get a clear look at my eyes. He's far too good at guessing what I'm thinking, and I can't afford that today. I'm already risking a little too much by carrying the cell phone around with me, since I refused to get one for years. Jadyn wanted to be able to check up on me no matter where I was, which I thought was too easy for her already. I switched the ringer off when I picked it up this morning, so at least that won't give me away, but bodyguards tend to notice things like bulging pockets. If he asks, I'll have to make up a story to explain where it came from. If I tell too many lies, I'll lose track, so I can't be too careful.

And, even with all the worries, my hand keeps drifting toward the pocket of my shorts, just to make sure the cell's there. I think I know what smokers must feel like on airplane trips; now that I couldn't possibly answer the cell, I want it to ring more than anything.

It's strange. I don't like Officer Carmichael, or being blackmailed

by her—no matter how nicely it fits with my own plans—and I have no idea how I'm going to get out of this when I've done what I need to do. But seeing Jadyn's face this morning made it all worth it. Let her feel cornered for a change; serves her right. Officer Carmichael's given me an idea. She's pretending she's blackmailing Jadyn, but I could really *do* it. I could follow her, watch Nadal, find out which rumors are actually true, and start sending her notes about them. Or e-mails. Or anonymous phone calls. I'm not even sure I'd ask for anything; it would be fun just to watch her try to find me. Or maybe I'd just send my findings straight to the papers...

An unexpected breeze makes the hair on the back of my neck stand up. Someone's standing behind me, flipping through a thick pad of paper. I glance back, irritated, only a little relieved to see that it's Peter. "What?"

Peter's gazing down at the open pad of high-grade drawing paper like he's found some kind of information-age Rosetta Stone. "So," he says, without looking up, as though he's continuing a conversation we never actually started, "there was a phone call for you last night. Some guy from your school."

"Oh?" I pull my sunglasses down a little, because a bar of light from the window is glaring across them and it's hard to see his face. "You didn't tell me."

"Well, no. He called around 9:45. I went upstairs to let you know, and you weren't there."

I watch him apprehensively. He's still looking down, which is good because I'm suddenly wishing I'd left the sunglasses in place. "Um..." I have no idea what to say. I haven't had much practice lying about where I've been, since it doesn't come up much, and, anyway, I don't like lying to Peter. If I didn't have to, I wouldn't. Why does he have to ask so many questions? "Yeah, I … I was … Uh, who did you say called?"

Peter turns a page of the pad, holding it carefully between his thumb and index finger. "Some kid. Aaron or Eric or something like that."

"Ari, maybe? Ari Foster?" Now I'm worried. Peter always remembers names, almost automatically. He had to have been pretty concerned last night to forget. The more worried he is, the closer he'll be watching me.

"Sounds right. Wasn't important, was it?"

"No, actually, I didn't want to talk to him." Good; it's safe to talk about Ari. Maybe if I sidetrack him far enough, he'll forget what the original idea was. "What did you tell him?"

Peter's eyes lock onto mine over the top of the pad. They're shiny and deep and much, much too alert, and I know right then that it won't work. "Just that you weren't taking calls. You were going to tell me where you were?"

"I was just—" My eyes slide away, desperately focusing on the sheets of paper draped over the rack. There's nowhere I can say I was. I'm never anywhere except home. "Out. It's not important." I glance up, meet his eyes again, and know there's no way he's letting it go at that. "I didn't want to bother you. You know, with the Excelsior samples and everything."

Peter smiles humorlessly. "I mailed those yesterday before dinner. That isn't my job, Natalie; you are. I get paid to keep you out of trouble." I stare down at the white polished straps of my sandals; I have no idea how he's going to end this. Something very close to dread settles into my stomach.

Peter smacks the pad lightly against his hand, then tucks it under his arm. When I risk looking up, he's staring out the window. "I trust you," he says, finally, and I feel the hard knot in my stomach start—very slowly—to unwind. "Don't know why, but I do. You've never given me trouble. You don't smoke; if you drink I've never caught you; and you don't have bizarre friends who abuse solvents."

"I don't have *any* friends, you mean," I mutter. It's a reflex, like saying *gesundheit* when somebody sneezes.

He shakes his head a little. "You've got a few. Not many, but some. Besides, it's hard to make friends when you don't really know who you are. Give it a year."

I stare at him in disbelief; where did *that* come from? "So you're a psychologist now, too?"

That comes out sounding nastier than I meant it to, but Peter only looks at me as though I should have known better. "That's about three-fourths of the job, Natalie." He takes a deep, steady breath. "So. I'm going to cut you some slack this time. You don't generally take off like that, and I assume you had a good reason for it. No one else knows you were out—" I let out a breath I hadn't realized I'd been holding, "—and I'm not going to tell them."

There's someone behind me, looking through the hole punches. I don't turn around, but I can hear the sharp clicks. Peter waits, patiently, until the noisemaker moves on.

"But," he continues, "if it happens again, I will."

I'm all ready to protest, but there's nothing I can tell him that would change his mind. I can't tell him the truth, but I don't dare lie, and so it's safest not to say anything. I shut my mouth.

"If there's a reason I shouldn't tell," he says, "you'd better fill me in. Otherwise, things may get sticky."

"That sounds like a threat, Peter," I say, flatly. *Not you, too.*

He sounds too much like Officer Carmichael, and I'm a little hurt.

"It's not a threat. It's a realistic assessment of the situation." Peter studies my expression—which is probably pretty strained by this time—and sighs. "Look at it this way, Natalie: things already have the potential to be sticky. Right now, I'm keeping them normal, but it's not really in my job description. Don't expect me to do it again."

I shrug, uncomfortably. The tiny cell phone feels like a brick in my pocket. Peter's obviously done talking; it's my turn to say something. My mind spins, frantically searching for a safe topic, but there's nothing. Nothing except… "Look… about Ari…"

Peter's silent, waiting.

"He, um… he was at my party, and I thought maybe he… you know." I glance at him to make sure he does know; he doesn't seem to. "Liked me," I say, quickly. "He looked like he did." Peter's eyebrows come together. "But then I overheard him talking to some friends, and he just wanted pictures."

"Of what?"

"I dunno… Me? The house? Some tabloid was buying. So I just—"

Peter's jaw tightens. "That stupid little—" Deep breath. "What did you do?"

"Nothing yet. Jadyn says not to let him push me around, but I can't just—"

"Will you let me handle it?"

This may have worked *too* well; Peter's eyes look dangerous. "He's a high-schooler. You can't just…" Even so, part of me is happy. If Dad was here, maybe he'd act like this. "I'll take care of it. Really. I just don't know how yet."

A little of the tension ebbs out of Peter's face. "All right. But if you decide you want backup, just let me know. I've been a high school boy. I know what scares them."

I give a crooked smile, in spite of myself. "Thanks. Um, did you find what you needed?"

Peter's mouth twitches humorously, but he nods, holding up the sketch pad. "This, and a few other things. It shouldn't cost more than two hundred dollars."

I shoot a skeptical glance at the Bristol board. "Two hundred dollars for that?"

"This and two jars of ink, three new pens, some quality brushes, and a good light box." He shrugs apologetically. "The light box is the expensive thing, but they're supposed to be worth it."

"It's fine," I tell him. I don't want him to think I'm a poor loser. Especially not now. "It's your money."

The first thing I do once I'm safely home and in my room is check the cell for messages, but there's nothing. I turn the ringer back on, trying out all the tones and songs and finally setting it to the *Mission Impossible* theme.

Downstairs, people come and go all day. Doors open and close and slam, and sometimes I hear voices echoing up the stairwell. I stay on the third floor, out of the way, feeling stifled and hot and irritable. For a while, I tell myself it's the weather. It's hot again, ninety-six degrees, with no clouds expected for at least a week. After an hour of sitting on a windowsill, trying to read, and dangling my bare feet over the air vent until they're so cold I can barely feel my toes, I have to admit that it's not the heat. It's the waiting. I feel as though I've lit the fuse to something gigantic and am trapped in the second between the spark and the explosion. I don't know whether this will be a success or a failure, but I know, either way, it will be frighteningly big. Once Officer Carmichael calls, I'll be okay.

She doesn't call until after 8:00. By then, I'm in the third floor rec room, watching *The Princess Bride* on cable. Westley and Inigo Montoya are just working up to their first swordfight—my favorite part—and I'm so tired of waiting for the call that I almost don't want to answer it, but I do. "This is Natalie."

"We got him," says Officer Carmichael, not bothering to say hello. "He had more than twenty thousand dollars worth of heroin in those chairs."

I shut my eyes, feeling relief start to soothe my tensed muscles. *Act cool. Don't let her know how important this is.*

"Did you see the papers, by the way?"

"Yeah," I say, trying to sound as though I'd been expecting the flood of articles for months. Then, on a whim, I add, "So did Jadyn." I want to see how she reacts.

"And?" Officer Carmichael's voice is perfectly neutral.

"She was upset." *Understatement of the year.*

"Understandable," she says, dryly, in a tone that makes it impossible to tell whether she's satisfied or resigned or just plain tired of dealing with prima donnas. "Tell her she's free to come help Monica out any time she likes."

Monica. "Right. What about Monica?"

"Excuse me?"

"What does she think she's doing? What did they tell her?"

Officer Carmichael hesitates. "She thinks she's fronting for Jadyn, of course. She doesn't know about you. Why?"

"Then there's no danger of her accidentally... talking to someone?"

She chuckles. "Not Monica. No, Monica wouldn't be a danger even if she *did* know. She's a very nice, well brought-up, and un-imaginative young woman. She's been told what to do, and as she's fairly useless as a strategist, I think we can count on her to do it." Good. That was the impression I got from the photo, but I wanted to make sure. Monica the spokesmodel.

"I'm going to need you tomorrow afternoon," Officer Carmichael is saying. "It won't be like last night; you're going to have to come down to the station. How long can you stay invisible?"

I'm not sure. "An hour or so."

"That should be manageable. I'll pick you up around three."

Yes! Something else to do. I'm about to hang up when an image of Peter flickers through my mind. It hurts to think of him as a threat. I don't think he'd intentionally do anything to hurt me, but he doesn't know how much damage this could do. And I still have nothing to tell him.

"Wait," I say, quickly. "There's something else. My bodyguard noticed I was gone last night, and he wasn't happy about it. He's starting to worry about losing his job. What do I tell him?"

I'm hoping maybe she'll have some miraculous code-word that I can say that will make Peter understand this is something he has no place in, but she's no help at all. "I don't really care, as long as you keep him out of it."

"Yeah, I know," I say, and I'm about to add, "but it's not like I can bribe him; he isn't that kind of bodyguard," but she's already hung up. *Thanks, Officer Carmichael. Very helpful.* I let the phone fall onto the cushy leather couch and drop down beside it. On the TV, Westley's finished the swordfight and is slowly but surely over-powering the strongman.

c h a p t e r   n i n e

I'm awake most of the night, trying to think of something to tell Peter, but it's no use. All Monday morning I work on plans to sneak out without him noticing, but that's no good, either. He's watching for that sort of thing now. Finally, around lunchtime, I think I've come up with a halfway-decent idea.

Peter is down in the kitchen, talking to the man who delivers our groceries. I stand in the doorway, trying hard not to fidget; I just want to get this over with. I'm sure Peter's noticed me, but he's finishing the conversation. Finally, the deliveryman shrugs and turns away, heading for the back door. Peter looks back at me, eyebrows raised questioningly.

"I wanted to tell you that I'm going to be gone this afternoon," I say, forcing myself to look him in the eye. Can he tell how hard it is? "Jadyn's meeting this guy for dinner, to talk about Isole, and she wanted me to come." The part about the dinner meeting is true; I heard her talking about it on the phone earlier this morning. Hopefully Peter didn't, since I wasn't mentioned. "She's going to be shopping for a couple hours before, though, and she isn't going to be home between the two, so ... " I shrug, trying to smile.

Peter watches me, and I can't read anything in his expression. He might believe me. He might know I'm lying through my teeth. He might be thinking about the samples he sent to Excelsior and not really be listening at all; there's no way to tell. I stand still, clenching my fists behind my back so my hands don't shake, and tell myself that at least I've found a good excuse for leaving him at the house—if I can make him believe it. Jadyn has always refused to hire a bodyguard for herself; she doesn't like them on principle. She insists she can take better care of herself than any bodyguard ever could, and she's probably right. It's conceivable that, if I were going to a dinner meeting with her, she'd make Peter stay behind.

"Where is this going to be?" Peter asks.

"At Tru," I say, honestly. It's a risk, because, if he calls down to check, I won't be there. But at least Jadyn will be.

Peter nods, somewhat sympathetically. Going places with Jadyn is always interesting, but rarely relaxing. "Have fun." And I still can't quite believe that he believes me, but it's the best I'm going to get, so I leave.

Officer Carmichael is only two minutes late, but by the time the grey midsize pulls up, I'm already feeling jumpy. I left the house early, not wanting to risk being late, and since I didn't dare stand in the street for half an hour in broad daylight in front of somebody else's house, I'm invisible. When Officer Carmichael finally arrives, she pulls up half a block away from where I'm standing. I jog down the block to the car, and, just as I come up to the door, I realize that it might not actually be her. I can't tell the car's color or who's in it when I'm like this, and the car's so nondescript I can't even remember its shape.

I hesitate, feeling myself start to panic; then I realize that the window is open a couple of inches. I can hear the radio, tuned to a talk show. I hook my fingers over the top of the window glass, squinting through the gap, and the chatter and static is enough to show me Officer Carmichael's familiar, frizzy hair. I yank the door open, slide into the seat and tug the door shut, unsnapping as I do.

There's a hiss of alarm from the driver's seat, which quickly turns to exasperation. Officer Carmichael rubs a hand across her shiny, sweaty forehead. "I *wish* you wouldn't do that," she snaps, shoving the car into gear.

"Sorry," I mutter. "Did you expect me to unsnap on the sidewalk or something?"

"Do what?"

"Um…change."

She just shakes her head, mumbling something I can't quite hear. I rest my chin in my hand, staring out the window. The sun is hot on my arm. Apparently, this is going to be one of those days. Then I remember something she said yesterday, when I was too excited to pay attention. "Uh…I don't actually have to go into the station, do I?"

Officer Carmichael shoots me a look. "Why not?"

"I just…" I could sit through a briefing and manage to stay invisible, but I'm tired. I didn't sleep much last night, and it's hot, and I'll be invisible for a long time anyway, and everyone's already cranky. If I have to sit through a meeting on top of it all, I'm going to scream. "I'm feeling kinda sick. I'll do whatever you want; I'd just rather not go in."

"So, instead, you're going to … ?"

"I could wait in the car."

"It's too hot."

"You could leave the windows rolled down. I'll be here."

"Visible, you mean? So, if someone comes out and wonders why you're in my car, you'll say … ?"

Drat. "I'm not going in there," I say, stubbornly. She can't make me. At least, I hope she can't.

"Well, then, what would you suggest?" Officer Carmichael is doing her level best to be diplomatic; there's only a slight hint of sarcasm in the words.

"I don't know. I just don't want … Couldn't you leave me in a room people don't use much, and come back for me after the meeting?" She's watching me, a little suspiciously, and I add, "Unless, you know, you need me to help you remember stuff." It's a cheap shot, but I'm hoping it will distract her. Being rude is one of the easiest ways to sidetrack people. It's hard to think in a straight line when you're angry.

She snorts. "I believe I can handle it, thank you very much." She drives for a minute in silence. "You know, I think you're trying to make life difficult." For a second, I'm sure she's going to add "like mother, like daughter," which sets my teeth on edge.

"I'm here, aren't I? I didn't ask you to blackmail me."

Officer Carmichael brakes for a red light. She shoots an odd, appraising glance at me, then looks away. For a second, I think she might be reconsidering the whole blackmail thing, and I swallow, wishing I'd kept my mouth shut. On the one hand, if I stop, I won't have to worry about being caught sneaking out by Peter. On the other, there's no way I can do the stuff I've been doing on my own; I'd be losing some valuable, protected practice, and I still don't know exactly what I'm going to do to Jadyn, let alone how. I'm just about to give in, tell her I'll go to the briefing and risk it, when she sighs.

"I'll see what I can do."

Apparently it isn't easy, but eventually—after we've wandered through most of the station, and I've spent about fifteen minutes trying to avoid bumping into people without stepping on Officer Carmichael's heels—she opens a door to a room that seems to suck sound in like a sponge. I step inside and look around, carefully. Even though the noise from our footsteps still echoes faintly in the hall, I can't see more than three feet into the room. If it wasn't for the muffled, enclosed feeling, I'd be afraid there wasn't a room there at all.

"It's a lounge," Officer Carmichael says, holding the door open because she doesn't quite know where I am, "but it's not a very good one. No one uses it unless they have to. The briefing will take between fifteen and twenty minutes. I'll come for you."

"Thanks," I say, meaning it. The click of the door shutting behind me makes the lines on that wall glimmer, then fade. I walk around the room, painfully slowly, whistling "Early One Morning." It doesn't feel safe. The walls and ceiling swallow so much of the sound that I have to make quite a bit of noise to see, and I'm not sure yet how much I can afford. By the time I see the open doorway on the other side of the room, and, through it, a faint smudge of stairs leading up, I'm feeling anxious enough that I stop whistling altogether. The last note melts into the room's deadness, and

I have to feel my way over to the wall and the nearest vinyl couch. The cushions make a squeaky whooshing noise as I sit down. I run my hand over the couch's material. *Yuk.* It's the stiff, vinyl kind they put in doctor's offices. No wonder people don't use this room much. I bet the lights are the hiccupping, fluorescent type. It's tempting to unsnap to check, but I have no idea where that stairway leads. With my luck, Officer Carmichael would come back and catch me, and then I'd *have* to go to the briefing, on principle. Twenty minutes isn't such a long time. I lean my head back against the top of the couch, and wait.

After five minutes, I'm starting to fidget. Waiting isn't easy when you can't see anything, and the only sound is an occasional rattle from the air conditioner, and your skin is so tight with goosebumps that it almost hurts. I start scuffing my shoe across the tiles, seeing how much of the room I can make out from just that sound. Not much.

After ten minutes, I've found a low table with some magazines and newspapers piled on it on it. I run my fingers over the papers, gently, realizing after a minute that I'm actually trying to guess which magazines they are by the feel of the ink on the covers. *Stupid. You're acting like a preschooler. If you can't handle sitting still for ten more minutes...* But my eyes are starting to ache from reflexively trying to focus on something, and I haven't heard a sound from the stairway or the hall outside since I've been here. Besides, I haven't seen today's papers yet; it's possible that there's another article about Jadyn, or at least Monica. I need all the information I can possibly get. I fumble my way across the room until I touch the wall beside the door; then I feel my way to the closest corner, where no one at the door or on the stairs can see me, and unsnap.

The fluorescent lights are as bad as I guessed they'd be, but they're bright enough to read by. It doesn't take me more than five seconds to realize that there won't be anything useful in the stack of magazines. The newspaper on the top of the stack is from mid-April, and it's the most recent one. Evidently people really *don't* come here that often. I shuffle through the rest of the pile, automatically trying not to disturb it more than I have to—although it obviously wouldn't matter if I did—until my fingers touch the cool tabletop. The last paper is a year and a half old, from two Decembers ago. I'm not even sure what I was doing then. Whether out of curiosity or boredom, I tug the paper out from under the stack and unfold it.

Most of the first section is holiday stuff: a Salvation Army fund-raiser, a section of recipes for fruitcakes "that your relatives won't have to lie about liking," an article on the Hanukkah services at Beth Israel synagogue, and a charity gala given by one of Jadyn's friends—which I remember, come to think of it, because Jadyn was gone until almost 4:30 AM, and I went downstairs in the middle of the night and made Peter come up and sleep on the couch in the rec room, because I'd been having nightmares and couldn't sleep if I was the only person on the entire floor. On page nine, there's an article about a failed assassination attempt on a diplomat in Colombia, and on the last page is a column headed, "Treadwell Death Declared Accidental." I barely glance at it, but as I'm refolding the paper, the name "Nadal" catches my eye. I hesitate, then unfold the paper again and read through the article.

> *The December 6th death of Ms. Sommara Treadwell was declared accidental today by a Cook County court. Ms. Treadwell's car ran off the road on Interstate 94, ten miles from Milwaukee, a little after eleven PM. Her death was*

initially thought to be due to foul play; however, the court has determined that the car was not tampered with before the accident, and eyewitnesses claim that no other car was involved. Ms. Treadwell died as a result of a broken neck, probably sustained when the car rolled over. An autopsy found no evidence of poison or drugs in her body, and, while there was a small amount of alcohol in her blood, the coroner states that it was not enough to impair her judgment or reaction time. Ms. Treadwell's partner, Mr. Javier Nadal, who had been considered a person of interest due to threats allegedly made against Ms. Treadwell after a recent quarrel, has not been accused.

I don't remember this. Two years isn't all *that* long ago; you'd think the fact that the man my mother is dating was suspected of murdering his last girlfriend would have stuck in my mind.

Neither he nor his lawyer could be reached for comment. Ms. Treadwell was twenty-seven. She is survived by her parents and a younger sis—

She's too quiet. The first sign I have that someone's there is the click of the doorknob turning; by the time I look up, she's in the room. I have half a second to decide what to do, which is just long enough for me to realize that, whatever I do, it's too late to snap invisible. Then there's a flicker of brown eyes and a startled double-take, and she's seen me. I stare at the girl, not really able to look away. I should know her. I know I've seen her somewhere before; her hair is the exact same brown as her eyes, and I remember that. As soon as my brain unfreezes, I'll know her name.

The girl recovers faster than I do. She takes a quick step back and covers her mouth with one hand. If I couldn't see the spark of humor in her eyes, I'd think she was embarrassed. "Geez, I'm sorry! I didn't think anyone was here; you're so quiet."

"It's okay," I say automatically. It isn't okay, not really, but she's already seen me. The damage is done. For a second I think she's going to duck back out into the hall, but then she hesitates, and, instead, pushes the door shut behind her. "Mind if I stay? I won't talk if you want to read. They won't let me in while they're briefing your mom, and I feel like I'm in the way everywhere else."

Of course. This is Monica. The fake me. It's good to know, but now I *really* can't think of anything to say. What's safe? How much have they told her? Monica misinterprets the look on my face as confusion; her forehead creases. "You *are* Natalie Irving, right?"

"Um. Yeah." Thank heavens she thinks I'm waiting for Jadyn. I nod, hoping I don't sound as uncertain as I feel. "Why won't they let you into the briefing?"

Monica shrugs, dropping onto the creaking vinyl couch across from the door. "Official police business."

They won't let her into Jadyn's briefing because Jadyn isn't there, but I want to see what she's been told. I can feel my synapses starting to fire again. This is the perfect chance to check Officer Carmichael's story. "Aren't you kind of 'official police business' yourself?"

Monica's already managed to tan more than I probably ever will, and her smile is startlingly bright against her golden skin. "Well, yeah, but I'm just Public Relations; I don't get to make policy." *Monica the spokesmodel*, I think again, then catch myself. Inwardly, I've already pegged her as silly, but it feels mean to think that while she's actually in the room talking to me, even if there's no way she could know. She sits back on the couch, crossing her arms against the air conditioning. "Actually, I think it's probably one of Jadyn's conditions. They want her to stay so badly they'll do anything she asks."

Has Jadyn thought of that? Odd, if she has; having that much leverage with the city sounds like her idea of paradise. "I guess so," I say, realizing right after I've said it that I can't remember how Monica ended the sentence, and that that might not have made sense.

Evidently it's good enough. Monica picks up an old copy of *Reader's Digest* and flips through it. She has beautiful hands; her nails are professionally manicured, but the skin around the edges is rough and pinkish. If she's going to be on TV as much as I think she will be, they'll have to make her stop biting her nails. "So," she says abruptly, "what brought this on?"

I blink, realizing I've been staring, and look away. "What do you mean?"

"You know." She glances at me over the top of the magazine. "With Jadyn. She hasn't wanted anything to do with the city for more than ten years, and now, suddenly, here she is. What happened?"

I shrug, all at once feeling very tired. "I have no idea. Who knows why she does anything?"

Something in Monica's eyes shifts. "You aren't … close, then?" I just look at her, and she hurries on; "I mean, she doesn't seem close to anyone outside her family, so I assumed …"

"No." *Moron.* How could anyone be close to Jadyn? Having her as a friend would be like owning a pet tiger: you think it's tame, just one of the family, and then one day …

Monica is watching me, measuringly. The sparkle in her eyes

fades, and I brace myself. I've seen this before. This is the part where she decides that personality defects are genetic and that I'm just an extension of Jadyn, then writes me off as a lost cause. *So what? Who cares what you think? Why should I—*

"It's hard, huh?" she says. I search her expression for sarcasm, but there's nothing. Her face is the most open one I've seen in months, and she's still looking directly into my eyes. Suddenly, my throat hurts.

"Yeah. Sometimes." *How did she...?* This is too weird. My eyes are starting to prickle; if I'm not careful, I'm going to cry. Over *Jadyn.* In front of a girl I don't really know, who is, essentially, my stunt double. I clear my throat, trying to rein in my slipping control, and deliberately change the subject. "What do you think of the job?"

Monica smiles bemusedly. She's noticed the subject change, but doesn't mention it. "It's... Wow." She shakes her head, slowly. "It's very weird. Awesome, but still weird. Sometimes it's like they think I'm Joan of Arc or something; I had no idea so many people thought this was important, that they cared this much. I..." She hesitates, staring at the generic floral watercolor on the wall by the stairs. "Sometimes it makes me feel guilty. I mean, I'm not what they think I am, you know? But even if I can't do the things they're counting on me to do, someone else will. I'm really glad Jadyn is doing this, and I can see why she wouldn't want her name used—"

"I can't," I say, impulsively. "Why?"

Monica looks at me as though she's surprised I have to ask. "Well, you know, all the pressure. All those people counting on her, and what if she fails? She put up with it for almost sixteen years. I don't think I could have held out half that long."

She means it. For a second I'm sure she's joking, but she's

perfectly serious. I don't know how she got that idea; everyone knows Jadyn stopped working because she didn't like being told what she could and couldn't do. But maybe if you didn't know her, and you were the kind of person who doesn't like to think bad things about strangers, you could pretend it was the strain. "So this way, if she fails, all those people blame *you*? And that's better?"

Monica pulls a wry face. "Well, not really… But if that's what she needs in order to come back, it's worth the risk. I think they need her."

I stare at her, wordlessly. How can she guess what it must be like to live with Jadyn and still think things like that about her? Jadyn's never been afraid of anything, as far as I know. She doesn't *need* anything. She doesn't care whether people like her or not.

And then the door swings open, and Officer Carmichael is standing there, staring at Monica, obviously taken aback. Monica stands apprehensively. "Is something wrong? I thought—"

As I jump up, Officer Carmichael's eyes flick across to me, then narrow slightly as she realizes she can actually see me. "It's fine," I say, as brightly as I can manage. "We were just talking about Jadyn. Is she done?"

I have to hand it to Officer Carmichael; she's a professional. She doesn't miss a beat. "Yes, and she's in a hurry. Follow me. And you," she barks at Monica, "need to report to the Chief's office; they're waiting for you."

Monica nods, a little sheepishly, then flashes me a quick smile. "Nice talking to you, Natalie. Tell Jadyn thanks from me, okay?"

I hesitate, then force myself to nod. "Of course." Then, because she seems much too decent a person to be a spokesmodel for either me *or* Jadyn, and there's no good way to say that: "I'll tell her not to mess up, too."

Monica's eyebrows shoot up, and she giggles. *Sure enough ...* Normally I can't stand gigglers, but Monica's laugh sounds like she really means it, and that makes it okay. "Maybe best not to, don't you think?" she says. Then she's slipped through the door and away, and Officer Carmichael is stalking down the hall in the opposite direction. I wait in the lounge until neither of them can see me, then I snap invisible and hurry after Officer Carmichael.

I don't unsnap as soon as I'm in the car this time; I don't dare while we're still so close to the police station. I wait until we're three blocks away before I let myself go, saying, "I'm coming back," right before I do.

"*Thank* you," Officer Carmichael says, dryly, but I can tell she means it.

"So what am I supposed to be doing?"

She's quiet for just a little too long. *Uh-oh. She really is annoyed with me.* I remember the look on her face when she saw me with Monica, and resolve to be extra-polite for the rest of the day. "You'll be down at Kinzie Marina," she says finally, "watching for a boat called *Estrella del Mar*. It's been used to run heroin across from somewhere in Ontario. The dogs have scented it on the boat, but so far, we haven't managed to find anything conclusive. The owner claims he has no idea why areas of his boat inexplicably smell like heroin; last time, he blamed it on a crew member and fired him."

She isn't expecting me to sneak onboard and look, is she? This would not be a good day for her to find out I can't see while I'm invisible. "Why don't you just search it yourselves? I mean, there isn't much I can do—"

"You can watch. They must be getting it off the boat somehow.

Our people are going to be busy searching the boat, so I want you to watch the crew. Keep an eye on every member, and if anyone starts to slip off somewhere, follow him. Just make sure you're not noticed."

"Will I be able to see if he's carrying anything? What kind of a package am I looking for?" Officer Carmichael gives a stiff half-shrug. "I have no idea. You may not be able to tell. They've probably got between one and five pounds; that would make a fairly good-sized package on its own, but it may be sewn into a coat, or carried in a spare gasoline can, or anything. These are very creative people. Don't look for anything in particular; just look for someone who doesn't want to be spotted, and who's being shielded by everybody else. It may be quite a wait, by the way," she adds, sounding grimly satisfied. "The boat isn't due in until five."

It *is* a long wait, but it's not as bad as being back at the police station. For one thing, I can see out here. The sound of the water hitting the poles of the pier and slapping the sides of the moored boats would be enough by itself, but there's also the sound of people talking and laughing, and motors out on the lake, and traffic noises from up above, on the street. Looking at the sliding, psychedelic surface of the water makes me dizzy, but if I avoid that, it's kind of nice out here.

There's a small cluster of police officers on the pier below me, Officer Carmichael among them. She stands next to a woman who's minding two restless German shepherds that are supposed to be able to smell heroin. The officers are wearing uniforms, which I thought was pretty dumb, considering. Officer Carmichael says it's because they want to attract attention. They don't expect to find anything on this search, and they want to be conspicuous, so that the boat's crew isn't cautious around everybody. If they think they know exactly who's an officer and who isn't, they might be more careless when they think the police aren't watching, which will give me a better chance to see something. The police are counting on me too, and *that* makes me nervous. Monica's voice drifts through my mind—*All those people, counting on her, and what if she fails…*—and I shake my head. *Concentrate.*

The police know I'm here. I waited down on the pier for a while, close to the cluster of uniforms, but it made them nervous. They couldn't see me, so they didn't talk to me, but since they knew I was close, they didn't say much to each other, either. The dogs could tell exactly where I was, and they didn't like it. The woman holding their leashes kept having to drag them away from me, and the dogs growled and whined and stared at me until I couldn't take it anymore. I went back up one of the sandpaper-floored ramps that lead from the concrete riverwalk down to the actual dock; right now, I'm sitting about halfway up, dangling my feet over the edge, trying to avoid the hot metal railing. I picked the ramp at the far end of the marina, so there aren't as many people trying to get up and down, and so far no one's tripped over me. This way, I've got a better view of what's going on down on the pier.

The ordinary boaters give the knot of police officers a wide margin, which is either respectful or wary. The German shepherds pace restlessly, getting underfoot. I can tell the sun is hot by what it's done to the railing, but it doesn't feel hot on my head and shoulders, the way it would if I unsnapped. The officers are probably severely uncomfortable in those dark, heavy uniforms. The water slaps and sucks at the concrete wall beside me. Thirty feet below, the lake smells like fish and algae and boat exhaust, but the air is wonderfully cool. If I'm not careful, I could fall asleep.

There's a swirl of movement down on the dock, and I sit up straighter. A small boat has broken away from the swarm on the lake and approaches the pier, while the officers get ready for it. I watch them, wondering where the logic is in this. If I were a drug runner, and I saw a group of policemen in full uniform waiting for me to moor at the dock, I'd turn the boat around and head right back to Canada. If the captain decides to do that, the police will be stuck; they don't have a boat down here. But the *Estrella del Mar* keeps coming, finally nosing gently into the pier.

A couple of figures jump onto the planks, tying the boat to one of the mooring posts. Two of the officers walk across to them, deliberately; the men don't seem happy to see them, but they step back, letting the officers on board. The woman with the dogs lets them sniff at the men on the dock, but they come up blank, and she takes them on board the boat. After a minute, only two of the officers are left on the dock, and, from what I can tell, the entire crew of the boat stands out on the boat's small deck, watching the officers.

I stand, carefully making my way down the ramp until I'm only about twenty feet from the pier, still far enough away to let me see over people's heads, but close enough that I can tell what's going on at the boat. I wish I could hear what they were saying.

The *Estrella del Mar* seems like a normal fishing boat, with a small, square cabin near the front, and a large expanse of deck behind. It's easy to tell which chalky images are crew members and which are officers; the uniforms make the officers look bigger, and some of the crew members don't even seem to be wearing shirts. Most of the crew stays where they are, just watching, but two of the men slowly edge toward the side of the boat nearest the dock. They pause at the edge, then, abruptly, they both jump, almost simultaneously. The boat dips visibly, and an officer on-board shouts. The ones on the dock cluster around the man on the left, but the one on the right edges away. I watch, incredulously, as the gap between him and the police widens from ten feet, to twenty, to thirty. Why are they letting him go?

Then one of the officers glances back, looking up at me, and I know. They're letting him go so I can follow him, maybe even see the drop. I look around until I find the man again. He's already halfway up the next ramp over, climbing fast. I hurry up the ramp, keeping my eyes fastened on the man. I don't dare lose him.

At the top of the ramp, he turns onto the riverwalk and heads for the street. I follow, keeping a few yards behind, even though there's no way he can see me. The light changes, and he starts across the street; I run after him, just managing to make it across before the traffic starts again. For someone who's trying to avoid the police, he has a very confident walk. I can barely keep up with him. It's as though he doesn't just *think* he can't be caught, but knows it. *Think again, mister.*

We walk for blocks, down a comparatively quiet side street. The man looks back a few times, and each time, I let myself fall farther and farther behind, on instinct. I know he can't see me—*I* can't even really see me—but maybe he can hear something, somehow. He's acting suspiciously like he thinks he's being followed.

After seven blocks, the man walks up to another, bulkier man who's standing with his back against the wall of a nearby building, waiting for a bus. The first man puts a hand on his shoulder, and the big man flinches slightly, then turns, surreptitiously hold-ing out a hand. Something lumpy and soft, the size of a couple of potatoes, passes from the first man to the second and into his coat, so smoothly I'm not sure I've actually seen it. I turn so I can see them out of the corner of my eye but don't look as though I'm looking at them, and pretend to examine a sign which I'm pretty sure has the bus schedule pasted to it. *You're being dumb*, I tell myself; *he's just paranoid. He can't really see you.* Even so, I keep my eyes on the sign. I don't like the way the first drug runner kept looking back at me. Maybe the drug runners are just as worried about Jadyn as the police are.

"Followed?" The big man is speaking, his voice low and casual, as though he's just asking the time, but the word yanks my attention back to him so fast he might as well have yelled *Fire!* "Who was following you?"

The other man's voice is even lower. I can't hear anything, even though it's suddenly very important that I do. He *did* know I was there, somehow. How did he know? Am I slipping? What did I do wrong, and … am I still doing it? I glance down at my hand, but it's just the way I'd expect it to be: chalky and vague against a faintly shining sidewalk.

The big man scans the sidewalk. "Don't see 'em." He pulls his coat closer around him, even though it's got to be more than ninety degrees out here and the heat from the sidewalk is burning my feet through the soles of the ballet slippers. "Maybe you'd better take a vacation," he jokes. "You're starting to get paranoid." They start down the sidewalk, the big man sauntering carelessly, the smaller one walking in a way I'm sure would attract attention anywhere. It isn't a paranoid walk. I stare after them for a long minute; then I shake my head, trying to clear it, and head back to the marina.

Officer Carmichael is waiting in the car by the time I get back. I slip inside, say "Coming back," and unsnap.

"Well?" she says. The air conditioner in the car is on full-blast, but she still looks hot and cross and uncomfortable; her frizzy red hair clings damply to her forehead. Obviously, if I haven't found anything, the day will have been a complete waste of time. I decide that, whatever I do after college, I will not be a police officer; I don't think I could put up with this kind of pressure every day.

"I saw the trade," I start, carefully, "but I don't know who did it. I'm sorry; I didn't get a good look at their faces—"

But Officer Carmichael is staring at me. "Stop. What trade?"

"The guy who got off the boat. He had something about this big"—I put my hands out, spacing them about six inches apart, fingers curled—"and he took it to this other, bigger guy, six blocks away."

"They stopped the man who jumped off," Officer Carmichael says.

"No, not him, the other one."

She looks at me as though she suspects I got a little too much sun this afternoon. "They jumped off at the same time," I tell her patiently, "They stopped the first guy, but let the second one go on purpose. One of them signaled for me to follow him."

There is a brittle look in Officer Carmichael's dark eyes. "They had orders not to let anyone pass," she says, slowly and carefully. "They said no one did."

"Well, they're lying," I say crossly, determined to end the conversation before she convinces me I'm insane. "I know what I saw."

Neither of us says anything for the rest of the drive.

It's even easier to get into the house this time than it was on Saturday. I have to use my key on the back door, but there's no one downstairs. Either Jadyn gave everyone the day off, or they're all sleeping; they don't need to worry about dinner, since Jadyn and I are technically both supposed to be gone. I grab a package of Pop-Tarts from the kitchen on my way through, just in case Jadyn doesn't come back until late and I have to hide in my room for a long time. The rooms are soft and silent, and I find my way upstairs mostly by feel.

I can't get the man out of my mind. How did he know I was there? Even if I made noise—and I'll admit I wasn't being particularly careful to avoid it—we were on a city street. There's no way he could have heard me, and obviously no way he could have seen me. And then too, why didn't Officer Carmichael see *him*? Something feels wrong. I open my door, quietly, slip through and shut it behind me. Officer Carmichael said drug runners tend to be ingenious people. Could they have found some way to detect Jadyn, and therefore me? That would change everything...

I unsnap, turn around—and freeze.

Peter is standing by my window, hands in his pockets, watching me.

c h a p t e r   t e n

I can't think. The walls and ceiling glow in the late sunlight, and the air is cold on my shoulders and neck. Peter is a weirdly incongruous silhouette against the pale window. He never, ever comes into my room. He shouldn't be here. It's policy. I feel shaky, not so much because he's in my room as because he's broken a routine. It's as though I've accidentally walked into someone else's universe. *He didn't see me,* I think hazily, because Peter doesn't look startled, or even particularly surprised.

Peter shoves his hands into his pockets, still watching me. "Natalie?"

I feel paralyzed by all the things I need to do in the next couple of seconds if I'm going to save this. I *can* save it. I have to. I don't know enough to be able to manage without... If Peter finds out ... Officer Carmichael ... Monica ... Nadal ... Jadyn—*Somebody's going to kill me, for sure.*

"*What* are you doing in my room?" I hiss, even as I realize that it's about ten seconds too late for that approach. Peter is unfazed. "You aren't supposed to *be* here!"

"I'm sorry," he says, but he's only being polite. "This was the only place I was sure you'd come back to. How long has that been happening?"

He's so calm it's eerie. How did he know? I don't answer. I can't. This can't be happening.

"Natalie."

My stomach has dropped into the stupid ballet slippers. I shake my head no. If I try to talk, I know I'm going to be sick.

In the end, Peter's the one who moves. Carefully, he steps around me and opens the door. Half a step into the hallway he hesitates, looks around, then motions for me to follow him. I do because the only other choice is slamming the door on him, and I'd have to open it again someday.

We don't go far; Peter opens the door right around the corner from my bedroom, which leads into the rec room. The walls in there are a deep red, almost burgundy, and it's a lot darker than it is in my room. Peter sits me down on the leather sofa in front of the TV, and pulls a chair around to face me. *This shouldn't have happened. I must have been careless, somehow. It doesn't matter now; I'm too close to quit. Peter can ask questions until midnight if he wants to.* I've decided I'm not going to say another word.

Peter gives a little cough, clearing his throat. "All right. For starters, it's obvious why you haven't told your mother. I'm not going to tell her, and I won't ask you to. I think, at this time, it wouldn't help." He hesitates, as though he hasn't quite decided

where he's going to go with this. "I don't even need to know when or how this started, although I've got an idea. I do need you to tell me where you've been going and why, and then I need you to stop."

Deciding it's safer to stick to my original plan, I don't say anything. Neither does Peter. He just sits, hands clasped, elbows braced on his knees. I watch a yellow band of sunlight creep slowly across the creamy carpet, moving inexorably toward the mahogany pool table nobody uses. As the minutes tick by, and he still doesn't say anything, it occurs to me that giving him the silent treatment is like challenging him at his own game; I can't win it. I've got to get out of this some other way... but what other way is there? How *could* I stop, anyway? Even if I wanted to, which I don't, Officer Carmichael would never... That's *right*. That's it. I'm being blackmailed.

"I can't," I say, staring down at my hands, clenched into fists on my knees. It's so quiet I can hear the pendulum on the wall clock by the stairs creak as it ticks away the seconds.

"Natalie..."

"You don't understand, I *can't*," I tell him, letting my eyes fill with all the frustration and anger I've been trying to stamp down, then snapping them up to Peter's face, letting him have it. He knows me too well for it to work, and doesn't flinch, but I'm startled by his face. He looks more tired than I've seen him in a long time.

"Define *can't*," he says, meeting my eyes. "What exactly does that mean?"

I take a deep, slightly shaky breath. "I was practicing, for... well, practicing," I say lamely, "and... um... a police officer saw me." Peter's eyebrows go up, but he doesn't say anything. "She said if

I didn't help her, she'd tell people. If she tells, Jadyn will find out, and she's already so mad about Monica ... I don't want ... "

There's something in Peter's eyes that I don't understand. He's thinking hard, but I'm not sure it's about what I've just told him. Somewhere in there, he's heard something he really doesn't like. "You're telling me you're being blackmailed?"

"I ... I guess," I stutter. He isn't reacting the way I expected. Whatever he's thinking about, it isn't covering for me.

"Who by, exactly?"

"A woman from the police station." I don't want to say her name. Especially not when Peter's looking like this.

I can tell we're talking about the same thing now, and I wish we weren't. Peter's eyebrows come together, ominously. "What does she have you doing?"

I can't hold his gaze any longer; I look back down at my hands. "Running errands, basically."

He isn't buying that. "Blackmailing is too serious an offense to risk for a glorified message-runner. What kind of errands?"

"Looking for things. Mostly."

"Where?"

"Different places. All over."

"And what exactly does she have you looking for?"

Cornered. "Drugs."

Silence. I don't dare look up. After a few seconds, there's a sharp smacking noise, and I flinch. Peter's just clapped his hands onto his knees. I glance up uneasily as he stands. "Well," he says evenly, "we'd better go. It's already after six."

"Go where?"

"To find this woman."

I shrink back into the leather couch cushions. This *really* isn't going the way it's supposed to. "No, I can't! She'll think I told. She'll ... she'll tell on *me*."

Peter shakes his head. "Natalie, you can't let her do this to you. I'd have thought your mother would have taught you at least that much."

I can't stop him. I'll have to go along with it and just hope I've done enough for Officer Carmichael that she'll come up with a way to bail me out. When I stand, my knees feel so weak I'm surprised they hold my weight. "At least let me go change, then. It's hot." It isn't hot inside—I'm actually shivering—but I don't want to confront Officer Carmichael, hiding behind Peter in the clothes I wore to help her out this afternoon.

Peter nods. "I'll wait for you here. What's this woman's name?"

"Officer Carmichael," I tell him, realizing a second later that I'm not hiding her first name on purpose. I've never heard it.

Officer Carmichael has, of course, already left work, but Peter tells me she said she'd wait for us at The Pastiche again. The cafe is much busier than it was a few days ago. There isn't an empty table in sight, and some of them have extra chairs pulled up to the corners. The room is a blur of lights in stained glass shades and sunburned, laughing faces. The noise hits me like an open hand the second I walk through the door. I stop just inside, taken aback by all the people. If Officer Carmichael decides she wants to out me, all she'll have to do is raise her voice. She couldn't have picked a worse place for this conversation. But Peter is already skillfully maneuvering through tables and chairs to the table in the corner, and I don't dare let him talk to Officer Carmichael without me there. I hurry after him, before the gaps he's made in the crowd close.

Officer Carmichael seems much more relaxed than I would be if I had an appointment with somebody's angry bodyguard. She has another mug in front of her, identical to the last one, down to the shade of the tea inside. The only difference I can see is that, this time, she's changed from her uniform into a pair of white jean shorts and a shapeless purple T-shirt. The color looks very odd with her bright hair, and I think she's a little old to be wearing shorts, but I'm currently in no position to make comments like that. I stare at her, hard, until she glances up and our eyes meet. I can't read anything in her expression, and my heart sinks, but I shake my head anyway, hoping she'll understand that I tried. She looks back at Peter, ignoring me. "Sit down," she says, calmly. "I managed to save you some chairs."

I sit, after a second, and so does Peter, although he hesitates as though he'd rather not. "Now," she says, "what's the problem?"

Peter leans forward, moving deliberately, and rests his elbows on the table. His face is, if possible, even blanker than Officer Carmichael's. Anyone else here would probably assume he's tired, but I know better. The angrier Peter gets, the harder he is to read. From the look of things, he's even madder now than he was when the paparazzi crew hid in the girls' locker room at school and tried to ambush me after gym class when I was in sixth grade.

"I caught Natalie sneaking in tonight," he says; "She tells me that you've … *asked* her to help you with some things that are, potentially, quite dangerous. As I'm sure you're aware, Natalie's still a minor. I don't like this situation at all."

Officer Carmichael empties a packet of sugar into her mug,

slowly stirring it in. "If you know that," she says quietly, "you must also know that your charge has an extraordinarily useful talent. This is a good cause, Mr. Maraszek. I have no control over Natalie's age, but she's shown herself to be quite capable so far. One of her errands has already led to a seizure and arrest for us." Officer Carmichael's eyes, unlike Peter's, are very readable; they're glittering like jet beads, and, slowly, I start to relax. She isn't going to let him win.

On the table, Peter's fingers tighten, and he laces them together to hide it. "Congratulations. If Natalie weren't a minor, or if her mother had been consulted, I would be the last person to stop her. As it is, though, you have to understand that I can't let this continue."

Officer Carmichael glances up at him. "With all due respect," she says, "you're being a bit naïve. Things like this don't stay secret without an incredible amount of effort. Either Natalie works for us of her own accord, or she'll be forced. She has a civic responsibility, and always will, wherever she goes. You can't deny that. At least this way she can stay anonymous if she likes."

Peter closes his eyes for a second. I watch him nervously, thinking, *Please, please don't do anything stupid...* There's a particularly noisy burst of laughter behind us, exploding above the chatter like a flare breaking through clouds.

"I don't see how she can have civic responsibility of any kind," Peter says, finally "She can neither vote nor be drafted for another year. This is illegal."

"You're entirely free to consult a lawyer," Officer Carmichael tells him dryly, "but I won't take responsibility for the consequences. If Natalie doesn't come in to work next time, I will report her."

"No one else knows about this, then?" Peter asks, his voice much too casual.

Officer Carmichael gives him a sharp look. "I haven't told anyone, no. But I *have* typed up a very detailed statement with my lawyer. If anything happens to me, it will be released." She wraps her fingers around the mug as if for warmth, although it has to be seventy degrees in the cafe. "Stop it if you like, but don't expect Natalie to thank you for it. You won't be doing her a favor."

Peter grimly nods. To my relief, he seems to be giving up. "And what happens to her if her mother finds out? You know her position on this sort of work."

Officer Carmichael snorts. "*I* know that? *Everyone* knows that. She feels so strongly about it that she resorted to child endangerment to ensure we'd never get help. I wouldn't think that would be a difficult home to leave."

Yes! Child endangerment. That's it! If Jadyn could do something like that, I'm definitely entitled to do this. I glance at Peter, hoping to see his expression change, but he's still watching Officer Carmichael.

"It's unlikely," she concedes, "but if it did happen, Natalie would certainly be provided for. Losing her wouldn't be in anyone's best interests."

Peter stands, a little stiffly. The conversation is over. "I'll be in contact about this," he says, and then he turns, wading purposefully through the tables toward the door. I shoot one last, apprehensive glance back at Officer Carmichael, but she's staring fixedly down into her mug of tea, as though she's trying to read her future in it. She doesn't look up.

The sunlight outside The Pastiche looks oddly flat and hard. I flinch at the unexpected heat when we leave the shade of the skyscrapers to cross Cullerton Street. It seems so unreal I didn't expect it to feel like anything. The words *child endangerment* spin through my mind, occasionally striking sparks off an insult or a comment: things said to my face or behind my back, on TV, about Jadyn. About me. I can win this now. I know I can.

Several times, I sneak sideways glances at Peter. He knew exactly what Officer Carmichael was talking about. I saw it in his face when she said it. Nobody—especially not Peter—could look me in the eye and tell me I couldn't do this. Not if they knew Jadyn and what she'd done to me. All I have to do is ask the right questions, get him to talk himself into a corner, and I'll be okay. I can't try it out here, though; it's too loud, too crowded, too strange. Much too distracting, especially for someone trained to watch everyone in sight. It would be too easy for him to avoid the question. Besides, I'm not really sure I *could* ask him now. He's squinting against the sun, and the strange, low light fills the creases of his face with deep shadows. Right now, I'm finding it hard to trust anybody.

So I wait. I wait while we walk the six blocks to the parking garage, and while we take the stairs up to the fifth floor (Peter doesn't like elevators, and I've never managed to find out why), and while he unlocks the BMW, lets me in and settles into the driver's seat. Then, for what feels like about fifteen minutes, he sits still, staring at the concrete wall in front of the car. Finally, I can't take it anymore. "Peter."

He doesn't look at me. Either he's ignoring me, or he didn't hear. "*Peter.*"

He glances at me. I realize, just a little too late, that he did hear me the first time. "What was that stuff about Jadyn and child endangerment?" I've thought the sentence over in my mind so often since we left The Pastiche that saying it aloud feels ridiculous, as though I'm repeating myself.

Instead of answering, Peter starts the BMW and carefully backs out of the parking space. I bite my tongue, forcing myself not to ask again. I can't tell what's going on. Maybe he's mad at me. I mentally run over the last hour, trying to figure out exactly what I should apologize for. Peter drives down through the garage in silence, pays at the gate, and eases out over the sidewalk, watching for a gap in traffic. Only after he's seen one and taken it and we're heading down State Street does he say anything, and then it's so out of the blue I'm sure I've heard him wrong. "Is that why you hate her?"

Hate who? Hate Jadyn? "I don't *hate* her," I say automatically, even as I realize that I might, actually. It's just that hating Jadyn feels so futile it doesn't seem to count as hate. "I mean—Geez, Peter! You know what she's like. What would you do if you were me?"

Peter's expression doesn't change. "Probably the same. Was the blackmail set-up your idea?"

I was afraid he'd think that. I stare through my window at the side-view mirror, watching the city slide backward, so that he can't see my face. "No. It's not really that bad, though. I need the practice." I shoot another sideways glance at Peter. *He's probably going to ask* why *I need to practice.* "Do you think I could do this at home?"

"Practice for what?" he asks.

I don't say anything, even though Peter gives me a good thirty seconds to explain.

He sighs. "Natalie, I'd be glad to cover for you while you practice, since you're going to do that no matter what, but I don't want you working with that officer. Under the circumstances, it's too risky."

It's not like I have many other options. I think. "What about child endangerment?"

Peter blinks, thrown by the non sequitur. "Sorry?"

"Officer Carmichael said something about Jadyn and child endangerment, and you knew what she was talking about. Tell me."

As we merge onto I-55, he won't look at me, instead checking every mirror twice, slowing to let a semi pull in front of us. Finally, he clears his throat. "I don't know that there ever was any 'child endangerment.' There were rumors…" He flips the turn signal on, edging into the fast lane. "When your parents divorced, they both wanted custody of you. You were only a year old, and no one knew whether you'd inherited Jadyn's skill or not. Your father's lawyers managed to get the court to rule that, if and when you *did* develop that particular skill, custody would automatically go to him."

I haven't heard this part before, and I'm not sure I want to. "Why?"

"You know why. Jadyn's always been very ... *reluctant* to cooperate with the city. With any government, really. They didn't want her to influence you."

I stare out through the windshield. Sparks of sunlight blaze off the car ahead of us, blotching my vision with violet afterimages.

"When you were two," he says, "there was a rumor that you'd started to develop Jadyn's skill, that people had seen odd things. And then, somehow, before anything could be proven, you hurt your head. Afterward..." He shrugs. "People didn't believe it, of course. Three court-appointed social workers lived at your house for a solid month, watching and listening for any signs that Jadyn had lied, and she had to let them stay. After a month, they were convinced that, if you'd had the skill in the first place, it was gone now. They passed their story on to the courts and the media, and the general public had to settle for watered-down versions of that. Some people suspected Jadyn had crippled you on purpose, so that you couldn't be taken away or used against her."

I can believe the last part, but I'm having a hard time with the first one. They couldn't have taken custody away from Jadyn just because of political reasons, could they? Not here... Besides, my dad would never have gone along with it. Not *my* dad, with his smile, that sunlight hair. "Is it true?"

Peter shrugs. "No idea. I wasn't living in Chicago then, and it isn't the kind of thing Jadyn would tell someone else about. If you don't know, I doubt anyone does."

I lean back in the seat, the leather headrest cool against my neck. *Dad can't be like that*, I think, *but then why did he give up on getting custody once I was useless? He could have gotten at least one weekend a month; no one would have denied him that. Why hasn't he ever tried to see me?*

Stop it. Stop thinking. "Would you really cover for me?" I ask Peter.

"Yes."

"Why? I mean, you said…" I can't think of a good way to say it. Even if Peter doesn't know exactly what I'm doing, he's got a rough idea. If he's any kind of loyal employee at all, he shouldn't be able to back me up.

"Because it's better than the alternative."

"But Jadyn pays you."

No answer. For a long minute, the only sounds I hear are the buzz of our tires on the Interstate and the faint hiss of the air conditioning. And then Peter says, "You know that I know exactly what you can do. And, yes, I *am* paid by your mother, and you know what would happen if I told her about this."

I turn to look at him, very slowly, hoping I've heard wrong. "What—"

"I'm just asking if you realize that."

"Yes, I do."

"Good. Then you know if you repeat any of what I've said in this car to anyone, you will be in a world of trouble."

I don't believe this. "Geez! It's not like I'd tell on you anyway."

Peter shoots me a small, crooked smile, which doesn't reassure me as much as it normally would. "Fine. As I'm sure Officer Carmichael has told you, people have suspected Jadyn of being involved in various less-than-legal projects for years. Since she began to be associated with Javier Nadal, they've concentrated on trying to link her to the drug traffic."

I stare at the much-too-clean dashboard, glad that Peter's too busy driving to see my face. Officer Carmichael didn't mention any of that, but, suddenly, the errands she's been having me run make more sense.

"The fact that Jadyn has never really gotten along with any government makes most people—especially the ones *in* government—very nervous," he continues. "Eleven years back, after she refused to spy for the United States during the war, the government put a tail on her so that they'd know if she ever did start working for someone else."

Ha! That's been tried about fifty times that I can remember, and no one's managed it for more than forty-eight hours. "Good luck. Did she kill them, or did they just 'disappear'?"

"Neither. Yet."

I glance up at Peter, eyebrows raised. "Do you know who—"

Then I see the tension in the back of his hands, and his white knuckles.

"It … it's *you*?"

Peter nods, so slightly that I'm not sure I've seen it. "The problem with the system is that Jadyn never really talks. Not to staff, not to the police, not even to you. She talks at parties and dinners, when she's expected to, but she rarely speaks about personal matters and I've never seen her even slightly drunk. She never lets anything slip. She's so good, it's no wonder everyone wants to recruit her for their side."

This creeps me out. Not the conversation itself, but the fact that I'm having it with Peter. He reaches over and switches the air conditioning to low. "However," he says, "if *you've* managed to get something on her ..."

I've known Peter for most of my life, talked to him far more than I've talked to anyone else, and I thought his biggest secret was that he wanted to be a penciler. Secret identities and spies ... No wonder he likes comic books so much.

"I haven't," I say. "but what if I had? Who are you with?"

"The CIA."

Geez! "So you ... weren't with the Secret Service?" What would have happened if I *had* managed to search his file last week?

"I was with the Secret Service for a year, but I started out with the CIA, and I went back afterward."

"Wasn't Jadyn looking at about a dozen candidates when she hired you? What if she'd picked somebody else?"

Peter chuckles. "Well, eight of the twelve were CIA. They would have made sure one of us got hired."

Of course they would have. How can this have been going on for eleven years without my seeing a thing? Without *Jadyn* seeing? Nobody should be this good. But if someone *is*, and if it's Peter ...

"If I find something," I ask, "what's going to happen?"

Peter flips on the turn signal, switching back to the right lane as we come up on our exit. "It depends on what you find. If she does have drug connections, she'll go to jail, probably for quite a while. If she were anyone else, they'd probably just let her post bail, but no one is going to go easy on Jadyn." He glances at me, checking my reaction. "Your officer was right about one thing. If that happens, you'll definitely be taken care of." He slows, looking over his shoulder, and lets a Cadillac pass us before we merge onto South

County Line Road. "Of course, since she's your mother, you don't have to do any of this if you'd rather not."

"But you just said...I mean...I'm dangerous now, right?"

Peter smiles. "Not really. At least, you're no more dangerous to me than I am to you. We're about even."

On Fieldstone Drive now. I stare through the windshield at the gigantic, eccentric mansions on their acres-wide lawns that, somehow, stay green in spite of the heat. "I'll help," I say.

Peter's quiet for so long that I start to think he hasn't heard. Finally, just as I'm about to risk saying it again, he nods. "Good. Now all we have to do is figure out how to keep Officer Carmichael quiet."

"That's all, huh?"

"It won't be hard. It's just a matter of finding the right thing. Shouldn't take more than a few days. In the meantime, do your best to keep her happy. I'll cover for you at the house."

I step out of the BMW thinking that it's lucky Jadyn won't be back until late, because I don't want to deal with her right now. I don't care if she hurt me so I wouldn't be taken away, or how young she was when she did it; nobody sane would have done that to a kid. And she's *Jadyn*. She could have found another way.

When Peter and I walk into the front hall, though, I realize it's even better than I'd hoped: Jadyn's secretary is waiting for us with a message. "Jadyn won't be home this evening."

"Why not?"

"She called just after you left. She's going to stay at Isole for a while."

"But she just came back." Not that I mind, but it's strange. Why so suddenly? Did she hear something?

The secretary looks faintly embarrassed. "She didn't explain herself, but as Ms. Aloia's publicity spreads...I assume Jadyn hopes it won't be quite so, er, dense at Isole."

Which means she'll stay there until things calm down a bit. Good.

Peter disappears into the kitchen to see whether they've saved us any dinner, and I head upstairs to call Officer Carmichael. If I plan to keep working with her, I have to apologize for this afternoon.

The third-floor rec room is almost dark. Deep, dying stripes of sunset-orange light streak the ceiling, and the walls below the windows are lost in shadows. I flip the light switch; the track lights snap on and the room is bright again, artificially safe. I switch on the TV, pull the curtains on the sunset, and collapse onto the leather sofa. *Deja vu.* The chair Peter sat in earlier still faces me, blocking the TV. I push it away with my foot.

What can I tell Officer Carmichael? That I'm sorry? That Peter ambushed me? That I tried to keep him from calling her? It's all true. It's hard to believe I'm nervous about lying after all the practice I've had lately, but tonight is different. Tonight, if I try to lie, I may accidentally tell the truth; it's getting harder and harder to tell them apart.

The channel that played *The Princess Bride* last night now runs a black-and-white movie I don't recognize. I flip through the channels, past a cooking show, an infomercial for a home gym, a cheesy movie from the eighties, a documentary on World War II, Monica on the Chelly Wright Show—

Monica?

I flip back. Chelly and Monica sit in overstuffed, red upholstered chairs under those extraordinarily hot lights. Chelly has found the perfect balance between poised and relaxed, but Monica seems a little uncomfortable, as though she's worried the chair might swallow her. It feels weird to see her on TV after I talked to her at the police station just a few hours ago. I've seen lots of people I know on TV shows before, but never one of my friends. *But Monica isn't your friend,* I remind myself. *She's barely even an acquaintance.*

Monica wears pink velvety slacks and a matching sleeveless top that makes her hair look silky and perfect, but clashes quite badly with the chair. When the camera pans, there's a man in a dark suit standing at the edge of the picture—an obvious bodyguard.

"...an incredible change for you," Chelly is saying, her voice filled with that bizarre mix of sympathy and intensity that only reporters and talk-show hosts seem able to pull off.

I'm stalling by watching the show, and I know it. I turn on the cell phone, then realize there's another problem. Officer Carmichael has always called me, so I don't know her phone number. If I'm lucky, maybe it's in the speed dial...

"Now, I've heard rumors that you're going to work with the police on narcotics cases. Is that true?" Chelly's voice again.

She can't tell you that, I think, as I find the number, the only one in speed dial. I enter it.

On TV, Monica says, "I'm sorry, I can't answer that."

Officer Carmichael doesn't pick up until the fifth ring. "*Yes?*"

She sounds more annoyed than I expected, and I wince. "I...it's Natalie."

"Of course it is."

"I just...Look, I'm sorry. I didn't tell Peter. He was waiting for me when I got back, and I didn't see—"

"Don't lie." She cuts me off so sharply that I barely avoid biting my tongue.

"Wha—"

"You told him. You thought you could hide behind him, that he'd snarl a bit and I'd just go away. Well, you're wrong. It's too late to get out now. I can't let you go any more than you can just leave."

Monica's voice filters through the haze of apprehension that's settling over my mind. "No," she says, "they definitely didn't want me to go. My mom was afraid they'd mess up, cut something important, and I'd end up a vegetable. But they knew it was my choice. They're proud."

I open my mouth, realize I can't make a sound, and clear my throat. "Officer Carmichael, I swear—"

"You—No. I don't believe this. You rich people just assume you own the world, but you don't. You aren't invincible, or immortal, or above the law. You're just like your mother."

My mother the child abuser? My mother the drug runner? Over my dead body! I can hear the blood pounding in my ears. "No! Listen to me, I—"

"*You* listen. If you try something like that again, I will turn you in immediately. In fact, I might just do it now."

She isn't bluffing, and suddenly it's hard to breathe. "But—"

"I will *not* be threatened, Natalie!"

I slide down until I'm lying on the couch, and shut my eyes. It isn't easy to be calm about this, but I *have* to. If I blow it now, I could wreck everything. I swallow, hard. "I know. I'm really, really sorry. I honestly didn't tell him. I didn't want him to find out. I was tired and careless and he surprised me."

"So you told him about me."

"Well, I... What was I supposed to say?"

"Anything except that would have been fine."

She's right, of course. Now that I'm by myself and Peter isn't staring at me, waiting for answers, it's obvious that lying was the only logical thing to do. Earlier, of course, logic was impossible; it was hard just to breathe, let alone form a coherent sentence. But there's no way she'll believe that.

In the heavy silence, Chelly Wright's voice sounds as thin as fishing line. "... the scariest thing you've had to do so far?"

"You're right," I say, finally. "I panicked. I couldn't think of anything else to say, and I—I was afraid he'd tell my mother. If she knew I was doing this, she'd kill me, I'm not kidding."

"You can't stop now," she says again.

"I know that. It's okay. It's interesting, and I don't mind... um, helping you. Please, can't we just forget about today? Peter won't tell. I swear he won't be a problem."

Officer Carmichael is silent. A burst of applause from the TV startles me; I glance up in time to see the camera pan back to Chelly Wright. "There have been several drastic comparisons drawn between the two of you," Chelly says. Her voice is even, but there's a hardness in her eyes that says she's going to believe every one of the comparisons, with or without proof. "Some people think she may be a threat to you. One of our callers earlier this evening thought she should be forced to relocate to another part of the country so that she can't sabotage your efforts. What do you think?"

There is a sharp, hissing sigh from the cell phone. "Fine," Office Carmichael says. " For today, I won't tell. But if one more thing happens—if I get so much as a single threatening phone call from *anyone*—that's it."

I stare up at the ceiling, gritting my teeth, forcing myself to stay quiet.

"I will be out of town for the next few days," she continues. "When I get back, I will call you. Do not try to call me before then."

"What should I—"

But she's hung up. The frustration that's been building up inside me boils over with a rush, and I slam my fist into the back of the couch as hard as I can. It makes a solid, stinging thwack that, under other circumstances, might have been satisfying. Today, it's going to take a lot more than that. Why can't this be simple? I need practice, Officer Carmichael needs help, and Peter's objectives match mine. It should be the easiest arrangement in the world, but somehow it keeps getting more and more tangled. If it gets much worse... It's not fair. I just want to be able to be me, to have that be good enough. Most people don't have a problem with that, do they? If only I'd been born somewhere else, as someone else...

"I think she should be able to do what she wants," Monica says. I turn my head, very slowly, to look at her face on the screen. The back of my neck is prickling. "We don't own her."

It takes me a minute to grasp that she's talking about Jadyn.

chapter twelve

he next few days are a nightmare. After that last phone call, I desperately need something to do to stop me from thinking about Officer Carmichael, and of course there's nothing. Peter is gone most of the day, off doing who-knows-what. He's probably looking for something to use against Officer Carmichael, but he hasn't said anything, and so far I haven't managed to ask. Since he isn't around to watch my back, I'm technically not supposed to leave the house.

The air outside is heavy and humid, prime thunderstorm weather, but it's nothing compared to the atmosphere inside. Everything seems to be waiting, watching me when my back is turned; even the walls seem faintly alive. I find myself taking the long way downstairs, just so I have a better chance of running into another living person.

I'm not the only one who feels nervous. Even people who couldn't possibly know a fraction of what's been happening—the landscaping crew, the man who washes the windows, the sisters who come in to clean the main floor—act edgy and uncomfortable. People are taking every possible opportunity to stay away, and the house feels emptier every day. It can't stay like this forever. Something's going to have to give, and soon.

I spend most of Tuesday upstairs in the rec room, flipping through TV channels, watching for Monica. She's currently my only link with the police. I don't dare count on Officer Carmichael to play fair just now; she probably won't break her side of the bargain entirely, but I wouldn't be surprised if she decided to make things harder for me. I tell myself that Monica might let some information slip and then at least I'll have some idea of what to watch for, but when I finally do find her, I forget what I'm looking for. I end up just listening to her voice, trying to figure out what she's trying to get out of this whole situation. I still can't find anything, and, after her segment is over, I can't even remember what was discussed.

Then, of course, there's Jadyn. She hasn't called, which isn't a problem as far as I'm concerned. I've got enough to worry about here; she can stay at Isole until I go to college for all I care. But there's something about the situation that bothers me, skittering in the blurriness at the edges of my mind, and I can't get rid of it. To make things worse, the stupid "Treadwell Death Declared Accidental" article must have gotten into my subconscious somehow, because Tuesday night is miserable. I keep waking up, and when I do sleep I have nightmares.

Me, getting up in the middle of the night and going into the rec room to scan the TV for Monica again, but finding Jadyn instead, lying in a field with a broken neck, her eyes wide and glazed and empty, as a man's voice drones on about statistics and murder and drugs ...

Jadyn's car, speeding down an inky-black highway, dangerously fast, until something goes wrong and it skids, swerves, bursts into flames and starts rolling ... and rolling ... and rolling ...

Jadyn and Nadal waiting for me at the house when I come back from one of Officer Carmichael's errands. Jadyn whispers something to Nadal, but she's looking at me, and Nadal pulls out a gun, pointing it at my face, and I can't move ...

On Wednesday, I'm determined to figure out how the drug runner knew I was there. Did I not go entirely invisible after all? Could he have seen something when I moved? I have to know. I practice for four solid hours, snapping and unsnapping in front of a mirror, trying everything I can think of, but it's impossible. Either I can see myself or I can't; there isn't any space in between. If Peter were here, I could ask him to watch and tell me, but he isn't; he's out investigating Officer Carmichael. By the end of the afternoon, I've convinced myself that the drug runner must have been paranoid, and that he would have had to be part bat to know where I was.

My head hurts so much it's hard to think, but at least that night I don't dream.

By Thursday, I'm about to go insane. Peter is gone again. Officer Carmichael hasn't called. Jadyn hasn't called. No one in the house will speak to me unless I speak to them first. To be fair, they don't really need to talk to me; Jadyn always leaves very clear orders, and she's gone so much everyone gets used to the routine. They probably have the patterns memorized even better than she

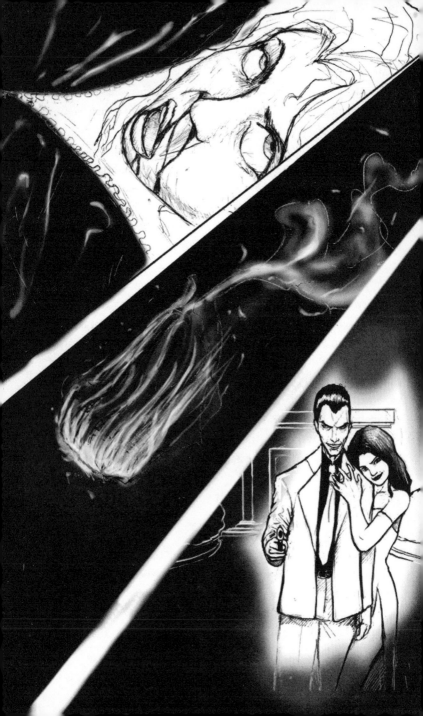

knows; I'm almost sure they don't dust her rooms until the morning before she's due back...

And that's when I get my brilliant idea. Jadyn is *gone*. Which means her rooms are empty. If Peter weren't looking for Officer Carmichael's secrets, he'd probably be looking for something against Jadyn, and since *he* isn't...

Well, it's something to do. Jadyn's rooms are on the second floor, on the opposite end of the house from mine. From her windows, you can see patches of Fieldstone Drive through the row of birch trees edging the front lawn. I curse myself all the way downstairs for not thinking of this way back on Tuesday, and it isn't until I'm actually standing in front of her door, fingers curled around the cut-crystal doorknob, that I remember why I didn't. Jadyn's rooms give me the creeps. They always have. They're perfect rooms for hiding in, even if you're aren't invisible, and whenever I go in there—which isn't often—I'm never quite sure I'm alone. I hesitate, trying to fight back the feeling that there's someone standing just on the other side of the door, waiting for the knob to turn. Just as I've almost convinced myself that Jadyn wouldn't be dumb enough to leave anything incriminating in her bedroom, I hear someone climbing the stairs, just one room over. I wrench the door open and slide through, wincing at the click it makes as it shuts behind me. I flip the lock, just for good measure.

The room is dark, and the air's so hot and thick it feels like I'm breathing smoke. It takes me a moment to realize that it isn't my nerves playing tricks on me: the windows haven't been opened since Jadyn left, and someone's closed the air vents. So they really *haven't* been cleaning her room. I grin, a little nervously, more because I need to prove it's possible in here than because I really feel like it.

I'm fairly sure I'm the only person in the room, but it's not easy to tell; there are too many large pieces of furniture, too many dark corners. There's a large armoire beside the rolltop writing desk, large enough for someone to hide in, and a window seat with shutters that can be—and have been—pulled across to make the seat into a closed cubicle. But the bed is the worst. It's a large, dark four-poster, so tall there's a stepstool beside it. A canopy of gauzy white material, almost like mosquito netting, hangs down to cover the whole bed. It looks like the bed is smothered under a very large spider web. Vague shadows of a pillow and the line of the mattress are visible through it, but I couldn't swear there's no one hiding in there. I flip the lights on, then go to the bed and shove the clingy material aside.

Nothing there. Just a large expanse of dark blue comforter and three beaded accent pillows. I leave the drapery pushed to one side, because it makes me feel a little less like I'm being watched, and start looking.

The walls are midnight blue, with tiny faceted crystals scattered across them in odd places; they catch stray sparks of light and gleam unsettlingly, so that you're always seeing weird, untraceable glints out of the corner of your eye. The furniture is all deep mahogany, and the curtains are heavy blue velvet. It's the kind of room where turning on the light makes you feel like you're in a spotlight on a darkened stage, staring out at an audience you can hear but can't see. I really don't like this room.

But Jadyn isn't here. There's no one to see me. I open the shutters and check the inside of the armoire. Then, opening the air vents as I go, I walk through Jadyn's sitting room and bathroom. I check the corners in the sitting room, and under the furniture, and in the magazine rack. I even check the medicine cabinet in the bathroom. I'm not entirely sure what I'm looking for, but there's nothing in there except an unopened bottle of aspirin, an almost-empty bottle of sleeping pills, and a flat tube of toothpaste; it's like she doesn't even live here. I stare into the cabinet, thinking that maybe I should take a picture of it and send it to Ari. I could write "So you don't have to bother asking me out" on the back, or something. As I close the mirrored cabinet door, the flash of my own grinning face startles me.

After half an hour, when I've exhausted all the obvious hiding places in the other rooms, I stand in the doorway, looking into the bedroom. This room's going to be the hardest one, and I'm not sure where to start. *It's just like cleaning your room. Start with the closest thing, and then go to the next closest thing, and the next, until you're done. Easy if you don't think about it.*

There's a small, framed photo on the polished accent table near the bed that I don't remember. I pick it up, gently, by the edges. The photo is of a little girl, maybe ten or eleven years old, wrapped around a tire swing like a contortionist; she's leaning back, bobbed dark hair flying around her ears as she grins at whoever's holding the camera. Her eyes are squinched up by the smile, so it takes me almost a full minute to realize the girl is Jadyn. I frown, tilting the frame so that the light from the window doesn't glint on the glass; the edges of the leaf-shadows on the grass are sharp then, and I can see a squirrel crossing the fence at the very back of the yard, but I still can't see anything of Jadyn in that girl's face.

I've seen pictures of Jadyn when she was younger before, but they're mostly from when she was twelve and older, clipped from newspapers, when she was already on her way up and had started to change. I've never seen her normal, although I know the basics: She was born middle-class, in Tacoma, Washington. Her dad was a nurse at St. Joseph Medical Center and her mom was a political activist. Her name was Janice until she turned eighteen and changed it because "Jadyn" fit her image better. Her parents still live in Washington, as far as I know; she used to take me to see them until they stopped speaking to her. I've never seen a picture of *them* here. I think she threw them away, just like she got rid of Dad's photos. She's tried so hard to erase the fact that she used to be someone else. You'd think, after all that, the last thing she'd want is a frozen fragment of her childhood by her bed where she has to see it every morning.

I set the photo down, gently, and turn to the desk. It isn't used much. Except for a clear space in the center about the size of a dinner tray, it's crowded with loose note cards and boxes of stationery, ornamental clocks and miniature crystal animals, unread paperback books and about three reams' worth of scattered paper. At first I shuffle through the papers quickly, sure I'll recognize what I'm looking for when I see it, but I stop when I realize even *I* can tell that the mess has been rearranged. Reluctantly, I slow down.

Near the center of the desk, face-down and pushed under the pigeonholes, is a photo in a heavy silver frame. Not a photo of Dad or of Jadyn's parents, but a studio portrait of Javier Nadal that used to be displayed on a shelf near the window. And now it's face-down and half-buried in her desk? Odd. Did they fight? I stare at the photo, wondering if he really did kill his girlfriend, if he really is involved in drugs. If I could punch through the thin veneer of charisma in those eyes, what would I find? I slide the photo back into place, then push some of the papers around it so that it isn't right on top of everything.

There has to be a day-planner or a journal in here somewhere, but there aren't any books in the pigeonholes; the only interesting thing in the top half of the desk is a stamped, addressed envelope lying on the slatted roll-top. Jadyn probably expected whoever cleans her room to find it and mail it when they came in to dust, so if I do it, Jadyn may never notice that no one cleaned her room while she was gone. I move the letter to the seat of the desk chair so I won't forget it.

I don't find anything even remotely useful until I'm on the third desk drawer. There's a blank manila envelope there, pressed flat against the side of the drawer. The metal catch is fastened but the flap isn't sealed, and the envelope is stuffed so full that it's starting to tear at the corners. I set it on the desktop and open it, gently, so it doesn't tear more.

Full of newspaper clippings. *Geez, how egotistical can you get?* I think, disgusted, but I pull the first few out anyway, just to see.

They aren't about Jadyn. They're about Nadal.

This is weird. Jadyn gets along with Nadal well enough, but I doubt she's this seriously in love with him. Even if she was, she's not the scrapbooking type. I scan the articles' headlines quickly, looking for a pattern:

"Nadal to Speak at UIC Commencement."

"Shipping Heir Funds Scholarship."

"Heroin Deaths on the Rise."

"Nadal Spotted at Madison Square Garden."

And even, "Treadwell Death Declared Accidental."

I pull the rest of the clippings out of the envelope and fan them out in front of me. There doesn't seem to be a common thread. Stories about charity functions and business functions are jumbled together with articles on murdered prostitutes and rising crime rates. Nadal isn't even mentioned in about a third of them.

I don't understand. This isn't scrapbooker behavior, it's stalker behavior. Jadyn has an article on what seems like every crime Javier Nadal has ever been connected to, even indirectly, including the one about his dead girlfriend. She's been collecting these for at least five years, maybe longer. She doesn't need to be warned about him; she knows he's dangerous. She must have known before she started seeing him. Is she crazy? Is that *why* she likes him, because he's dangerous?

I glance up at the desktop. From where I'm sitting I can just see the sharp silver edge of the half-buried picture frame. If she knew he was dangerous ... if she knew about the drugs ... What did they fight about, anyway?

It's probably pointless to try to figure it out. Peter will want to see these, though; maybe they'll mean something to him. I scoop the clippings back into the envelope as carefully as I can, without crumpling them or ripping the envelope. I pull the drape back around the bed and close the shutters, but I leave the vents open. Then, feeling like a professional, I take the letter from the chair, pick up the manila envelope and slip out the door, turning off the lights as I leave. Funny how normal the room feels, now that I'm walking out of it.

For the first time in almost seventy-two hours, I feel myself relax, just a little. I've done something. I can afford to spend the rest of the day doing whatever I want and not feel guilty. The light flooding the outer rooms isn't as hard as it felt before, and if the walls are still waiting for something, they're ignoring me. If I'd only done this on Tuesday ...

Once I'm safe in my room, with another locked door between me and the rest of the house, I open all the windows, even the one in my bathroom. We do have air conditioning, but it isn't very good up on the third floor, and I like outside air better anyway. I turn on both the ceiling fan and my desk fan, grab a paperback copy of *I, Robot* off my bookshelf, and flop down on my bed. As I do, something crackles under me, and I realize I've forgotten to put Jadyn's letter in the mailbox. I'm sure the mailman's already come today, anyway; I'll just put it out tomorrow. *If she left it in her room for someone else to mail,* I think, *it can't have been urgent.*

I glance at the address, just to double-check. It's addressed to a Mr. and Mrs. Samuel A. Irving; I don't immediately recognize the names as either friends or business contacts, and I tug the letter closer, skimming the rest of the address: Mr. and Mrs. Samuel A. Irving in Tacoma, Washington…Wait. This can't be right. I must have read it wrong. Jadyn wouldn't write to her parents. As far as I know, she hasn't so much as sent them a birthday card in eleven years, or, for that matter, gotten one from them. They probably wouldn't even read this if they got it. Why would she…

The envelope is ripped open before I have time to think about it. *Well,* I tell myself, *it doesn't matter. You're mailing it before Jadyn gets back, so she won't notice. She hasn't written to them in years, so they won't recognize her handwriting anyway. Just address another envelope and mail it in that.* To make up for being careless, I handle the letter as though it's been written on rice paper.

Monday, July 26th

To Mr. and Mrs. Irving,

By now, you will have heard the news. It's the only reason I expect you to read this letter instead of burning it unopened. I promise to explain exactly why I did what I did, if you'll promise to read to the end of this letter. You are the only ones I've told.

Please believe that I'm sorry about the past few years. I do not apologize for what I've done—or have not done—but I am sorry to have disappointed you. If I had been someone else, it would have been easier to be what you wanted. Sacrificing time and energy to help another person is hard for anyone, but most people who do so gain honor by the action. When you are expected to sacrifice everything as a matter of course, there is nothing to be gained by fulfilling expectations except still more expectations. In refusing, of course, you are branded a traitor and a coward, but at least your life is your own. I know this is not a view you agree with, and I don't expect you to understand now. It's just part of the explanation.

Even refusing isn't safe. I frighten people; you know I always have. (Remember the preschool worker who said I was Satanic? I do.) Frightened people want nothing more than to feel safe, and so, given a chance to remove the threat, they will. Hiding from them would have the same effect as being openly antagonistic, but if I can keep them uneasy, just worried enough that they think they stand to lose less by tolerating me than by making me angry, it's possible to live an almost normal life.

As you've seen, things have changed. They've found a champion, one who doesn't understand what she's risking, too young to know that, eventually, they will eat her alive. She knows me too well to be intimidated. They wouldn't have a chance without her; with her, they can't lose. I prefer not to fall quite as far as they'd like me to.

You won't see me again. I need a change of scene, and I doubt I'll ever be back. People will say this fiasco has backed me into a corner, but it's a corner I've seen coming for years. I'm not proud of everything I've done, but there have been reasons.

Try to believe that for Natalie's sake. I would like you to contact her at least once after you receive this letter. You'll like her; she's nothing like me. I don't think my leaving will disturb her much, especially now, but she has very few allies here. She's quiet and won't try to stand up for herself in public; that tendency could prove fatal in the situations she'll be in. She's been under a lot of stress lately. I don't know whether she has emotional scarring; but I do know that, most of the time, she's very afraid. Give her as much room as she wants and don't ask too many questions, but please be there. This is the first favor I've asked of you in eleven years, and it's also the last. She's your blood as well as mine.

J. Irving

Halfway through the letter, I lose focus and have to start over again. Then, when I still don't understand, I go back and read it again. And again. As I read, the air in the room slows, crystallizing into one unending second. The illusion is so complete that when the breeze from the ceiling fan tugs at the stationery in my hands, it startles me. I lay the letter face-down on the bed, holding it down with my palm. My heart pounds.

Who wrote *this, anyway?* It can't have been Jadyn. Jadyn sues people; she doesn't run. Jadyn *can't* write to her parents when she's in trouble; it would be asking for help, or at least admitting that she was wrong, and either way her pride wouldn't allow it. Jadyn isn't afraid of anything. Most importantly, Jadyn doesn't like me.

To her, I'm either a disappointment or a possession. She hated me enough to hurt me, just so she wouldn't have to give up custody of … *No. That doesn't make sense.*

I stare down at the paper under my hand, not really seeing it. I feel a little sick.

The house is too quiet. By 5:00, most of the staff that came at all has gone home; since Jadyn isn't here, the handful that actually live at the house have the evening off, with the result that, at 8:00, I come downstairs and find the house empty.

I walk through all the rooms, just to make sure I'm really alone. The sun won't set for another hour or so, and the jewel-toned downstairs rooms glow like paper-bag luminaries. It feels sad, somehow. Lonely. I turn on a few lights as I go, because sooner or later it *will* be dark, and I may still be the only one home.

The cook has left dinner in covered dishes on the kitchen counter: pasta primavera, orange-glazed chicken, green peas and a note that says "Ice cream in freezer." I take some of everything except the peas, grab a can of Coke, and take my plate into the main dining room. As usual, it *is* dark in there; the shades are kept drawn on days like this to keep the sunlight from fading the Oriental rug. The table is a long, black shape, gleaming faintly in the dimness like a deserted ice rink. I don't normally eat here even when the house is full of people, but right now it's a strategic location, just down the hall from the front door, and close enough to the back that I'll hear if anyone comes in. I turn on just one of the wall-sconce lamps and sit on the window seat at the back of the room, bracing my plate on my knees. The manila envelope from Jadyn's room is sandwiched between my leg and the window; I didn't bring the letter downstairs. For some reason I don't even want to show it to Peter, at least not yet.

At 8:45, the latch on the front door clicks, and the knob rattles. The sound echoes coldly against the marble, and I flinch; I hadn't realized until now just how spooked the emptiness is making me. It's tempting to snap invisible, just until I'm sure it's safe, but at the last second I remember that the light's on, and that my plate won't turn invisible with me. I don't want anyone to see anything strange, especially while Jadyn's not here. I hear footsteps in the hall, amplified for a second as whoever-it-is passes the stairwell, and a light outside the dining room clicks on. I slide my hand down, getting a good grip on the manila envelope, and wait, staring at the doorway. A man's form walks across the space, silhouetted against the light; his head turns toward the dining room reflexively as he passes, then hesitates and looks again. It's Peter.

"Natalie?"

I let out a breath I don't remember taking. "Yeah. Hi."

He steps into the room, putting a hand on the chandelier's light switch. "Is it dark in here for a reason?"

I shake my head, leaning down to put my mostly-empty plate on the rug. "Not really. You can turn the lights on if you want." When he does, it's brighter than I expected. I rub at my eyes, blinking blue spots away. I feel disoriented, as though I've just woken up. "Long time no see, huh? Did you find anything?"

Peter pulls a chair out halfway down the length of the table and sits, slipping his notepad onto the table in front of him. Even from where I'm sitting I can tell that the top page, at least, is full. He nods. "Nothing substantial enough to use yet, but I've got a couple of leads." He crosses his arms, leaning on the table; he's wearing a long, drab coat that isn't quite a duster, even though it's hot enough outside that people in T-shirts and shorts are probably overheating. "Did you know your officer's been married three times? Widowed once, divorced twice. She was born in Chicago but moved to Springfield when she was twenty-nine and lived there for fifteen years before moving back. Interestingly, the man she was married to when she lived there owned and operated a garage which was tentatively connected to a rash of car thefts during her last year in Springfield."

I feel my eyebrows lift. "Was he the one who died?"

The corners of Peter's mouth twitch; it isn't quite a smile. "No. And the garage connection was never proven. But that doesn't mean it can't be looked into, or that, proven or not, she'd want it brought up again." He flips the top page back, scanning the page beneath, then glances up at me. "Have you been home alone all evening?"

"Um, yeah."

"I'm sorry. If I'd remembered, I would have been back sooner."

I shrug, trying to look like one of those people whose life's ambition is to live in a cabin a thousand miles from anything. "There are always too many people here anyway. It was kind of nice. Very quiet." Peter raises an eyebrow quizzically, and I change the subject as quickly as I can. "There's food in the kitchen, if you're hungry."

"No, thanks."

I stand, barely avoiding stepping on my plate. I've been holding onto the envelope so hard that the patches under my fingers are damp. "I … um, I found something, too. I think."

"You think?"

"Yeah." I shrug uneasily. "I mean, I know it's something. I'm just not sure what it means."

Peter's eyes drop to the envelope; I realize I'm still holding it close to my leg, half-hidden behind me.

"Um, here." I hand it to him, a little embarrassed, and glance down at his notepad so I don't have to watch his face. Peter's handwriting is unbelievably messy; I can't even begin to read it. With most people, you can at least tell the *t*'s, *r*'s and *p*'s apart from each other, but Peter's notes seem to be one long scribble. It reminds me of an EKG printout.

I hear papers rustle as he opens the envelope and shuffles through the articles. The edges of the clippings flicker in and out of my peripheral vision, and I stare down at the illegible notes, trying to focus. *Maybe he used shorthand?* He's doodled a brick wall all the way up the left side of the notepad; there's a small sketch of a man lying at the base of the wall, hands covering his head, and a scarily well-muscled man in a cape and spandex, climbing a rope which snakes around the top of the notepad to snag on the top of the wall. I've just discovered that one of the worst smudges in Peter's notes is actually a tiny figure he's drawn behind the words, running toward the back of the notepad, when Peter sets the clippings down on the table.

"Where did you find these?" he asks.

"Jadyn's room," I say, still not looking at him. "I had to do *something*. And I was careful not to move things around too much."

Peter doesn't say anything. He starts to lay the articles out on the table, methodically, side by side.

"Why would she do this?" I ask.

"Hmm?" Peter doesn't look up.

"I mean, she's dating Nadal, whether or not she's involved in his 'business' in any way."

The articles are now spread over as much of the table as Peter can reach from his chair. He stands, moving down the table, and starts a new row.

"And," I say, "she's got all kinds of articles in there, gossip columns and business articles and profiles of crimes that he might possibly have had a connection to."

"Sure. Why wouldn't she want to know if he was involved in anything illegal?"

"That's not the point. Some of those are more than five years old. She wasn't even seeing him then. She knows all this stuff, or at least suspects it, and she's still involved with him?" Peter doesn't say anything. "Or... is that *why* she likes him? Because that's sick."

Peter puts the last article down. The table is seventeen feet long and five feet wide, and there's only about a yard of clear space at the end. The rest is covered with scraps of newspaper. "I think your mother is the kind of person who tries to avoid being caught off-guard at all costs. She ran into Nadal pretty frequently even before they started seeing each other, and he's prominent. She probably thought it would be a good idea to keep an eye on him."

"Well, if she's been keeping an eye on him, she knows he might be in big trouble in the very near future. Why wouldn't she drop him before it hits?"

Peter shrugs. He's still scanning the articles, not looking at me. "Maybe she's afraid he'll implicate her."

"Then..." I hesitate, remembering just in time that I don't plan to tell Peter about the letter. But there's no reason for him to suspect it isn't just a random question. "If he really can implicate her, do you think she'll run? Leave the country?"

"Maybe. I doubt she'd do it until something definitely threatening happened. If she ran, and for some reason Nadal wasn't arrested, he'd be pretty upset with her. She may stay out of Chicago proper for a while, but I don't think she'll leave the country, or even the area, until this is settled somehow."

I curl my fingers over the back of the nearest chair. There's an unusual, twisted-spiral design carved into the wood, and my fingers trace it. "You make it sound like she's afraid of him or something."

"She might be." Peter is restacking the articles again, I suspect in chronological order.

"But she *can't* be. She's not afraid of anything."

Peter's hand hesitates, and he glances up at me. "No? Everyone is afraid of something."

"But she isn't—"

"Isn't what?"

I realize I've almost said isn't human, and I shut my mouth quickly. After a few seconds, Peter continues as though I haven't interrupted. "He doesn't seem like a safe person to cross, and if he's involved in the drug trade, he probably has some very good international connections."

Treadwell Death Declared Accidental. This conversation isn't helping at all. "But she knew that *before* she got involved with him, remember? Why would she … ?"

Peter shakes his head, slowly, not bothering to look up. "Why do people have affairs? Why do they do stunts that could paralyze or kill them, just for fun? Why do some people commit suicide over something that would have blown over if they'd held out another week or two? Some very bad ideas sound good at the time. Often, by the time they realize the idea isn't so good, it's too late to stop."

c h a p t e r   t h i r t e e n

On Friday morning, I wake up to a tinny rendition of *Mission Impossible*, shrieking right next to my ear. I make a grab for the cell phone, hitting the talk button almost before I'm conscious. "H-hello?"

"I'm going to need you today."

Officer Carmichael. The fact that she's calling now probably means that she hasn't told on me, at least not yet, but...I'm so tired. My head feels fuzzy, and, after yesterday, I'm a little afraid to try to clear it. I squeeze my eyes shut against the glare from the window, struggling to collect myself. *Keep her happy. It doesn't matter what it takes; you won't be doing this for much longer. Just don't give her a chance to get mad again.* "Sure. What am I doing?"

"Kidnapping."

I freeze; for a second I'm afraid she's gone over the edge and wants *me* to kidnap someone.

"Do you know Mr. and Mrs. Bartolon?" she asks.

I've seen them at Nadal's place once or twice, but I've never actually spoken to them. "Sort of."

"Their six-year-old son, Tavey, disappeared on Wednesday afternoon. His nanny, Pilar Alvarez, took him downtown to the Field Museum of Natural History, and neither of them came back. According to the museum, they never got there. There was a ransom call on Thursday morning at 7:30, and Mr. Bartolon kept them talking long enough for us to trace the call to an apartment complex. We've had people watching it since 8:30 yesterday morning. We know which apartment they're in, and that there are three men at the site."

"What about Tavey and the nanny?"

"That's where you come in."

"I don't understand," I say, although I'm afraid I might.

"It isn't that complicated," she says with a sharpness to her voice that makes me wince. "You're going to go find them."

No! A kidnapping? I'm not trained for this. People might die if I mess up. She must know that. Is she doing this on purpose? "First of all," she continues, "you'll need to find out exactly where they're keeping Tavey and Miss Alvarez. There will be a team standing by to help when the time comes, and one of them will get you inside, but from there you're on your own. After you find them, get them away from where they're being kept. Make sure you get Tavey whatever you do; the boy is top priority. Try to keep him where no one can get a clear shot at him. Once you're in a relatively safe place, you will call my cell phone. The number is the first speed dial setting. To get it, you have to—"

"I know how," I tell her, hastily. "And, um, when you said, 'so no one can get a clear shot at him ...'?"

"That shouldn't need explaining."

"There are going to be guns there? Men with guns?"

"I wouldn't be surprised."

The sarcasm in her voice is so thick it's a wonder the phone doesn't overload. She's *enjoying* this. She knows I can't afford to say no, that, since everyone will expect Monica to be involved, if I mess up or refuse to help, they'd have to do so much explaining that she'd be duty-bound to tell on me. Personal vendettas aside, how could she trust something this important to *me?*

"Look," I say, as reasonably as I can, "I'm not trained for this. You really need a professional. Somebody could get killed, and I won't…I don't want to be responsible for that."

Officer Carmichael sighs, and for a moment I can tell she knows exactly what kind of a risk she's taking, and that she's not much more comfortable with it than I am. "Frankly, you've got as good a shot at beating these people as anyone we've got. Kidnappings are ugly. Sometimes the ransom is paid, and no one on either side tries anything stupid, and the victim is killed anyway. But I'm not asking you to negotiate for us. I want you to give us the advantage of surprise." She hesitates, and I get the uneasy feeling that she's deciding how much to tell me. "When the Bartolons called us, they specifically asked that Monica be involved. If we didn't have her, they didn't want us to do anything."

His parents requested me? Do they trust Monica that much? Are they that desperate? If this goes wrong, and Tavey gets hurt, or worse, it'll be my fault. "I…Do I have to do this?" My throat is so tight the words come out in a whisper. "You tell me, Natalie." Officer Carmichael's voice is hard again. "I could care less whether you like it or not, but if you don't show up, you'd better be willing to face the consequences."

The phone beeps irritably and goes dead: she's hung up on me. I flop back onto my pillow, staring blankly at the bright ceiling and the slowly spinning fan. *She isn't stupid*, I think. *She may be mad at you, but she'd never be mad enough to risk someone else's life just to make you look bad.*

"I'll be there," I say, into the emptiness. "But you'd better be right."

At six o'clock in the evening, I pull on the ballet slippers. They aren't meant for street use—professional ballerinas wear theirs out in a night, just from dancing on a varnished stage—and I've been walking on gravel, kicking at things, and running in mine. The leather is so scuffed and fragile around the edges that I'm afraid I'll poke holes in it just pulling the slippers on, and the sole of the right one has been rubbed much too smooth, its stitching starting to come undone.

Peter's gone again, trying to officially connect Officer Carmichael's ex with car theft. I haven't told him about the phone call, since knowing what she wants me to do this time would only make Peter mad. I did call Isole around two o'clock, because, even though Peter's probably right about Jadyn not going anywhere until the Nadal thing is resolved, something still doesn't feel right. She wasn't technically there, but the man at the desk told me she'd left at one o'clock to meet some prospective investors and wouldn't be back until late. I didn't dare ask many questions, but in any case, she was there this morning, and the letter I found was written at least three days ago. She hasn't disappeared yet. She's waiting, like Peter and me.

The elastic on the left ballet slipper snaps, stinging my ankle. I stare at it, feeling a superstitious shiver prickle up my spine. Is that supposed to mean something? Maybe I'm forgetting something important, or not seeing something I'm going to need, or

maybe I should have told Peter about the call... *You're being dumb.
It's not an omen. It means you need better shoes, that's all. Peter's fine,
Jadyn's fine, you're fine. Heck, even Tavey's probably fine. Get a grip.* I
get a safety pin out of the bathroom and fix the strap, and then I
go downstairs and slip out of the back door.

Officer Carmichael picks me up on the usual stretch of Fieldstone
Drive. I expect a silent, frigid ride, but instead she talks constantly,
reminding me that everyone on the SWAT team we'll be meeting
is going to think I'm Jadyn and not Monica, so not to answer to
the wrong name, and that I'm supposed to be as fast as I can when
I'm inside, but I need to avoid causing a disturbance, no matter
what. If I think I've been noticed, should get out safely, if possible,
or hide, but it is crucial that I not blow my cover or theirs. If the
police are forced to come in too early, the kidnappers will start
shooting. And one of them will probably go straight to Tavey to
make sure he can't identify them.

These people have most likely done this before. They're pros,
and this is not a game or a TV program. It's not even planned
ahead. People could die.

By this time, I think all the blood in my body has drained into
my shoes; I can feel my hands shaking, but I don't dare say anything. Officer Carmichael's voice is as hard and brittle as sheet ice,
and I know she's just waiting for me to say something out of line,
so I stare out my window without saying anything. There's no way
I'm giving her the satisfaction of yelling at me. I snap invisible
near the end of the trip, just to be on the safe side, and the last
few blocks are a shaky, faded blur of the car's interior. Opaque, the
windshield feels much, much closer to my face. Claustrophobia
squeezes at my throat as, underneath me, the car slows and then

stops outside a run-down apartment in one of the dingy, neglected projects sandwiched between Oak Park and Chicago proper. Officer Carmichael opens her door and gets out. Shakily, I swing my feet over onto the sidewalk and stand up. The world is abruptly gigantic; I'm so relieved at the sense of space that the two dozen officers standing in the gravel lot beside the car, who have turned and are staring at the spot where logic tells them I'm standing, barely even register.

Fingers fumble at my shoulder, getting a firm grip on my arm before I can pull away. Officer Carmichael isn't taking any chances today. She tows me across the sidewalk and onto the gravel lot, right through the middle of the group of policemen who part hastily, giving us much too much room.

"Curtis!" she snaps, and one of the officers tenses, trying to freeze in the act of stepping back.

"Present," he says; his voice sounds young and slightly wary.

"Do you have everything you need?"

"Affirmative."

"Good. Jadyn's here, and she's going to follow you. Get her into that apartment."

"Yes, ma'am," he says, and starts across the lot; to his credit, he doesn't even try to make sure I'm following him.

Curtis—I have no idea if that's his first name or his last—isn't hard to see. He wears a humongous T-shirt, a backward baseball cap, and jeans so baggy it's hard to resist stepping on the cuff just to see what would happen. The denim makes a rough, rasping sound every time he takes a step, and the chain that joins his waistband and wallet clinks. It's the audio equivalent of wearing a fluorescent safety vest.

We quick-march down a block, then cut diagonally through the yards and alleys of a second one, then walk, slightly more slowly, along half of a third. The vague shapes of the projects loom on my left, blocking out the emptiness of the sky. Against the darkness, the sturdy, U-shaped buildings seem solid and secure, like medieval fortresses, but I've driven by them before, and know better. The paint has been peeling for so long that all that's left is shreds of bleached white on bare boards. The ragged patches of grass that pass for lawns are either knee-high or so full of clover and weeds that they don't need cutting anymore. Useless cars rust in the parking courts, and every available surface has been tagged with gang signs.

I'm so busy scanning the buildings for movement that I don't notice Curtis has stopped until I run into him. "Sorry," he whispers. "Stairs here."

"I know," I whisper back, irritated to be caught off guard. "I can see them. I just wasn't looking."

"Oh. Sorry," he says again, and I realize he's a little afraid of me. It makes sense. I've lived with Jadyn my entire life, and *I'm* wary around her. But I don't like this. I don't want people to be afraid of me on principle. "There are fifteen steps up. Don't make a sound."

I follow him up, staring at the bright points where his feet scuff against the wooden treads, until we reach a tiny landing tacked onto the back of the second story. When we reach the door, Curtis does something to the knob, turns it gently, and pulls. It opens out onto the landing with a shuddering creak. "Go," he whispers, and I slip inside.

The room is empty, except for an armchair in the middle of the peeling linoleum floor. TV noise blares from the apartment next door, through a wall so thin it might as well not be there. Behind me, Curtis eases the door shut. "Okay," he mutters, his voice pitched just low enough that I can hear it under the noise from the TV. "The apartment you want is next door. The floor plan is a mirror image of this one. See the patio door in the next room?"

I look, following his pointing finger; there's something shaped like a shower door set into the far wall. "Yeah."

"It opens onto a balcony that this apartment shares with the one next door. Their patio door will be the next opening on the right, and next to that there's going to be a bedroom window. You'll have to get in through one of those, and I think the bedroom might be the safest bet. Come here." He crosses the room with the patio doors and turns left, into an even smaller room. "You'll have to do this from the outside, and I can only show you from this side, but it will work the same way." He pulls out a short, thick-bladed knife and shows me how to jam it into the window sash beside the catch, and how to lever it back so the catch loosens and unlocks. Then he hands me the knife. It feels strangely light and flimsy in my hand, and I feel anxiety crawl down my spine.

"Can you see it?" I ask.

"Sort of." I can't read anything in Curtis's voice. "Not the handle, and only an inch or so of the blade."

I close the knife. "How about now?"

"It's gone."

I slip it into my jeans pocket. "Now?"

"Still gone."

None of this seems real at all. Any second now, someone is going to yell "Cut!" and the apartment will be dismantled around us. I take a deep breath. "Is that it, then?"

"That's all I know. Carmichael briefed you in the car, right?"

"Yeah." Although I can't remember any of it.

"Then, good luck. Get him out alive," he says. He slides the patio door open for me, and I step through onto the balcony. I might as well have stepped into another dimension. Feelings that were numbed in the relative safety of the vacant apartment are suddenly, terrifyingly sharp. Instincts I didn't even know I had trigger reflexes that I follow without thinking. *Stay down. Keep quiet. Stick close to the walls. Move slowly. Breathe through your mouth.* Someone somewhere is smoking a cigarette; the smell is so acrid it makes me want to gag, even though I know the source has to be across the parking court, fifty feet away. The boards under my feet vibrate faintly, and the sound from the TV in the next apartment is painfully loud.

A second later, I realize that the other patio door is cracked open a few inches. Not enough to let me through, but more than enough to let me see the inside of the room. Two men sit there on what appear to be beanbag chairs, yelling at the TV. "Whaddaya *mean*, foul? He was totally gone!"

I tiptoe past the blank rectangle of glass, running my fingers lightly across it until they hit the hot aluminum edge, then the splintery wall. The window is only a couple of feet from the patio door, much too close for comfort, about four feet off the ground. It didn't seem that high in the other apartment. Even if I manage to get it open, I can't possibly get through it quietly. I squeeze my eyes shut—which, unfortunately, doesn't affect the lines at all—and think, *I could go home. This isn't really my problem. They've got an entire SWAT team here; sooner or later they'll have to do something, and Tavey would probably be better off if I left...*

But I don't.

As I'm wavering, it dawns on me that the half of the window I'm staring at looks funny, sort of hazy, not as sharp as the glass in the other half. I put my fingers up and touch window screen.

They don't have air conditioning, so, naturally, they've opened the windows. *Easy.* I don't even have to break in. Getting in and finding Tavey will probably be easier than trying to explain to Officer Carmichael why I ducked out. I cut the window screen quickly, not giving myself time for second thoughts. It's flimsier than I expected it to be—probably some kind of fiberglass, instead of wire—and the knife only makes a faint tearing noise, instead of the sharp pinging I was afraid of.

When the sides and bottom of the screen hang loose, I hook my hands over the top of the sill and pull myself up, realizing when I'm already painfully balanced on my stomach, with the aluminum track cutting into my middle, that the only thing I can do is slide through. There's no way to get my feet under me. I push myself forward, tipping just a little farther, and then farther. The blood rushes to my head, and then I'm slipping, falling, and my hands meet the floor with a thud.

My wrists burn, but I force them to hold me up until I've managed to let my knees and feet slide, more or less quietly, down the wall to the floor. I sit on the carpet for a minute, massaging the aching, tingly patches on my wrists. The air in the room is thick and stale, as though someone used a deep fat fryer in here for about a year and never bothered to open a window.

I squeeze my eyes shut, and feel my heart struggle to settle into a normal rhythm. In the next room, one of the men shouts. I shrink back against the wall, staring at the door, and then I realize, with a relief so sharp I feel almost sick, that they're yelling at each other, fighting about the game. They haven't heard anything. The TV must have covered for me.

The sooner I've gotten my bearings, the sooner I can find Tavey and Miss Alvarez, and then I can leave. *See? Not hard at all. You're doing fine.* I stand, shakily, then slide through the bedroom door, into the frenzied, floodlight-bright noise of the TV room, and from there into the slightly dimmer, quieter kitchen.

A third man is in this room. He sits at the table, half-screened by the newspaper he's reading, with a thick glass tumbler by his elbow. Something strangely compact sits between the paper and the glass. Not a shape I recognize. I take a step closer, leaning down to see, then freeze.

It's a gun.

As I stand there, mesmerized, the paper rustles. When I lift my head I find myself looking straight into the man's eyes. For a second, I'm sure he can see me, and I can't even breathe, let alone run. Then the man's focus shifts, lazily, until he's looking past my right shoulder, and I remember the gun, only a few inches from his hand. If he really had seen me, I probably wouldn't even be here anymore.

Goosebumps prickle up on my arms. I would give anything— and I mean *anything*—to have Peter here, right now, but that's not going to happen. *If you get shot, it will be your own stupid fault*, I tell myself, and I back slowly away from the table. The man's face is still tilted toward me, and it's making me nervous. The air in the room is heavy with heat and sweat, and I slip away, down the hall that gapes on my right.

The apartment is small, and there are only three doors opening off the hall. The first is a bathroom, with no towels, no toilet paper, no toilet seat, and a dripping tap. The second, across from the bathroom, is closed, and I don't dare open it with the man sitting only twenty feet away. The third, at the end of the hall, is just an empty doorway. I lean into the room and look around quickly.

There's a king-sized mattress on a metal frame in the middle of the floor, with a rumpled sleeping bag on top of it, and a door that's probably a closet set into the wall closest to the bathroom. I back into the hall, biting anxiously at my lip. *Come on, where are they?* There isn't room here to hide *anyone*, let alone do it well. If they aren't in the hall closet, or in the bedroom closet, I don't know where they would be. And I don't dare open the hall closet to check.

But if I don't ... *I have to find Tavey. He has to be here. Why would they go to all the trouble of kidnapping him if they weren't going to keep him? Maybe they were just trying to throw the police off their track by making the ransom call from here, but then why would they still be here? Tavey has to be in the closet. Maybe, if I'm quiet enough, I can open the door an inch or so.*

I dart a glance down the hall at the man behind the table. His head is bent over the table, even though he's laid the paper down, leaving both hands free. *If he decides to go for the gun ...* But the TV is pretty loud. It *must* be loud enough to cover any noise I could make opening a door. I wrap my fingers around the knob on the hall closet door, slowly, gingerly turn it, and pull.

The door gives a stiff, unoiled shriek. I let go of the knob as though it's been electrified, and, in the kitchen, a chair scrapes across the linoleum. Fear sheets through me like heavy rain. The man stands now and takes a step toward me, around the table. I back away, and the only thought in my head is *Pleasepleasepleaseplease ...*

He bends down to pick up something from the floor behind the table, and I turn and run for the bedroom. I've already blown my cover, but if I leave before I get a look inside the bedroom closet, and Tavey's in there, they'll kill him for sure, and then I'm finished too. I'm too close not to try. Once I know for sure he isn't there, that's enough; I can get out, call the police in. Officer Carmichael can't be mad at me then, not for anything. If I'm quick…I run into the bedroom, not bothering to avoid the creaky floorboards, yank the closet door open, and—

Nothing. A rod full of jangling, motion-blurred wire hangers.

And then, behind me, the apartment explodes.

By now I'm so wound up that I scream; I feel my throat tense, but I can't hear myself. The room becomes a blinding, sleeting blur of white and pale grey, sliding into a color too bright to name. *Not a real explosion*, I realize. Somebody's playing a heavy-metal album at top volume on a very good stereo system, and it *hurts*. Even if I were normal, it would hurt. As it is, I'm clutching my head, afraid it's going to crack open. I shift my hands back to cover my ears, but it doesn't help. The sound resonates in my bones, and although everything's so bright it hurts to look at it, there's no way to shut my eyes. I stumble back toward the place where I'm pretty sure the door is, unable to think past getting away from the noise and the tearing brightness.

I run smack into a body blocking the doorway, hitting him so hard I bounce off his chest. He flinches, and his fingers rake across my shoulder, but he's too startled to catch me. I stagger backward. The mattress catches me across the back of the knees and I sit down hard.

They knew, I think, dazedly. *They didn't just know I was coming. They knew I couldn't hear if I couldn't see.* Funny. You wouldn't think that was the kind of information Jadyn would share with anyone, even Nadal. Especially Nadal.

Close to me, a person screams in anger, not in fear. "No, here! Right here, where I'm pointing!"

My feet are still touching the floor, and I feel it vibrate as someone comes closer. It's getting harder and harder to pay attention, as if the sound is burning my mind away.

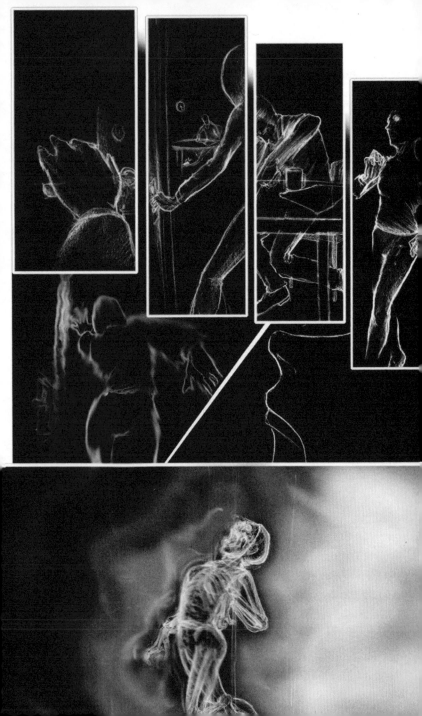

"But if it's Nadal's, won't he—"

There is one explanation why the kidnappers would call from a place they knew the police would find, then stay there and leave a convenient window open.

"Doesn't matter. He wants this over."

They might even have told the Bartolons to specifically ask for Monica. But why would anyone go to all this trouble to—

I don't know what makes me realize what's happening. Maybe there's something about the way the air swirls around the men, or maybe the quality of the suffocating flood of noise shifts just a little, or maybe I've somehow heard the hammer click back. In any case, when the man at the door fires over the dent in the mattress where I should be, I'm on the floor, struggling to pull myself under the bed.

They didn't want Tavey at all. They wanted me.

chapter fourteen

O lie in the claustrophobic space between the bed frame and the floor, hands covering my ears, face pressed into the musty carpet. This has to be what hell is like. Every sense I have is overloading. I keep expecting to black out, but it doesn't happen. Figures, since it's all I want. Anything to make this stop… *If you black out, you'll unsnap, and they'll see you. You have to get away from the noise. Now.* The floor shakes under me, but I can't tell whether it's because of the men or the music. I have to *focus*.

I put one hand out, groping across the carpet until my fingers hit metal. One of the bed legs. There's about two feet of space between me and the edge of the bed; if someone's kneeling on the floor already it won't be enough to hide me, but at this point it's no less risky than any of my other options. I unsnap.

Instantly, the noise is a little more bearable, its edges dulled, bruising instead of cutting. The floor in front of me is clear, but I've gotten turned around so that I'm facing the open closet door. I twist sideways until I can see the door to the hall, and the pair of shiny black combat boots standing in it. They're weirdly blurred, and it isn't until then that I realize my eyes are tearing up. My head hurts so much...

Left. Go left.

A scuffed khaki sneaker hits the floor in front of my face and I snap invisible again, whimpering as the pain shrieks back in. The air around me surges upwards and a dangling spring scratches my cheek; they're tipping the bed frame over... Away from the door. That's good. I put a hand on the underside of the mattress, feeling it rise; when the angle is sharp enough, I push myself to my hands and knees and scramble for the nearest wall. I hit it just as the bed frame crashes down again, and for a second I just rest there, eyes shut, cheek pressed to the cool wall. The paint still smells new. *Just a little farther. You'll be fine.*

The men are shouting; I hear it as a sort of echo at the edges of the stereo's din. *What next? Focus!*

I need to get past the man in the doorway, or make him move out of the way. I push my fingers into my pocket and work the knife out. If I don't do this right the first time... My fingers clutch the knife so hard that the plastic grip digs into them. It hurts. *Everything* hurts.

Someone brushes past me, so close that I can't tell whether they've touched me or not. I cock my arm back and throw the knife as hard as I can. The floor in front of me shakes violently as someone stumbles, and I push off from the wall, running for the door. If I'm lucky, the knife either made it past the man into the hall, or it grazed him and he's distracted, trying to see what hit him. If I'm *not* lucky…

The doorway is empty. I tuck my head down, keep my hands in front of me, more to cushion the impact if I hit something than to feel where I'm going, and run.

The stereo is in the hall; I can feel it as I dash by it, a molten ball of noise. Evidently it's just a portable one; the man probably had it with him in the kitchen. The fact that it's facing the bedroom, and that I'm no longer in front of it, should mean the pain gets better, but it doesn't. The apartment is too small. The noise fills every corner and crevice, saturating the air, smothering me. The surface under my feet shifts from carpet to linoleum to carpet again as I run through the living room, heading for the patio doors. It doesn't matter how much noise I make now. I could break the window and no one would hear. But I'm not familiar enough with the apartment to navigate it blindly; disoriented, I feel my way along the wall.

Just when I think I've made it, the floor drops out from under me.

I'm too startled to scream. I manage to hook my left leg over the edge of the hole as I fall, and my elbows and back slam into the rough rim so hard the tears are jolted out of my eyes, running back into my ears. I'm not falling anymore, but I'm far enough in that I'm not sure I can pull myself out. My shoulders ache from trying to support my weight at this angle; my one dangling leg flails uselessly, trying to find something solid. A very small part of my brain knows that if I panic I probably won't ever get out of here, but I'm beyond rational thinking by now.

Then my foot hits the wall, slides down a few inches…and sticks. There's something solid there. I stop struggling and put

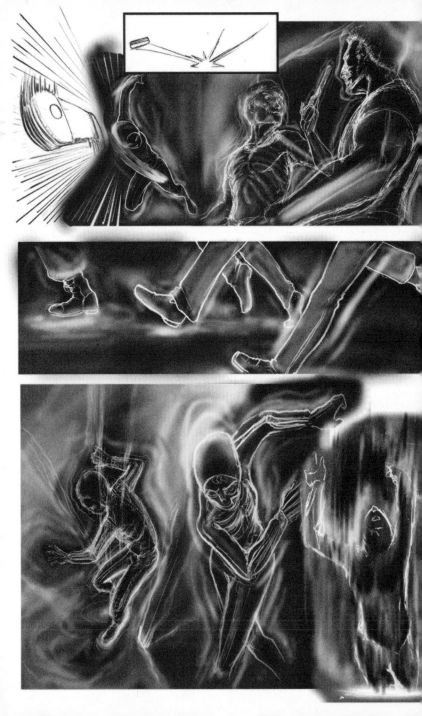

one hand on the wall, feeling across it. My shaking fingers catch on a smooth, narrow ridge, then find another about a foot below the first. *A ladder?* I've fallen into some kind of trapdoor. From the sharp feel of the edges, it's new.

Forcing myself to move slowly, I brace my dangling foot on the closest rung, grab the ladder with both hands, and maneuver my other leg through the trapdoor. I don't dare breathe until both feet are solidly on the ladder, and then I rest there for a moment, clutching the rungs. I could go up, but I might run into one of the men. I have no idea what's on the other end of the ladder, and I don't want to go anywhere unfamiliar when I'm blind like this, but...I don't think anyone's down there. And I still have the cell phone; I could call Officer Carmichael.

And maybe it will be quieter.

That's enough of a reason. I start down the ladder, slowly; it's shaky, not attached to the wall the way I thought at first. My senses are melting together. I'm not sure whether the rungs are truly solid or just jarring beats from the stereo upstairs until I've put my weight on them, and once I shift halfway onto a rung before realizing it isn't there at all. After that, I unsnap. The floor below me is a patch of dingy brown carpet, identical to the floor in the bedroom. Beyond that, everything's black.

I drop to the carpet as soon as I can, falling to my hands and knees. I still can't see. The room around me feels big and musty. I back out of the patch of light, shut my aching eyes; I hold my hands over them for a few seconds, then open them again, staring at the wall. There are windows, but they're covered with plywood. Why? Were they planning to keep someone here? If I was wrong about Tavey...

It doesn't matter. The situation is far out of my control. The only thing to do now is get the police in here as soon as possible. I yank the phone out of my pocket, and, although my hands are so shaky I almost drop it, I manage to activate the speed-dial. Did Officer Carmichael say to talk to her, or just call? I can't remember. I'm not even sure yet whether I *can* talk.

I hang up and put the phone away; it's so hard to move my fingers accurately, I know I'll never manage to form words. If I feel my way through the darkness, trying not to hear the heavy, running footsteps upstairs or the numbing shriek of the music, until my fingers fumble across a doorknob. I pull the door open, stumble inside, and drag it shut behind me. The air is thick with dust, and the carpet crunches softly under my ballet slippers. *Dead bugs, probably.* I'm tired enough that I sit down anyway, leaning back against the wall.

I'm in the hall closet. It's exactly the same as the one I tried to open upstairs, only this door is quiet. *Well, of course. They probably made sure the upstairs door was good and loud. How else were they supposed to know when you got here?* I pull my knees up to my chest, wrap my arms around them, and rest my forehead on my arms; my face feels too hot, but I'm still shivering. My head hurts so much... I shut my eyes and let everything around me fade.

Noise washes over me without touching me. I hear the police come, and a few gunshots, very close together. Then there's only the music, until somebody turns off the stereo, and, finally, it's very, very quiet. There's a high, keening ringing in my ears and I pull away from it, trying to draw back into my mind so far that I can't hear it. *You're almost out of here*, I tell myself. *It has to get better. It* has *to.*

Faintly, I hear a tinkly, video-game version of "Mission

Impossible." I listen blankly as it plays once, then again, and again. On the fourth ring, I force myself to answer. "Hello?"

"Do you have him?" Officer Carmichael's voice is tense.

"No."

There's a crackling pause. *She isn't going to like that,* I think, sluggishly. *She said to*—

"I told you to make sure he was safe *before*—"

"No." I take a deep breath, forcing myself to concentrate. "He isn't here. I would've found him. He was never here."

"So you're saying our surveillance got it wrong." Her voice is flat. Why can't she just accept this and take me home? I can't keep this up for much longer. "They ... I ... Monica ..."

"What are you talking about?"

I can't finish. Even stringing words together is too hard. "I want to go home," I tell her. "Take me home." I hit the "End" button, cutting her off mid-sentence. Then I curl up again, head on my knees, trying to avoid the sizzling ache in the center of my skull, and let the phone fall to the carpet.

In the car on the way home, we don't speak. I'm not sure I could, even if I wanted to. I feel numb and heavy and very, very far away. My head swims with formless worries, but only one stays long enough to sink in, and, weirdly, it's the least important one. What am I going to tell Peter? I don't even want to try explaining. All I want to do is sleep and forget about everything.

I shouldn't have worried. Peter isn't home when I get back. The only sound in the house is the hum of the air conditioning. I think I hear a vacuum cleaner somewhere on the second floor, but I'm not sure. If it's there, it's very faint, and my ears are still buzzing. I drag myself upstairs, feet scuffing across the steps. In my room, even though it's nearing sunset and the light outside is growing softer, I pull the curtains across the windows. The darkness is wonderfully gentle. In my bathroom, I have to turn on the night-light to make sure it's the Ibuprofen bottle I've grabbed. Even the nightlight's a little too bright.

I shake two pills into my hand, staring at them for a long time in the gold-tinged glow. They're so small. It's tempting to take about half the bottle, but I don't. I wash the pills down with warm, vaguely rusty water from the bathroom tap, then cap the bottle and put it away.

As I close the mirrored cabinet door, I catch a glimpse of my face. I don't even recognize it at first. I feel like I'm a hundred and ten, but I look about twelve years old, panicked and dazed, like a little kid who's woken up at a sleepover and can't remember whose house she's at or how she got there. There's a glassy look to my eyes that I don't think I like, and I turn away from the mirror, shivering a little. *Eventually, they will eat you alive ...*

Where did I hear that?

I crawl into bed, not bothering to change out of my work clothes. Even though I'm already too hot, I pull the sheet up to my ears. It helps take the edge off the fear that still shudders through me every few minutes. *Maybe this is a nightmare. Maybe as soon as I fall asleep, I'll wake up and all this will be gone.*

Just before she'd dropped me off at home, Officer Carmichael had grudgingly admitted that things at the apartment had looked a bit odd, and that they were checking into the possibility that I'd been ambushed. She said she'd call me tomorrow and let me know what they found. I don't even want to think about there being a tomorrow. I want to stay here forever, just like this. It's safe here. I squeeze my eyes shut and wait until the minutes start to run into each other, then slip away entirely.

Downstairs, a door clicks. Through half-lidded eyes I see Jadyn standing two floors below on the green marble floor of the entry hall, staring up at me with eyes like frosted peridots. I'm aware that I wouldn't normally have this kind of vision, but somehow it doesn't feel strange. Maybe it's because I know Jadyn can see me too, that she's been looking for me.

"Why did you tell him?" I whisper. "Do you hate me that much?"

But she's still watching me, only watching, and the words echo in the space between us until I'm not sure who really said them.

Jadyn looks down at the floor; all I can see is the top of her head and her cold black hair. *"It's a corner I've seen coming for years. I'm not proud of everything I've done."*

I raise myself up on my elbows, staring down at her over the edge of the bed. Maybe she knew there were going to be problems, but she couldn't have seen *this* coming. Not all of it.

"Nobody's normal anymore," I tell her. "You're gone. Nadal's a drug lord. Peter's a spy. The police are blackmailing me, and I..." I can't finish that sentence, even in a dream. Not to Jadyn.

Jadyn raises her head slightly, looking at something at the end of the hall. *"Did you ever fight as long and as hard as you could to destroy your worst enemy, and then realize, at the very end, that you'd been fighting yourself? Sometimes..."* She doesn't finish. Instead, she turns and walks toward the front door, out of my field of vision.

"Wait!" I say, or I try to; it's getting very hard to talk. I'm so tired. "What are you talking about?"

She's not there anymore, but I can still hear her voice, very small, very close to my ear. *"Eventually, they will eat you alive."* I stare down at the distant marble, trying to catch her reflection in it. Where did she go? Why would she...

Something's wrong. The polished surface is growing dull, then there's a shadow... And then something black and liquid rushes over it, covering the marble licking hungrily at the foot of the stairs. It's rising rapidly; the hall is disappearing under the blackness. There's a weird, acidic quality to it that somehow reminds me of the feel of that music inside my skull, and I try to shrink backward onto the mattress, but I can't look away from the liquid below me. I can't tell what it is. I *do* know that I've never been more scared of anything in my life...

Abruptly, my eyes fly open. The air is dark and hot. For one endless second I'm positive that the black liquid has made it to my room, that it's much too late to get away. I reach out, shakily, and snap on my bedside lamp. The darkness pulls back, leaving me in a bubble of light, but I know it's normal darkness. That other darkness would never have given up so easily. I rub my eyes with the back of my hand. It's 1:20 AM.

Jadyn. I glance over the edge of my bed, but all I can see is the dusky carpet. *Eventually, they will eat you alive...* Of course; that's where I saw it. It was in the letter she wrote to her parents.

I slip out of bed and remove the panel from the back of the closet, fingering the scraps of paper and photos until I feel the letter's torn flap. It's out of the envelope before I'm back on the bed, and I scan through it quickly, holding it close to the bedside lamp. The line I remembered is there, and so is the one about her feeling cornered. The middle one, though, the one about fighting yourself—where did that come from? I lie back on the bed, tucking one arm under my pillow, and stare up at the ceiling.

Fighting yourself... Could that be about my being blackmailed by Officer Carmichael? What else could she have meant? Trying to take it literally doesn't make sense; how either of us actually be—

And then it hits me. The drug runners jumping off the boat almost at the same time. The police stopping the one man but letting the other go. The way the drug runner looked back at me like he knew I was there, but walked as though he wasn't worried about being seen. The fact that although he somehow knew I was there, his partner didn't see anything.

Not *his* partner. *Her* partner. Jadyn is tall; she normally walks as though she isn't afraid of anything, and details vanish when I'm seeing by sound. When Jadyn's normal, she can't see me any more than Officer Carmichael can. When she's invisible, we see the same way, which means …

I squeeze my eyes shut. *Of course.* I really should have seen that sooner. Peter will want to know. But … Wait a second. That's not all it means. I open my eyes slowly, staring into the shadows on the ceiling.

If I can figure that out, after less than a month of experience, Jadyn definitely could. Come to think of it … Maybe she has already. The day I went to Kinzie Marina was the day Jadyn left for Isole. She hasn't tried to call home since then. And she wrote that letter just before she left … That's too many coincidences. Even if she isn't sure I'm the one behind Monica, she has to suspect it. If she tried to cripple me when I was little, she would have known this was a possibility, might actually have been watching for it. If she told Nadal, told him how to hurt me …

But then the letter makes no sense at all. I hold it up, above my face, so that it catches the light from the lamp. In the letter, she sounded as though she was giving up, not as though she planned to have me killed. *She's your* mother. *Jadyn Irving is a lot of things, but she isn't the Devil incarnate. Get a grip.*

If she isn't, though, how would Nadal know about me? Jadyn wouldn't tell anyone that she *had* a weakness, let alone describe it. He couldn't force Jadyn into anything…unless…maybe he drugged her?

Something in the back of my mind is coiling around an idea, trying to make me look at it, and I'm suddenly afraid to. If I've been fighting Nadal…and if Jadyn's been working for him…and if she hasn't told him about me…If he somehow found out that Monica was a fake, then he'd have to think—

I've got to get out of here.

The darkness is smothering me. I stand, heading for the door; I'm so afraid that it's hard to move. The only reason I *can* move is that nowhere feels safe. *Why* does it have to be so dark? *What if someone's watching me?* The darkness under the ornamental teak table seems thicker than normal. There's a strange, lumpy shape against the wall a few yards away. My hands clench into fists, fingernails biting into my palms. *Don't think about it, there's no one here, you're just—*

But as I'm passing the open rec room door, I hear an odd creak. I freeze. I don't want to look. People in horror movies always look, and they always pay for it. But there's really nowhere to go; if I start running now I know I'll never stop. My feet feel like sacks of cement, but I take one step back and cautiously peek around the edge of the doorframe.

It's Peter.

He's lying on the leather couch, using an afghan as a blanket; his arms are crossed on top of it, and the hand I can see is curled into a loose fist.

I sag against the doorframe; I have no idea why he's here, but it doesn't matter. Peter means safety. He's back. More to the point, he's obviously been in the rec room for a while; if someone else really was here, he'd know. He would've woken me up.

"Natalie?"

He's so still I assumed he was asleep, but now that I'm really looking, I can see the gleam of his eyes in the darkness. "Um. Yeah."

"Everything okay?"

Everything today has been so far from okay that I don't know where to start. I don't have the energy to go into it at all, anyway. Tomorrow, maybe. But not now.

I shrug noncommittally, curling my fingers around the silky wood of the doorframe. "Yeah, I just…I don't know. I guess it was a nightmare. It's not important."

Peter's nod is a shadowy movement against the pale leather of the couch. "Sorry I woke you up," I say.

"You didn't," he says, settling into the sofa again. The leather creaks under his weight; the same sound that scared me out of my wits a minute ago is now as comforting as a nightlight.

I walk back to my room, shut the door behind me, and crawl into bed. I didn't wake him up. He really is keeping watch. I shut my eyes, and this time I don't feel any need to open them again, to check the shadows one more time.

By the time I remember Jadyn's letter, I'm too tired to get up; I push it under my pillow. It crackles faintly when I move my head, but it isn't loud enough to be annoying. The sound could be anything: dry leaves, the wind blowing candy wrappers down the street, or faraway firecrackers…

This time, when I fall asleep, I don't dream.

When I open my eyes again, the ceiling is a flat, dull grey. I gaze up at it, not sure whether I'm awake or still dreaming. The room is absolutely silent; the curtains muffle any noise from outside, and if anyone's moving downstairs, I can't hear it. The ghost of a headache hangs around my temples, and I reach up to touch them, gingerly. *Something happened yesterday...*

I realize a split-second later that it's something I've been trying to forget, but it's too late; fragments of memories float to the surface, and I can't stop them. I sit up, wincing at the raw line of pain across my back. *How did...?*

No. Don't think.

I swing my feet over the edge of the bed, and, as they touch the carpet, I see something: eyes like frosted peridots, drowning in oily, liquid blackness…I flinch back, jerking my feet up onto the bed again as the last slivers of memory click into place. Jadyn's back, or she was, and something's downstairs…

Wait. It's just a memory. No, not even a real memory. A dream.

I curl up and squeeze my eyes shut, but the fear I'm expecting doesn't come. Now that I know what I've been avoiding, the uneasiness is draining away, leaving me empty and as grey as the ceiling. I don't want to get up. I don't want to do anything, or talk to anyone, or even *see* anyone. I just want to sleep, or better, be unconscious so I can't dream again. But Officer Carmichael is going to call today to tell me whether she's decided that they were wrong or that I'm delusional. If I fall asleep, the call might wake me up, and I don't think I can stand being yanked back into this again.

So I compromise, and stall. I take a long shower, washing away the grit and sweat and fear from yesterday. I spend close to an hour picking out clothes to wear, even though, if everything goes right, I won't be going anywhere today. I tug the sheets back into place, rearranging the comforter, even though I don't usually make my bed at all. Then I remember I slept in the clothes I wore to the projects last night, and I strip the bed down to the mattress. When I open the curtains, the sky is the same lifeless grey as the ceiling, and the air is heavy and still. *Everything* is grey today.

It's noon before I get hungry enough to decide that venturing down to the kitchen is worth the risk. The hallway seems fuzzy, as though the air itself is congealing; I turn on the lights as I go, but it feels like trying to fix a broken arm with a Band-Aid. I glance into the rec room, but of course Peter isn't there. There's nothing to show that he ever was. How did he know I needed someone close by last night? I haven't even told him I was out yesterday, let alone what almost happened. Sometimes Peter just seems to know when he's needed. Unlike *some* people I'm related to.

The kitchen is mercifully empty. I grab two bagels and a jar of peanut butter, and slip out again, into the hall. As I turn the corner, I almost bump into Peter. For a minute I just stand there, staring at his shirt collar. It's not that I'm mad at him. I literally can't talk. My mind is blank, words aren't coming, and there's a thick lump in my throat. Neither of us move. The silence stretches out, ridiculously long.

Finally, I step around him, awkwardly, ducking my head so that he'll know I'm okay and just don't want to talk. As I pass him, he catches my shoulder. "Natalie, wait."

I stop, still not looking at him. *Don't talk to me. Please. Not now.*

But he only slips a thin envelope into my hands, wedging it between the bagels. I stare down at it, dumbly, then glance up at him. His eyes are fatigue-tarnished and—I think—a little sad, but he smiles, nods, and continues down the hall.

Why couldn't Peter have been my dad? He wouldn't have given up on me. He never has, and he's not even related to me.

I tighten my hands around the bagels and peanut butter, to make sure the envelope doesn't slip, and manage to get upstairs without seeing anyone else. Once I'm safely locked into my room—and have managed to butter one of the bagels with a nail file from the bathroom cabinet, since I forgot to grab a knife—I open the envelope.

There are two pieces of paper inside: a full-sized letter, and, fastened to it with a paperclip, a small page that looks as if it was ripped out of a spiral-bound notepad. Which, since it's from Peter, it probably was. There's a short note penciled on the smaller sheet, in Peter's handwriting, which he's tried his hardest to keep legible: *Natalie—This will do it, I think. I've kept a copy as well, for security reasons. Put yours somewhere safe.* I smile ruefully and fold the note back so I can read the letter.

It's a long, reassuringly dense summary of exactly what Peter's found on Officer Carmichael. There's a surprising amount of stuff, most of it fairly minor—a cousin in another state who was convicted of robbing a 7-Eleven, scattered cases of insanity in her mother's family—but there are other things, too. Peter's managed to connect the second husband to the chop shop, and has determined that Officer Carmichael didn't divorce him until two months after she discovered what he was involved in. There's even—ironically—a provable instance of drug abuse in college.

I take a big bite of the bagel and chew, eyes still fixed on the letter. *This is it,* I think. *My ticket out of this whole situation. No more getting shot at, or chasing Jadyn around, or being pulled in different directions by Officer Carmichael, Peter, Jadyn and myself.*

But the knowledge doesn't help. Anxiety is a leaden lump in my chest, and the bagel doesn't taste good anymore. I flop back onto my bed, squeezing my eyes shut. *Seriously, calm down. There's nothing to worry about. You're safe today. You don't have to go anywhere. If Officer Carmichael calls, all you have to do is tell her what you've got on her. Peter can even take you out of town for a few days, until things quiet down. Jadyn will be fine on her own.*

Jadyn. *She's* what's bothering me. The images from last night are branded into my mind, like smoke stains after a house fire. *All that blackness ...*

Stop it. You're being stupid. If it bothers you that much, just call Isole and ask whether she's there. It's not that hard.

The closest house phone is on a table in the hall, but I don't want anyone else to hear me making this call. The cell phone is lying on the floor by my stripped bed, where I tossed it earlier. I pick it up, sit down on the edge of the mattress, and punch in Isole's number. The phone rings three times, and then a friendly, smooth, and obviously prerecorded woman's voice speaks. "Thank you for calling Isole Resort and Spa. If you would like to place reservations, please press one. If you are interested in hearing about our weekend packages, please press two. Isole is proud to house *Alfonso's*, a five-star bistro. If you would like to hear today's menu, please press—"

I don't have time for this. I tug the phone away from my ear and press o as fast as I can for about ten seconds, a trick I learned from Jadyn's previous secretary. Automated systems like Isole's can't handle it, and your call automatically switches over to a real person. Sure enough, when I put the phone back to my ear, the canned voice has been replaced by a flustered-sounding and obviously live young man's. "Hello, I'm sorry, could you hold for just a—"

"No, I can't. This is Natalie Irving. Is my mother there?"

The voice hesitates, then reluctantly shifts into conversational mode. "Natalie. Right. I'm sorry. We're swamped right now and things are just insane."

So Jadyn *was* right about business picking up. "This won't take long. I just—I called yesterday, but Jadyn was out for the afternoon and they said to try again today. She's back, isn't she?"

"Uh…Hang on a sec." The man sets the phone down, but doesn't put me on hold. Close to the mouthpiece, I hear paper rustling, and, in the background, a steady murmur of voices. It sounds a little like the ocean. Then the receiver clatters, and the man is back. "No, actually, I'm afraid she's not."

"But ... she was supposed to come back, wasn't she?"

"Looks like it," the man agrees. "She was due back at ten last night, but someone called around eight-thirty and said she'd run into some friends and would be staying at their place for the night."

Last night, at eight-thirty ... ? *No, it's possible. Coincidences happen.* I clear my throat, hoping I don't sound nervous. "Um, who called? Was it Jadyn?"

"Her driver, I think."

"And who was she staying with?"

"The Bartolons. Emile and Katharine Bartolon."

The Bartolons? My stomach gives a sick little lurch. *No.* There's no way they'd invite friends over on Friday night if their son had been kidnapped on Wednesday. Someone is lying.

"Did you want me to see if I can get hold of them for you?"

"No," I say, "I can call from here. Thank you."

The line goes dead. Gently, I place the phone on the mattress by my leg.

She might just have dropped out of sight, the way her letter said she planned to.

But if Peter's right about her, it's too early. She wouldn't risk disappearing while Nadal was free to hunt her down. It wouldn't be safe. So where *is* she?

Why do you even care? You don't have to be involved in this anymore. Jadyn's an adult. She can handle it.

But what if she can't?

She wouldn't want help, especially not from you.

She wouldn't *ask* for it. That doesn't mean she doesn't *want* it.

What was it Peter said? *"She doesn't trust anyone enough to be that transparent."*

But he isn't related to her. He can afford to say stuff like that.

"All the pressure; all those people counting on her…" No one besides Monica would say that. No one else in this city would even think it. How *could* they, when she's so… She even said in her letter that she wanted to keep people worried.

"That way, it's possible to live an almost normal life…"

She only has that problem because she's her. Anyone else could do this right.

Like your dad, who wanted you so badly he sued for custody but hasn't so much as checked on you since you turned out normal? Like Officer Carmichael, who's willing to ruin your life if it will help clean up the city? Face it. What's the real *reason you don't want to go public? So they don't make you into her?*

Someone raps on my bedroom door, firmly and so abruptly. Warily, I stand. "Who is it?"

"Well, it isn't the President." Peter's voice is muffled by the door. "It isn't Interpol, either, so it must be—"

I flip the lock on the door. "The CIA?"

Peter raises an eyebrow at me. "Doubtful. No, actually, it's the Chicago Police Department."

"The…" I force myself to focus. "Officer Carmichael?"

He nods.

"Why didn't she call the cell?" I glance back into the room, realizing I don't remember ending the call to Isole. "Um. Right. Should I call her back, then?"

"She's still on the line." Peter steps back to let me through the door. "Use the phone in the rec room. I'm going to listen in on the hall extension, but pretend I'm not there. And, for now, don't mention anything from that report I gave you. Find out what she wants first."

I nod, glad for the orders, which help me force my thoughts into a straight line. I stand by the antique-looking upright phone, hand poised over the receiver, until I see Peter start to lift his receiver in the hall. Then I pick up my end, rattling it just a bit more than usual to cover any noise Peter makes. "This is Natalie."

"Why was the phone I gave you busy?"

"Oh, I …" *Why can't she ever just say* hello? *I don't have an excuse ready.*

"It gets better reception than the house lines on long-distance calls," I say, "so I just—"

"That phone is for business calls only. If you are not using it to talk to me, I expect the line to be open."

"Right. Okay." *She can't have called to yell at me for wasting her long-distance minutes.* "Um, what's going on?"

They have to have confirmed the ambush by now; I expect her to try to admit she was wrong without actually apologizing. Instead, she's silent for almost thirty seconds, and there's a tension in the empty air that I don't like. Peter leans around the edge of the door and catches my eye. I shrug helplessly; I don't understand this, either.

"Well," she says, finally, "which do you want first, the good news or the bad news? I will warn you, there's more bad than good."

Umm … "Good news, I guess," I tell her, just as Peter mouths "bad."

"Tavey is safe."

"Oh." After everything that's happened in the last twenty-four hours, this seems strangely insignificant. "Where was he?"

"At a hotel in Detroit with Ms. Alvarez, the nanny." Officer Carmichael sighs; she sounds worn thin, as though she worked straight through the night. "Apparently, they checked in at

9:00 PM on Wednesday. On Friday evening, Ms. Alvarez took Tavey down to the main desk and told them to call the Bartolons' number, and to let Tavey talk to them. She said he missed his mother and wanted to say good night to her, and that she was going outside for a cigarette."

"And ... she left?"

"Of course. It took the hotel staff a good ten minutes to figure out what had happened, and by the time they did, she was long gone."

"So, neither of them were ever at the apartment, which means ... it really was an ambush."

"I thought we'd decided that last night."

We did? I think, but I don't say it. I don't have enough spare concentration to antagonize her right now. "So, Tavey is found, but we obviously didn't find him, and we didn't even have the right city, let alone the right apartment. How are they explaining yesterday?"

No answer. We've evidently come to the bad news.

"What's Monica telling people?" I ask.

"Monica is in the hospital with a broken wrist, a broken collarbone, two fractured ribs and a concussion."

Officer Carmichael's voice is so flat and measured that it takes a few seconds for the actual words to sink in. When they do, it's as though the air in the room has thickened. It's hard to breathe. "H-how did she ... Why? What happened?"

"No one knows. She's still unconscious, so we can't ask her. She was checked into Northwestern Memorial Hospital a little after six, by a man who left no impression on anyone. He signed her in under another name, so we didn't even know she was there until eight."

No. This is … *No.* I shut my eyes, but it doesn't help. All I can see is Monica in the police station lobby on Monday, defending Jadyn to me: *It's okay if they blame her mistakes on me. She wants to be anonymous, and if that's what it takes to get her to come back, it's worth it.* It can't be worth this. Monica had brain surgery done recently; the fact that she's still unconscious is not a good sign. She couldn't have expected to be attacked like that. She probably can't even fight. It must have been so easy for them to … "Where were her bodyguards?"

"Again, no idea. We found one of them this morning."

"Alive?"

"No."

Silence. I blink, trying to clear my vision, and realize that Peter is watching me. When he knows he's caught my attention, he raises his left wrist and deliberately taps his watch. I lift my own wrist, not sure what he's trying to say, but my watch is still in my room, on top of my bookshelf.

And then I get it.

"Wait. What time did you say Monica was checked in?"

"A few minutes after six."

"And we didn't get to the apartment until … about six-thirty, right?"

No answer.

"So people can prove Monica was at the hospital when she was supposed to be with your team?"

"She isn't checked in under her real name. They may not know yet."

"But they *will* know. Soon."

"Natalie, I didn't plan this, all right? I don't want your cover blown any more than you do."

It's too late for that. Somebody already knew Monica wasn't for real. Someone mugged her, and half an hour later someone tried to ambush me. And Jadyn didn't return to Isole last night.

"There is one thing," Officer Carmichael says, a little more briskly. She seems relieved, as though the worst is over. "We caught all of the men who were at the apartment, and one of them has agreed to talk in exchange for a lighter sentence. Care to guess who hired them?"

I don't have to guess; I know. Who else could it have been? Who else outside the government would have been worried about the existence of another Jadyn? My head is clear, but my heart is pounding so fast it's making me feel shaky. I lower myself to the carpet, holding on to the edge of the table for balance. The raw line across my back stings. "I don't know." I lie.

"Javier Nadal." She doesn't add, "your mother's friend," but she wants to. I can tell. "We've never managed to pin anything on him before, but this will stick. We'll arrest him tonight, and you can get some of your own back then."

If Nadal hurt Monica that badly when he was fairly sure she *wasn't* the person who was trying to undermine him, what would he do to Jadyn? "I can…what?"

"I want you to come along tonight and go ahead of us. You can make sure we aren't walking into anything unexpected, and that Nadal doesn't run. He may be expecting us by now, but I doubt he'll be expecting you. And Jadyn is still in Michigan, correct? If worse comes to worst, we can just say you're her tonight and deal with any backlash later."

"But she's not—" I say, just as a crumpled wad of paper bounces off my shoulder and skitters across the carpet. I glance up. Peter is watching me, motioning urgently in the paper's general direction. It's rolled out of reach. I push myself to my hands and knees, careful not to knock the receiver against anything, and crawl until I can snag the wad with my fingers. Unfolded, the paper says, *Say yes and hang up.*

I look up again to find Peter still looking at me.. I cover the mouthpiece with my palm and start to say "But…" He shakes his head emphatically and mimes hanging up a receiver. I shoot him a *You'd-better-know-what-you're-doing* glare, and uncover the mouthpiece. "I have to go. What time will you come by for me?"

"Three," Officer Carmichael says. She sounds vaguely taken aback, as though she was expecting a fight. "At the same place as before."

"I'll be there," I say, and hang up before she can ask any questions. I hear the receiver in the hall click down as I drop my receiver into its cradle, and I've barely managed to stand before Peter comes in, shutting the door tightly. "What was that about?" I ask.

I'm upset, not so much because of the note as because, if he gives me one more thing to worry about, I'm going to explode. Peter sits down on the couch, and motions for me to sit down too, but I don't. "What was that?" I ask again.

"You don't have to go," he says. "I can call your Officer and tell her what we have on her. She can't force you to do any of this."

I start to interrupt, but he holds up a hand, stopping me.

"I'm not saying you *can't* go if you don't want to, but you need to think very carefully before you decide."

I know that. What does he think I've been doing? "Peter," I say, "Jadyn isn't at Isole. The guy I talked to said someone told them she was staying with the Bartolons, and she *can't* be."

"Then you know where she probably is."

"Of course I do. You heard what she said about Monica, If Nadal didn't know where Jadyn was yesterday, then—"

"Then nobody will suspect you. Yet. But if you help the police arrest Jadyn tonight, while Monica's in the hospital, don't you think people will start to wonder?"

I open my mouth, but the perfectly logical answer I'm reaching for doesn't come.

Peter's still watching me. "If you decide you want to do so," he says, "tonight would be a good time to publicly announce yourself. By helping to arrest Jadyn, you'll automatically put yourself on the general public's good side." He pauses until he's sure he's got my attention. "On the other hand, if you'd rather keep things quiet, staying here tonight is probably your last chance."

He's right. And I *don't* want Jadyn's job, not really. Not like this. *Can't trust ... All those people ... Eat you alive ... No one will go easy on Jadyn ...*

Still, you shouldn't have to spend your whole life dealing with decisions you made when you were twelve. No sane person would have planned to end up like this. Maybe she *is* a jerk and a criminal and a not-so-great parent ... But if no one gives her a chance at a way out, I can't hope for one either.

If I get to Nadal's before the police do, I can try to fix things, somehow. But if I go, Peter has to go, too ... and he's also being paid to find evidence against Jadyn. I need to talk to her before anything else. Would he let me?

I glance up at Peter, realize I'm chewing my lip, and force myself to stop. "You didn't let me finish, Peter. I'm not sure Nadal knew where Jadyn was last night. If he thinks she's turned on him ..." I watch Peter's face so closely my eyes ache, desperate for some kind of signal, but he doesn't even blink. "It could be dangerous. For her."

"Does that matter? If it's a choice between the two of you…"

A flash of anger sizzles through me. *Of all the times to be sarcastic…* But he's serious. It was an honest question. And as soon as I realize that, my mind goes blank. Is that what I'd be doing, choosing between her and myself? "If she's there, do the police have enough evidence to arrest her?"

"If they don't, I do. It won't be a problem."

So, no help from Peter this time. Or from Officer Carmichael, or anybody. *Can't do a thing without help, can you?* If she were here, Jadyn would laugh.

I sigh, annoyed, and shove my hands into the pockets of my shorts. "I'll stay," I say. "I'm tired, anyway; I don't think I'd do them much good." Peter's eyes are unsettlingly steady, but I manage to hold his gaze. "I'll stay," I say again, a little louder, and I take a step toward the door.

"Fine," Peter says. "I'll call the Officer, then."

"Okay," I say, but he doesn't move. I've got the uneasy feeling that he's waiting for something. I take another step toward the door till I'm past him. "I'll be in my room, if you need me. Yesterday was pretty rough, and I need a nap. Would you tell people not to bother me?"

He nods. "Can I use your cell phone? In case someone picks up one of the house phones."

"Oh. Right. Just a second." I duck through the door and hurry around the corner to my room, forcing myself not to run. Running looks suspicious. I think I've got him fooled so far—if he believes I wouldn't mind Jadyn getting worked over or killed, he won't think I've got any reason to sneak out—but I don't dare risk it.

The cell is still on my bed. I snatch it up and walk back to the rec room as quickly as I can. Peter stands near the sofa, looking out the window. As I come in, he turns, hand held out for the phone. I give it to him and turn to leave in the same motion.

"Natalie," he says.

I stop, but don't turn around. *Just call, okay, Peter? Leave me alone.* "What?"

"How long has it been since the last time you drove?"

Since the last time I... "Um, excuse me?" I don't dare turn around now; I can't look at him.

"I'm not sure I trust you with the BMW, is all."

Did I miss something? "I'm not going to be driving the BMW."

"Yes, you are. You can't drive stick shifts, and the BMW is the only automatic car Jadyn owns."

"Peter, I'm tired. I'm going to take a nap."

Peter sighs. "No, you're not. You're going to *pretend* to go take a nap, then sneak out when no one's watching."

I shoot a shocked look over my shoulder at him. How on earth did he...

"I've had this job for eleven years, Natalie. Give me a break."

I swallow hard. "Look, I—I don't want you to come this time, okay? I want to do it myself."

"Why?"

I just watch him. I can't say, *I don't want her arrested.* He wouldn't believe me.

"I can't let you go by yourself."

Then what am I supposed to *do?* "Fine," I spit, "Then stop me."

The blackness crashes down around me so fast I feel dizzy, but I take three or four steps along the wall, away from the door, before I can even see outlines. I look back, straining to make out Peter's form by only the soft third-floor noises. He hasn't moved. From what I can tell, he's managed to track my position, but he's not trying to follow. I hesitate, unsure what to do.

"Natalie, I'm not going to arrest her," he says.

I don't buy it. Why wouldn't he? He *has* to. Everyone wants to. I can't even blame them. And he said...

"I'm not in charge of that. My job is to gather information and send it back to the people who *are* in charge of it. You're going to go whether or not I let you, and my immediate obligation is to keep you safe."

I take another small step away from him. "If Jadyn's arrested for smuggling drugs, aren't all bets sorta off?" His head turns, ever so slightly, but he still hasn't tried to come closer. "I mean, you don't really want protecting a drug runner's daughter on your resume."

Peter's quiet for so long I think I must have called his bluff. It hurts more than I expected it to, even though I was the one who said it. This is insane. I can't choose *Jadyn* over Peter. I don't even want to. But...

A quiet beep close by makes Peter's form flare white for a second, so sudden it makes me jump. It isn't until I see him lower his hand that I realize the beep came from the cell phone as he turned it off.

"Natalie," he says, "my parents are both dead. I haven't heard from my sister since I was eighteen years old, and I have no idea where she is. If I have cousins or nieces or nephews, I don't know about them. I've held this job for over a decade. You are the closest thing to a relative that I have. Even if you were running drugs *yourself* I wouldn't let you get shot."

Silence. I unsnap, staring at Peter. He looks right at me, with no trace of emotion in his eyes, as though he's only stated a fact. And

Can't trust ...

Eat you alive ...

All those people ...

No one will go easy on Jadyn ...

he's not lying. I feel tears sting my eyes, unexpectedly. Was I not the only one pretending Peter was my dad?

As I watch, he turns the phone on again and nods toward the door. "If we're planning to beat the police to Nadal's, you'd better get ready now," he says. "I'll call Officer Carmichael first and let her know."

"Peter…" He glances up, finger poised over the speed-dial button. I have no idea what to say, and I settle for the first thing that pops into my head. "Um. Okay. Look, when you call her, tell her… Tell her that she has to *keep* pretending that Jadyn's been the one helping her. Jadyn, not Monica. No matter what. If she says otherwise, we'll go public."

"Any particular reason?"

I shrug. I'm not sure yet myself.

c h a p t e r   s i x t e e n

By the time I've changed clothes, Peter has finished his phone call to Officer Carmichael, but he doesn't say anything about how it went, and I don't ask. On the way out of the house, he stops by Jadyn's study to tell her secretary that we're going downtown to the library for a couple of hours.

The air outside is a blank, humid grey. It feels urgent, somehow, as though if it doesn't rain soon something will explode. Like me.

It isn't until we're on the freeway that I get up the courage to speak. "Um… What should I do when we get there?"

"You didn't have a plan?"

I'm watching Peter as he says it, and his eyes don't flicker. He knew I didn't have one. And he's still… "No," I say, a little defiantly.

At this point, it feels as though any answer will be the wrong one, so I might as well tell the truth.

"Why are we going, then? What do you want to do?"

"I...I want to find out what's really going on. And I need to see Jadyn before the police get there."

"Fine, but how are you going to do it?"

"I don't know. There's got to be a way...I'll know it when I see it."

"Not good enough," Peter says. "You may have to improvise, but planning to make things up as you go is no kind of strategy." I suspect he's going to turn around and take me back home, that he's just been humoring me so far, but then he says, "Just think about it."

So I do. It takes two hours to drive from Burr Ridge to Nadal's house, and neither of us says more than a dozen words the whole time. Nadal's estate is huge, acres wide, surrounded by a ten-foot-high stone wall. I'm so mesmerized by the grey blur of rock rushing by outside my window that it's several seconds before I notice that Peter's missed the entrance. "Peter, you just—"

"The police are coming in an hour or so, and you aren't supposed to be here, remember? We're parking out here."

"Oh."

"And it might be a good idea to go invisible now instead of later."

"Why?"

"If Nadal is into smuggling of any kind, he's probably got eyes much farther out than he'll admit. Better safe than sorry."

I snap invisible. The white-traced blackness is a relief after all the grey, and even inside the car things look surprisingly sharp. Peter slows the car, pulling over onto the gravel shoulder. "All right," he says, turning to face me. "Do you have a plan yet?"

He's looking right at me, and I can't convince myself he can't see me. "I … No." Then, because it's worth a shot, "Do you?"

"A plan for what?"

"For … Well, for beating Nadal."

"There's no way you can do that."

"But—"

"Listen to me. I do have a plan, but you're going to have to promise to follow it. To the letter. Do you understand?"

"I can't promise anything until I hear it, Peter."

He chuckles, humorlessly. "Like it or not, Natalie, you're definitely related to Jadyn." I'm trying to figure out whether I can afford to take issue with that, when he continues. "Nadal's house is in no way safe territory. I have no idea who or what is going to be there, or what they're expecting. That being the case, your best advantage is invisibility. If you can keep from being spotted, they won't be able to touch you."

There's logic behind that. Sort of. "But then I'm no good at all. What if I have to defend myself?"

"You'd better hope you don't. You won't be armed."

"But you brought your gun…"

"No. That's for emergencies only. You don't even know how to handle it, let alone fire it."

"You could show me." I don't like the idea of carrying a gun, but I like the idea of going into Nadal's house completely vulnerable even less.

"Natalie, let me put it this way. *If* you are found—which, remember, you want to avoid—you are several times more likely to get shot if you're waving a gun around than if you're unarmed. You're seventeen; you don't look like a Navy Seal. It's very unlikely that

SARAH NEUFELD

they'll think you threatening enough to shoot on sight, without asking questions."

They shot at me on Friday, I think, but I don't say it. "So, I'm not armed, and I'm not supposed to be seen. What's the point of going in, if I can't do anything?"

"Find Jadyn. Find out where she's being kept, whether she's been hurt, and, if possible, how she got there."

"Oh, and then I come back and tell you, and you go get her?"

"No. Then you tell her what's going on."

"*What?*" I'm so startled I lose the invisibility for a second. Peter flickers into color, then back to black and sketchy white. Feeling lightheaded, I put my hands up to my temples. "Why the heck would I—"

"Because we can't beat Nadal. Neither of us. This whole mess is built on other peoples' misunderstandings, so if you really think Jadyn is worth rescuing, and you believe it enough to do this, then clearing up one or two of those misunderstandings might be enough. If it isn't, then you will have tried, and your conscience will be clear. There are no other options."

I'm silent for a full ten seconds, until the quiet sounds of the car don't provide enough contrast, and then I unsnap. He's watching me, quietly; he's got the same look on his face as he did when I found him waiting in my room a few days ago. Not surprised, not expectant, not uneasy. Just waiting. "Will that do it?" I ask, finally.

"It will if you're right," Peter says.

I snap invisible before I get out of the car. Peter has me keep a hand on his shoulder the whole time we're walking, so he knows where I am. He's said he'll get me into the house. Inside, and getting out, I'll be on my own. The guard opens the front gate for him, as they

268

know each other, and he's seen Peter and me with Jadyn occasionally. He asks Peter why he's there, and Peter tells him something, but I don't hear what it is. The air out here feels so heavy it's like being underwater, and I'm suddenly glad Peter hasn't let me borrow his gun. It's hard enough to stay calm as it is.

I follow Peter down the drive, navigating by the feel of the ground under my feet and my hand on his shoulder. The ground changes from gritty asphalt to loose gravel that crunches under Peter's shoes, and I realize we've made it to the parking circle in front of Nadal's house. The front door is just on the other side, but Peter heads off around the house instead. We walk for so long that I'm not expecting it when Peter stops, and I almost run into him. He stands in front of another door, this one a service entrance of some kind. My fingers tighten on his shoulder, but it doesn't really register until Peter slips his hands into his pockets and says, quietly, "You don't have to do this, you know."

I don't think I can pull off sarcasm right now. Instead, I smack him on the shoulder—lightly, so it won't show if anyone's watching—and take my hand away so he can't tell where I am. Peter sighs, and presses the buzzer by the door.

It's about twenty seconds before the door opens, which is pretty long by Nadal's standards. I can tell right away that the person standing there is tall, but it isn't until he speaks that I realize he's not much older than me. "Yeah?"

"I need to talk to Brendan. Is he in today?"

"Brendan who?"

"Brendan Gutierrez. Is he in?"

"Oh, him. Maybe. Who are you?"

I shift uneasily from one foot to the other. How much time do I have until the police come?

"Peter Maraszek," Peter says. "I told him I was going to come by this week to return his sketches."

"Now's not really a good time," the kid says. Has he been told not to let anyone in? How many people here know—really *know*—about Jadyn and Nadal?

"Would you ask him?" Peter says. He doesn't seem concerned. "I'm not out this way often, and he did say anytime was okay."

"Fine," the guy says. "Hang on." He steps back, away from the door.

Peter stays where he is, waiting politely. After a couple of seconds, he reaches over and gives me a small push forward, startling me. I stumble a little, feet scuffing on the gravel, but manage to get through the door and into the kitchen before the boy is more than ten steps away.

The room is full of odd noises, rumbles and gurgles and spitting hisses, and, although I recognize all of them as normal cooking noises, it doesn't feel safe. I edge around the walls, even though I have the feeling no one would notice if I just walked straight through. There are only a handful of people in the room, and they're all absorbed in whatever they're doing. Even so, it's a relief to reach the quiet hallway on the other side of the kitchen.

I've always been nervous in Nadal's house. Even when I was invited and there were other people around. Even when Peter was there. Now that I know what Nadal's been doing, I expected the air to feel positively sinister… but it doesn't. It's hushed and empty, like Isole during the off-season. And I don't know what to do or where to start.

Just find Jadyn.

Where would they be? Not in the parts of the house that I know, the ones that get used for dinners and dances. Upstairs? At the far end of one of the wings? In the cellar? Does this place even *have* a cellar? I glance at my wrist, uneasily, but I can't see the hands on my watch. I know I'm running out of time, but I can't tell how fast.

As I reach the foot of a spiral staircase, the door across from me flies open and someone dashes out. I jerk backward, heart hammering, and crouch against the paneling under the first curve of the stairs. The footsteps pound past me without slowing, making the floor under me vibrate. I stay pressed against the paneling, letting my heart slow. *I need a system. I need to think.*

Just then, right behind me, someone whispers, "In an hour."

I freeze. The situation's straight out of a horror movie; I'm sure there's someone right behind me, just waiting for me to turn around. The voice is both very distinct and much too quiet, and it's a full five seconds before I realize that it isn't actually right behind me. The person speaking is somewhere above me, his voice traveling down through the stairwell. I squeeze my eyes shut, gritting my teeth, and then I realize why the voice still bothers me.

It bothers me because it belongs to Nadal.

I lean back, staring up through the stairs' center well, trying to see where he really is. "No," Nadal's voice says, still eerily close. "I seriously doubt it. It's nothing to worry about."

If anyone in this house knows where Jadyn is, it's him. Maybe if I follow him, he'll take me to her. I start up the stairs, carefully, sticking close to the wall to avoid creaking treads. Halfway through the first turn, I see a flicker of motion on the next floor.

Nadal rests his hand on the balcony railing. He's talking in clipped sentences, so quietly that, now that I've moved from the echo spot, I can't make out the words. I can't even begin to guess who he's talking to.

By the time I'm five steps from the top, Nadal's pocketed his cell phone and has started down the hall. He isn't walking very fast, but it's not easy to walk noiselessly down a strange hall and I'm having a hard time keeping up with him. About four doors from the head of the stairs, he stops, unlocks a door, and steps inside. I follow, hesitating just outside. He hasn't really shut the door, just pushed it on his way past so that it's started to close. I put a hand out, gently, stopping it so that I can see through the crack.

Nadal definitely isn't hiding from anyone. He walks solidly, and I can track his progress by the way the floor creaks. "Well, that's taken care of," he says. He slides something out of his pocket and sets it on a low table a few yards inside the room. At first I think it's the cell phone, but the sound it makes when it hits the table-top is much too heavy. *It had better not be a …*

I narrow my eyes, squinting at the object. *You're being paranoid,* I tell myself. *You've only seen one gun the whole time you've been with the police, and now you're seeing them everywhere.* But from where I'm standing, the shape looks disturbingly familiar. I push the door open just far enough so that I can slip through; if that's a gun, I want to know about it.

"The police will be here in half an hour," Nadal says. I glance up, distracted, but there's no one else in the room. Is he talking to himself? He hasn't gotten the cell phone out again.

I'm near the table now. I stretch my hand out, and my fingers brush across metal. It *is* a gun. "This will all be over soon. Aren't you happy?"

"About … ?" says Jadyn.

My head jerks up, and I nearly stop breathing. She's here? Where? I can't see her.

I take an uneasy step backward … and the floor creaks.

Nadal spins around before I've finished shifting my weight; he's jumpier than his voice lets on. He seems to be staring right at me. "Who's there?" His voice is clipped. He sounds more angry than nervous.

"You said you got rid of Monica," Jadyn says. I still can't see her.

"*You* said she was never the real problem," Nadal says, staring in my direction. Or maybe he's looking at the gun.

"I'm here," Jadyn says. "There's nobody else."

"Are you sure?"

Silence.

There *is* somebody else. She knows about me. Why doesn't she say...?

Finally, Nadal turns away from me, walking toward the back of the room. And then there's a sharp, ringing slap. I jump. Nadal lowers his hand, slowly. "I said, are you sure?"

Silence.

Did he just...?

"You said earlier it wasn't you, and you said Monica wasn't real. There has to be someone else. Who *is* it?"

"Wasn't it you who told me secrets made me beautiful?"

He slaps her again, harder this time. My breath is coming so fast now I feel sick, and before I know what I'm doing, I've grabbed the gun off the table. "Stop it!"

Nadal jerks upright as though I've jabbed him with something sharp. He takes a quick step toward the table, then notices that the gun's not there and stops. I realize that, to him, the gun is hanging in mid-air, and I unsnap. I want him to see *me*. The way I feel right now, my eyes might be able to turn him to stone.

At first I think I might actually have managed it. Nadal's face is frozen in shock, caramel eyes wide. The gun wavers a little in my hand—the thing is *heavy*—but there's no way I'm lowering it. I can see Jadyn now, or at least where she is. She sits in a tall-backed wing chair, facing away from me. All I can see is the top of her head. Is she...

Nadal laughs. It's an honest-to-goodness laugh, as though he's just heard the best joke in the world. I raise the gun a little, but he doesn't come any closer. "Oh, Lord..." he says. "Natalie?"

I step backward, carefully, until I can push the door shut, and flip the lock.

It isn't until then that I remember I'm doing exactly what Peter told me not to do. At least no one's going to shoot me. I have the only gun in the room.

"Oh, for—" he says again. "Jadyn, did you know about this?"

Jadyn is silent.

"Does it matter?" I ask him. He takes a step toward me, and I shake the gun at him. "Don't move."

Nadal raises his hands. "Calm down," he says. "I won't hurt you. And yes, it does matter, because if it's you, then you've just—"

"Just what?"

"Just taken your mother clear out of the picture. Funny coincidence. Or did you plan it that way?"

"How did I? Jadyn's got nothing to do with this."

"I wouldn't blame you if you had planned it," he says, thoughtfully. He doesn't seem very unnerved by the gun. Can he tell I don't know how to use it? "She almost crippled you. On purpose. Just to avoid a court battle. You did know that, didn't you? All this time, you could have been somebody, and you've been stuck being Jadyn Irving's shadow. If I were you, I would have taken her down first chance I got."

"You're not me," I tell him, but my voice is shaking. Does he know how close to the truth he's hitting? Even now, hearing about what she did makes me feel sick. "And don't tell me to relax. You tried to kill me last night."

"I apologize. You were interrupting some very important things, and I was pressed for time."

"But you almost *did* kill Monica. You knew it wasn't her. Who did you think you were shooting at, Jadyn?" It isn't until after the words are out of my mouth that I realize they might be true.

"I wasn't sure. I'm glad to see that it wasn't."

"Let her go," I tell him. I'm starting to feel a little out of my depth—*why isn't he more worried about this gun?*—and I want to hurry up and finish this. "If it wasn't her, you don't have any reason to keep her here."

"Well, you see, I can't let her leave. The police would be very upset with me."

The police would…*what?* "Not likely. They're coming to arrest *you*."

"Why? They don't have anything on me. All they can prove is that drugs have been coming through my shipping lines."

"*Your* shipping lines," I point out. "That's kind of incriminating."

"Not really. Your mother and I have been involved for over a year, and I trusted her. She took advantage of my connections. When I found out about it, I put her under citizen's arrest and called the police."

He's got to be kidding. "Nobody's going to believe that."

Nadal shrugs. "Of course they will. Why wouldn't they? Last year, I paid to have a library built and stocked for a middle school that hadn't had a decent one in fifty years. I don't know even a fraction of the people who draw their paychecks from me. If I were arrested, my money would go to pay lawyers and courts, and who would keep up the scholarships I sponsor? I do enough for this city, goodness knows. They don't want me gone; they can't afford it. Your mother has never really been into altruism. Most of the people in the city would rather have her safely locked away somewhere, guilty or not. It won't be a hard choice."

I shoot a startled glance past Nadal's shoulder, toward Jadyn's chair. She hasn't moved. I can't believe he's saying this where she can hear him, but it's even harder to believe that she's just sitting there, taking it. She knows people think stuff like that, but whenever anyone so much as hints at it out loud, she calls her lawyers and takes them to court. And that's the total strangers. Hearing this from a man she's been seeing for more than a year … I would have expected her to physically attack him. It's as though she isn't even listening. I lick my lips. "But, if you turn her in, your, um, 'side-business' will fall apart."

"Doubtful."

"But you won't have Jadyn any more … "

"She was only a courier. Very convenient, of course, but not irreplaceable. I only needed her for some of the runs. And I've got you now, so that won't be a problem."

I almost choke. This from a guy who's got a gun pointed at him. By *me*. "Yeah, right! There's no way."

"I'd take some time to think about that, if I were you. Working for me could be just what you need."

Officer Carmichael was bad enough. "I'm not working for anybody anymore. Ever."

"Then you're planning to sell yourself out again? You can't keep going on the way you have the past few weeks for very much longer, you know. Monica will be in the hospital for a while, and Jadyn will be under observation, if not in jail. You'll be found out."

"Not if I don't do anything."

"Oh, I'll make sure you're found out."

A nervous little flutter starts in the pit of my stomach. "You can't—"

"*When* that happens," he continues—he has control of the conversation now, and he's not letting go—"you'll have a choice. Should you cooperate with me, I will make sure that your reputation is comfortably high, and that you don't run into any of the problems your mother did. You'd be surprised at the number of people who'll agree with what I say, and how much of a difference that makes to the media. When I'm through, no one will even think to suspect you of anything." He takes a deliberate step toward me. I'm so confused, I don't even remember to raise the gun and tell him to stop. "If you don't cooperate … "

"What, you'll kill me?" There's a shaky edge to my voice that I don't like. I shoot a nervous glance at the back of Jadyn's chair, but I can't even see the top of her head any more.

He shakes his head, slowly, never taking his eyes from mine. "That would be a waste. What good would killing you do? If you don't cooperate, I will make sure you never have a single decent day. I can make your life hell. I can pay people off, people you'll never suspect until they've stabbed you in the back. I can make sure the wrong articles get published at the wrong times and that the wrong things get the most publicity. In the end, you won't be considered even semi-human any more. I'll turn you into more of a monster than anyone ever dreamed your mother could be. Why would I settle for killing you?"

The shakiness is turning into panic. "Did you forget I'm working with the police? They know—"

"Exactly as much as they think they do. They'd be the first to doubt you, considering. No one really trusts you; you are Jadyn Irving's daughter, after all. I'm not asking for much, Natalie. Just a fraction of your time. You can do whatever you like with the rest, so long as it doesn't interfere with my business. I'll make sure everything goes smoothly for you. You can't expect even half that from the police."

It's a little hard not to laugh, not because I think the conversation is funny, but because I'm sure that the minute I start, things will go surreal on me. Flowers will grow out of the walls, and Nadal will turn out to be riding a unicycle, and then I'll wake up. "Let me get this straight. My mother damaged me when I was little because, otherwise, I would have been taken away, and you say that's bad. Now you're threatening to damage me if I don't do what you want, and that's *not* bad?"

"It's life, Natalie." Nadal doesn't blink. "It's in your genes, along with the rest. You were born into it. People want what you have, and if they can't have it, they'll want to control it. There will always be someone behind you, watching you, waiting for you to make a mistake, and eventually you'll slip. Best to keep as much control as possible, I'd think. While you still have the option."

While you still have the option... *It's a corner I've seen coming for a long time.* When did Jadyn decide she'd run out of options? Does anyone ever really do that? I'm getting sick of this, and I realize, abruptly, that I've let Nadal get much too close. I raise the gun, although my wrists ache from holding it so high for so long. "You're talking pretty big for a guy with a gun pointed at him."

"That thing won't fire with the safety on."

What? I look down, realizing even as I do that it's a mistake, but it's too late. Before I can recover, Nadal's grabbed the barrel of the gun and yanked it out of my hands. All I see is a blurred metallic streak, and as I reach toward him, instinctively trying to grab it back, he swings it back down toward my face.

My legs collapse under me and I fall to the floor, snapping invisible by pure reflex. *What do I do?* There's nothing. I force myself to my knees and scramble backward as quickly as I can. The room is a jagged mess of black and white, and I can't tell where Nadal is. His house, his people, his terms. His gun. *He* knows how to use it, obviously. I can't remember what I thought I could do here.

The floor shakes under my hands. Someone's running. Toward me? Away? I can't tell. I crawl back until I hit the wall, then cover my head with my arms. Above me there's a startled yell, and then the world flashes white and cracks apart. He's fired the gun. At me? Did he miss? I can't tell. I'm not sure I can move. The blind whiteness fades into grey, then black.

Then someone says "Natalie."

I hug my knees, curling up, refusing to move. Somewhere, I know I'm thinking like a three-year-old: *he can't find me if I don't move.* The room smells like spent fireworks, and something else I recognize but can't put a name to. Footsteps cross the room toward me, and then someone's pinching my shoulder, hard, right by the base of my neck. It *hurts.* I yelp, trying to wriggle away, but the pressure makes the muscles at the back of my head go weak, and I unsnap.

Nadal lies a couple of yards away, his back to me, and there's something funny about his shirt. In the split-second it takes me

to realize that there's still a hand on my shoulder, and that, when I went invisible, Nadal's shirt was steel grey, not burgundy, Jadyn has unsnapped, and crouches in front of me. "Natalie, get up."

I gape at her, stupidly.

She shakes my shoulder, hard. *"Move."*

She's holding the gun. It isn't exactly pointed at me, but it's close enough to make me very, very nervous, and I pull away from her, struggling to my feet. "You just…"

"Good. Now get out."

"But…" She's killed Nadal. With that much blood outside of him, he's either dead or he's going to be very soon. I don't want to stare, but I can't look away.

Outside, very faintly, I hear the crunch of gravel under car tires, then the sound of voices. Jadyn's eyes flicker to the window. She swears and stands up, this time pointing the gun right at me. "Natalie," she says, "if you don't leave, he's going to win you. Do you want that?" I shake my head, dumbly. "Then get out of here."

"But he's—if they find—you're—"

"Why should you care? Javier isn't your problem. Now get out, or I *will* shoot."

"Fine," I say, as steadily as I can manage. I think she might actually do it. "I'm going. See?" I take one uncertain step backward, then another. The police are finally here. They'll find Jadyn with a gun and the corpse of the man they were planning on arresting, and I realize, abruptly, that Jadyn's eyes aren't reflecting. They're bright, almost too fierce to look at, and, somehow, familiar. It takes me a second to realize what I'm recognizing. I've seen it in the mirror about a million times in the past two weeks. She's afraid.

I close my eyes, briefly, and take a deep breath. "Mom." I haven't called her that since I was about ten, and she doesn't reply. "I'm leaving, but … look. Don't say anything when the police get here. Don't run, and don't say anything. Only the media thinks I'm Monica, The police think I'm you. If you stay quiet and let my … my contact explain this, you'll be fine."

The strangeness in Jadyn's eyes shifts, but I snap invisible before I can see what it's turned into. I don't want to know. She doesn't make a sound, but she lowers the gun, slowly. The footsteps come down the hall faster now. The room's outlines shiver rhythmically, and I lower my voice. "You can still win, if you want to."

Behind me, the door swings open. I slip past the first officer, pushing through the press in the hall, not caring who I bump into. No one will notice now.

After the first shocked second, the room behind me is strangely silent. I feel my way down the hall, fingers on the balcony rail, where Nadal's were just a few minutes ago. My head feels strange; too light, much too focused. *Too quiet.* Finally, as I step down onto the first stair, I hear a voice. It's Officer Carmichael.

"Jadyn…" she says. Then, in a strange, flat tone of voice, "He's dead." I stand frozen on the step, squeezing my eyes shut. *Please, Peter, whatever you told her, let it work …*

She clears her throat, and, slowly, I feel myself relax; I know that sound. I can picture the expression that's settling itself into Officer Carmichael's face. "Why did you have to go and do that? Do you have any idea how hard this is going to be to explain to the press?"

Slowly, the people in the hall above me start to move again, fanning out to check the other rooms. I even hear someone mutter, "Well, *that* was easy. I go downstairs in a daze, and it doesn't register that I'm on the main floor again until I've turned a corner and am walking through the sunroom. The staff on the ground floor are too busy gawking at the officers guarding the exits to notice me. When I leave through the front door, someone simply pushes it shut behind me.

The muggy air outside does nothing to clear my mind. I walk past the police cars parked in the long driveway and under the tunnel of birch trees, which seem to whisper to each other restlessly as I pass. The front gates stand open, although there are two officers guarding them; I walk past the men as though they aren't there, and then out onto the road.

I open the BMW's door without warning, sliding in and shutting it behind me before I unsnap. Peter's only response is to start the car. I lean back against the headrest, and close my eyes. Peter reaches over, flips the air conditioning on, and pulls out onto the highway. "Are you okay?" he asks.

I nod as well as I can without moving more than an inch or so. "Yeah."

No response. I glance up; Peter's watching the road intently. "Um…" I start, then pause. Still no reaction. "Aren't you going to ask how it went?"

"How what went?"

"The—" He still isn't looking at me, and I finally get it. "Oh. Um. Nothing."

"Good girl."

Of course. He could lose his job over this, be fired by the government. Aren't the penalties for disobeying orders more severe if you're supposed to be spying on someone? Eleven years, wasted… When did he decide it was worth the risk?

I lift my head, looking through the windshield, just as a big, fat raindrop spatters against it. Then another. And another. *Finally*, I think, dazedly, and roll my window down; the warm wind ruffles my hair. "Peter?"

"Hmm?"

I hold my hand out the window, letting the soft wind push against it, filling it with August rain. There's no photography equipment in the back seat, and the sun's definitely not shining, but, somehow, this feels very familiar. I lean back in my seat and watch the rain wash the windshield clean.

"Never mind."

he hall outside Monica's hospital room is so thick with flowers that I don't see how the medication carts manage to get through. The spicy, sweet scent is so strong that when I shut my eyes, it's hard to remember I'm even inside, let alone in downtown Chicago. I take a deep breath—more to steady my nerves than anything else—and tap on the wooden door, tentatively.

"C'min," says someone inside. I turn the knob, gently pushing the door open. A small fan sits on a high table by the door, set on low and locked into place, facing the door. A youngish woman with long, light hair lounges in a chair near Monica's hospital bed, reading a magazine. She glances up as I step in, smiles briefly, then returns to her magazine. *Guard,* I think. Not anyone I know.

"Natalie," Monica says. Officer Carmichael told me how badly she'd been injured, but somehow I hadn't visualized so many bandages. Or the bruises…Her left eye is still swollen almost shut, but she's smiling. Then—and I can't believe this—she starts lifting herself up onto her elbows.

"Hey," I say, batting a cluster of heart-shaped Mylar balloons out of my way and hurrying across the room toward her. "Don't! If you do stuff like that, they're going to kick me out."

"It isn't as bad as it looks," Monica says, although she's given up, wincing. "I'm on pain meds. When I'm lying still, nothing hurts at all. Then I forget and do something dumb like that, and it *all* hurts."

"I could come back some other time."

"No! Don't you dare. I've been waiting for you to come by. I wanted to talk to you."

I feel my heart sink. In this situation, there's only one thing she could want to talk to me about. It's odd that she's smiling, but then, she did hit her head.

Gingerly, Monica reaches back and presses the switch that tilts the top half of her mattress up. "Angie? Could you wait outside for a while? Please?"

The guard shoots her an appraising glance, then rolls up her magazine and slips out into the hallway. I watch her back until the door's shut behind her.

"Why do you have to go? You're fine here, Peter. I won't tell. Jadyn doesn't know. There's no reason to leave."

He gave his notice this morning. I sit at his oddly empty artist's table, watching him take the drawings off his wall and stack them carefully in a shoebox. He shrugs. "I do have my limits. If I stay here, I'll have to do my entire job; I don't want to risk seeing something that requires action."

He's not telling the whole truth. His having been here for eleven years cuts both ways: I can read him, too. He's leaving, maybe not because of me, but for me. Somehow. The only thing I can do is try to talk him out of it. "You won't. I mean, there won't be anything to see. I'll make sure."

Peter shoots me a look. "That's another problem, Natalie. Be careful. You can't stop everything. I don't see her wanting to get mixed up in that again, but if anything does happen, treat it as though you were a normal kid and go to the police. Don't try to stop her yourself. You aren't a one-person SWAT team, no matter how much practice you've gotten lately."

"Okay then, what if I get shot because you're not here?"

"That would mean I should have left sooner. You used to know better."

"She could have stayed," I say. "I'm not planning on discussing anything classified."

"Me either," Monica says, "but I don't like being watched all the time. It's a little creepy."

Considering what's happened to her, I would have thought *not* being watched would be creepier, but then, not everybody has Peter. I poke the closest balloon with my fingertip, and it bobs away to the end of its ribbon. I know I'm just stalling now, but I can't quite make myself stop. "You're pretty popular, aren't you? They couldn't even fit all your flowers in here."

Monica smiles ruefully. Her face looks a bit strange without makeup—either naked or younger, I'm not quite sure which. "Actually, there aren't any flowers in here because I'm allergic."

"Oh. Ouch." Hence the fan...

"Yeah. I wish I wasn't, They're so pretty. The balloons are fun, though."

"Um... You aren't allergic to chocolate, are you?" My peace offering. The heads of the men who beat her up would have been better, but they're out of my reach. I didn't even get Nadal. So: chocolate.

Monica's eyes widen. "You didn't actually manage to smuggle some *in*, did you?"

"Smuggle? I just carried it. Nobody stopped me."

"Oh, *yay!* No, I'm not allergic; can I..."

I hand her the box, and she breaks the seal with her thumbnail. "I wasn't sure what you liked, so it's a mix," I tell her.

I swivel the chair from side to side, restlessly, tapping at a crumpled wad of paper with my toes. "Seriously, Peter... You do know it's going to be miserable around here without you, right?"

"Who's going to be here? You'll be going to college next year, remember? And they do have telephones in New York."

I glance up at him, frowning, but I can't see his face from where I'm sitting. "Um... and that matters because...?"

"Because that's where I'll be. That's where my next job is."

"Oh?" Somebody already hired him? I feel my stomach clench. Not fair. "Who are you working for?"

"Excelsior," Peter says. He's trying to peel an especially stubborn strip of tape away from the wall.

For some reason, my mind is blank. "As security?"

"As a penciler."

"Okay," Monica says, staring down at the chocolates as though I've given her a boxful of diamonds. "Which ones are the best?"

"Depends on what you like. I think the white-chocolate-rasp-berry ones are really good, but ... "

She lifts one out of the box and takes an experimental bite, then stuffs the whole thing in her mouth. "Wow. Oh, yum. Thanks so much. Here, take one."

"They're yours."

"Exactly. Take one."

For a while, it's quiet and my gaze drifts to the wall nearest the bed. Monica's only been here for five days, but the paint is comp-letely hidden by cards and photos. There's a two-foot-square drawing by the second-grade class at somebody's school, an el-egantly plain card which I know for a fact only comes from the mayor's office, and a photo of about fifty people standing on a soccer field, holding a banner that says "Get Well *SOON!!!*" So many people... "I'm sorry," I manage, finally.

Peter's laughing at me. He hasn't turned—he won't let me see—but his shoulders are shaking. I can't seem to make my mouth work right. "I ... you ... they ... They hired you?"

"That's not very flattering, Natalie."

"No, I don't—I mean—When?"

"Yesterday," Peter says, studying one particular drawing for a long moment. "Yesterday morning. They're going to have me work on the Domino Rey book, for starters."

"Omigosh, that's GREAT! Geez, you're going to be famous!"

"Um, nooo ... But it should be fun. I'll mail you the issues, if you like."

"No way! I want to go buy them, so I can tell everyone in the store I know you. But you said you didn't have to move for this job. You could at least stay in Chicago."

"Sometimes it's easiest to change everything at once. You'll see what

291

I mean when you leave for college. Speaking of futures…Do you know what you're going to do with yours yet?"

I've caught Monica in the middle of putting the lid back on the chocolates; she looks up. "Pardon?"

"You got hurt pretending to be my…my mom. It's our fault you're in here."

"Natalie, since when are you your mother? Anyway, Jadyn didn't do this. They found out about her because I got hurt, and she said she isn't going to help anymore. I should be the one apologizing. It doesn't look like she might change her mind, does it?"

I shake my head, slowly. "No, it really doesn't." *Monica isn't mad at us? Why not?* "She doesn't like this stuff much."

Monica grimaces, "I don't blame her. I didn't think it was going to be quite this dangerous."

I shoot her an incredulous look, "You signed up for brain surgery, and you weren't expecting 'dangerous'?"

"That's different." Then, quieter, "Is she okay?"

As far as I know. Jadyn left for Seattle two days ago; she said she wanted to be alone for a while, and she's planning to drive down the coast from Seattle to Los Angeles. She didn't say anything about stopping in Tacoma, but it's right on the way, and I'm keeping my fingers crossed. "She's taking a road trip," I tell Monica. "She said she needed to get away for a while."

"Lucky," Monica says.

"You know," Peter says, "you don't ever have to use invisibility again, if you'd rather not. You can still pass yourself off as normal."

I shrug half-heartedly; somehow, even after everything, that doesn't sound appealing at all.

"And, if you decide otherwise," he continues, "call me first. It would probably be best to keep things quiet, but if you'd like to make a career out of invisibility, I'm sure something could be arranged. I know some people ... "

"In the CIA?"

Peter hesitates; then he quirks an eyebrow. "I'd tell you," he says, "but—"

I throw his pencil case at him.

"So, when is your mom coming back?"

"Not for a week or two."

"Are you staying with somebody?"

"I don't need to. There are always people around." *Although they still don't talk to me.*

"That's no fun." Monica tugs at the edge of the sheet, irritably. "Look. I'm going to need a nurse for a while, but they're letting me go back home in a few days. Why don't you come stay with me until your mom gets back?"

She's serious. This is what she wanted to talk about? "I ... You're hurt, though. You don't want company."

"No, I'm hurt, so I *do* want company. I won't be much fun, but I'd love to have somebody around to talk to. We can talk about guys. You've got somebody, right?"

I pull a face. I'd rather not go into it, but she presses me for an explanation and I'm afraid she'll forget and hurt herself again, so I tell her about Ari and the photos. She stares at me for a long moment, then almost shrieks with laughter, bracing herself against the bed rail. "Oh—*ow*—Ha ha ha! Okay, that settles it; you're coming over. First, we get rid of him. Then we find you a real guy. I've got a cousin you might like; he's kinda geeky, but really cute. Just

don't mention foreign policy around him, or you'll never get him to shut up."

"I... Are you serious?"

"About my cousin?"

"No, I mean, about me coming over."

"Of course," Monica says. "Why wouldn't I be?"

"Well, I..." Years of being Jadyn's shadow and scapegoat, the face the public is given when they ask for her... I hated it, but I've never been able to explain it well. "I'm *me*."

Monica blinks. "Yes? Me too. Most people are." I don't answer; she has to know what I mean. "Or are you really saying *you* don't want to be seen with *me*?"

"No!" I say, almost panicked.

Monica rolls her eyes. "*Well*, then. Tell you what. You come over, and if anyone gives us trouble, we'll sic my guard on them. That's what she's here for, right?"

"But... Most people don't like my mom, and they love you. What if they decide you've sold out because I'm there?"

"Then they need a better hobby. I think I'm old enough to decide who I want to associate with. So lighten up, okay? People will think whatever they want. The important thing here is what *you* think. Are you coming or not?"

In the light from the window, her bruised face is beautiful in a way I've never seen before. No lies, no ulterior motives; if she didn't like me, she really would tell me so. An actual friend? I'd all but decided those didn't exist. But if they do... If this is real...

I'll always be different, and I'll always know it.

That doesn't mean it has to matter all the time.

"I'll come."

The End.

Sarah Neufeld

…is a home-schooled world traveler who is heavily in-fluenced by her time living in Japan. Her admiration for the artistic storytelling in graphic novels, combined with a love of manga, served as inspiration when writing *Visibility*. Sarah currently works as a freelance Japanese translator. When she isn't busy writing, she can be found learning more languages, hiking in the urban forests around Portland, Oregon, and enjoying manga over a cup of tea.